F

D1625416

WITHDRAWN

COLD DECK

West Word Fiction

COLD DECK

H. LEE BARNES

UNIVERSITY OF NEVADA PRESS ▲▲ RENO | LAS VEGAS

West Word Fiction

University of Nevada Press, Reno, Nevada 89557 USA
Copyright © 2013 by H. Lee Barnes
All rights reserved
Manufactured in the United States of America
Design by Kathleen Szawiola

Library of Congress Cataloging-in-Publication Data
Barnes, H. Lee, 1944–
Cold deck / H. Lee Barnes.
p.   cm. — (West word fiction)
ISBN 978-0-87417-884-5 (cloth : alk. paper) — ISBN 978-0-87417-888-3 (ebook)
1. Card dealers—Fiction.   2. Single fathers—Fiction.   3. Casinos—Fiction.
4. Las Vegas (Nev.)—Fiction. I. Title.
PS3552.A673854C65   2013
813'.54—dc23   2012038422

The paper used in this book is a recycled stock made from 30 percent
post-consumer waste materials, certified by FSC, and meets the requirements
of American National Standard for Information Sciences—Permanence of
Paper for Printed Library Materials, ANSI/NISO Z39.48-1992 (R2002).
Binding materials were selected for strength and durability.

FIRST PRINTING
22 21 20 19 18 17 16 15 14 13
5 4 3 2 1

To Tonja Page, 1954–2008, with thanks for your
friendship, your humor, and your encouragement
when I needed it.
The casino story you wanted me to write.

ACKNOWLEDGMENTS

I wish to express my thanks to all those who have contributed to this book. My special thanks go out to Mary Sojourner and Deke Castleman, friends and remarkable readers. I will forever be indebted to the University of Nevada Press and the fine staff who have championed my works for more than a decade, with particular thanks to acquisitions editor Margaret Fisher Dalrymple and director Joanne O'Hare.

COLD DECK

1 The shift neared the morning hour we called the hump. A deck of cards lay idle at the far end of the table in the center of the break room, where the usual aggregation of dealers sat dour faced, some sprawled out in chairs watching television, volume turned low, others gathered around the table, cigarettes in hand. Smoke orbited the heads of those seated around the table as they puffed away and recycled a list of familiar gripes, one complaining of being screwed out of an early out, another grousing about being stuck on a table with a drunken chain-smoker, a third bitching about some guy who'd caught a run, won more than two grand, and stiffed him. None of us had an inkling that the day would become one of the pivotal moments in our lives. Until then, it'd passed no differently than any other.

I sat alone at a side table, head resting atop my arms, trying for a couple of winks and wishing, as I often did, that I was anywhere but inside a casino. Sleep, since the birth of my son, Lucas, was hard to come by. My wife, Anne, desperately needed a vacation from mothering. We'd learned to parent in shifts. If the day went as normal, in a few hours I would get home and find her waiting on the living room couch. She'd promptly surrender Lucas to me, peck me on the cheek, and head for the bedroom. Then I'd spend the next four or five hours being daddy-mom while she slept. When my turn came, I'd get five hours on the mattress before it was time to again get on the daily casino roller coaster, a ride of constant motion and incessant noise that offered little joy. Keep the roulette balls on the rail, the dice rolling, and the cards in the air.

Fortunately, soon after she'd told me she was pregnant, I'd landed a job at the MGM. Anne and I never could have made ends meet on what I'd earned dealing at the Mint. Tokes or zooks, as we called our tips, were steady, and the job paid the household bills with a little left over here and there for savings. Money aside, I was unhappy and losing my sense of self. I'd long resisted the cynicism that often affected dealers, but lately I'd found myself falling into the trap. I needed to get out of the casinos before I became absorbed by self-pity or anger, or began numbing myself with drugs or alcohol, or gambling away my tips the way some did. Drugs were out. That much I knew. I had a son now. Truth was, I seldom drank more than one beer on my days off and hadn't touched a joint since Anne had informed me she was pregnant.

Still, in Las Vegas a degenerate lifestyle was as easy to slip into as an air-conditioned theater, and willpower holds up only so long when you feel you're at a dead end. Those rare moments when Anne and I were together and Lucas was asleep, we argued about my quitting the casino, her expressing worries, me insisting I was losing my self-respect. I too needed a vacation. Hawaii, Siberia, Mars, it didn't matter.

Leona, who'd been dealing to a super tipper, left her seat in the corner and stood at the far end of the table. She said, "I've got this George, tips every fifth or sixth hand. Down to his last six hundred, he puts me up for a hundred, catches a cold twenty, and don't you know, I hit six cards to a twenty-one. What a bitch!"

Iris said, "My George went bust too. Won four hands in an entire shoe. Four grand gone."

"Hell, Iris," Rick said, "should'a sent him to my game. I gave enough away to support a few foreign dictators. And no one, not one of 'em on my game, put us up for a buck."

"Renzloe doesn't care for male dealers," Iris said. "He only plays with a woman."

"That can be taken two ways. Women dealers! Iris, they only hire women 'cause you'll never unionize," Rick said.

"Oh, here we go," Iris said and gave him a deadly look.

Oddly enough, the labor of dealing cards or turning dice seemed both to numb and arouse them. Bitching about the job, which often included a compendium of imagined dooms from being fired to the casino shutting its doors, served them as a kind of group therapy—that along with chain-smoking, drinking coffee, and talking of forming a union.

Iris took a long draw and blew smoke at the ceiling. "Yesterday, Ricky, you said they hired us because the bosses wanted to fuck us."

He yawned, then said, "No, it's not what I said. I said they hire the *pretty* ones, hoping to fuck them."

Edna discharged a lung full of smoke and said, "Ricky, you're a pig."

"Name's Rick, and oink, oink," he said, aiming the tip of his cigarette in my direction. "Jude, you think we need a union? I mean, look at the change management wants. Is them tellin' us to split tokes shift for shift fair? It's our money, ain't it?"

I knew better than to look up, but I did.

Ever since the night I pitched my first card on a blackjack game, I'd heard arguments for unionizing. I could reel off the reasons by rote—low wages, tips declining, management stinks, no job security. Voting in a union, some believed, would fix everything. It was their version of praying to the saints.

Shift after shift, my fellow dealers calculated their misfortunes, never factoring any blessings into the equation. None ever seemed to consider walking away from the business as an option. It boiled down to the three-by-five-inch envelope stuffed with cash ranging from fifty to two hundred dollars they opened at the start of every working day, a good buck or two for someone who wasn't even required to earn a high school diploma to hold the job. Me, I had plans to get out.

To pacify Rick, I said, "Why not?" I hoped that would satisfy all of them because I didn't want to be further drawn into the discussion.

"See," Rick said. "Even Jude agrees. Splitting tokes around the clock is bullshit. Look at the few scores we make. They makes up for the days zooks are lame and the shitty graveyard hours. We split what?—twenty to twenty-five ways? Day shift splits over fifty, work gravy hours and . . . Why don't we petition the Dwarf? You for that?"

That was the worst idea passed around so far. Denny Ellis, the Dwarf, the man who hired and fired dealers, ran the blackjack pits. He hated tall men, which meant every man compared to him. I back-doored my way in, all six-foot-two of me, because some crusty bosses in the joint knew my father from the old days. As the story went, Bernie the casino manager had hired Ellis in that position to give the dealers a boss to look down on, as if we didn't look down on most of them anyhow.

"I'll write up a petition and we'll all sign," Rick said. "Whatta you say to that?"

A few nodded, perhaps in agreement. More likely just to silence Rick. Petitioning for or organizing a union was the least of my concerns. Mine transcended all the crap at work. Postpartum blues, the doctor called it. To me, it seemed Anne's mood after giving birth was no different from what I'd evidenced ever since she told me she was pregnant and wouldn't consider an abortion. Two days later we married. Since then she'd parked herself in the house, eleven months now, alternately lost in the flickering images on the television screen or absorbed to the point of obsession with Lucas. I wanted something more normal in a family life and hoped, without great expectation, that a patio might pull her out of her funk and into the sunlight. Yesterday, I'd set forms and rented a cement mixer. Today, I intended to make the pour and trowel the surface. Weathermen predicted a high of sixty-five degrees, ideal for pouring and finishing cement.

Rick was still soliciting support for a petition as I stood. I stretched, then crossed the room to the door, where I paused. "If you think signing a petition or organizing a union'll do anything other than get us fired," I said, "you're nuts. If the Dwarf'll fire a dealer for being six foot three or for bitching about overtime, you can bet he'll fire twenty who signed a petition. A hundred like us are waiting for our jobs. And he knows it."

"That's the whole point. We need a union," Rick said.

"I hate to admit it, but I agree with Ricky," Edna said. "But he's still a pig."

"Don't call me Ricky."

I shrugged and stepped into the hall. Calculating the time it would take to mix, pour, and finish the patio without help, I headed for the casino toward the daily grind, four more hours of it. I was resigned to it for now.

As I walked the hall to the casino, I dreamed of my two-year plan, a masonry business. Until I could save enough to start it up, pumping cards provided stability for the homestead. In the interim, I'd somehow block out the slot machine buzzers and bells, players' insults, and the heat of a boss's breath as he stood a step away, sweating the outcome of a hand. Despite Anne's concerns about us losing health insurance and a predictable daily income, I had to try making it on my own before I sank into the abyss that consumed too many dealers. I needed to see something to completion, even if it was just laying a level course of cinder block for a wall. Naturally, it was a difficult idea for a wife to grasp when her concerns were sleep, doctor appointments, and dirty diapers.

And I had another concern. Early death ran in my family. I worried that I might go out like my father, who at fifty-one, while supervising blackjack games at the Sahara, collapsed on the carpet after suffering a coronary attack. For three crucial minutes he lay unnoticed. At twelve I was left fatherless. I didn't want that for my son, who was much of the reason for my getting out of bed at 1:15 a.m. on that November 21, 1980, and driving to the MGM. The date marked the third year to the day of my working in casinos. Now hours into the shift, as I neared the door the leading to the casino, I got a whiff of something smoldering. I paused and looked about, but I saw nothing.

I stopped at the security desk on my way to the pit. "I smell smoke back there." I pointed beyond the casino cage.

The bored guard looked down from his podium. "You sure?" he asked, his expression apathy and skepticism in equal proportions.

I said, "Pretty sure."

He scanned the casino and sniffed the air. "Don't smell nothing. You see any smoke?"

I shook my head.

"A porter probably emptied an ashtray in a wastebasket. Happens," he said and added that a small fire would set off the alarm. "Got the best system in town. I'll check it out, though."

I shrugged and left the matter at that. The guard was probably right. After all, the MGM had state-of-the-art everything. I'd seen it all on my hire date—palatial penthouses with Jacuzzis, French-mirrored ceilings, Grecian-marble floors, and Italian-tile bathrooms. The chic brass-and-crystal casino was the world's largest. Its several restaurants served food in near-limitless variety. One showroom headlined celebrity entertainers, a second a Hollywood-theme extravaganza with a faux yellow brick carpet leading to it. A shopping arcade on the lower level featured a theater and women in skimpy uniforms serving cocktails during the movie.

A number of late stayers and early risers were eating breakfast in the coffee shop. In the casino, business was slow, a scattering at the blackjack tables, a few cranking handles down on the slots, four diehards hanging over the rail of a crap table. As we lined up to enter the pit, Iris and Rick complained to the boss of smelling smoke. When my turn came, I mentioned the smell.

Deadpan, Artie gazed up and said, "Jude, I've got important stuff to do. Table 8."

"These new high heels," Edna said, "are killing me. I smelled it too."

"You're here to pump cards." Artie waved her off and said, "Table 14."

I went to table 8 and greeted the lone player, a man in his midthirties. He wore a cream-colored Armani suit and a black silk shirt unbuttoned to midchest. Stacks of hundred-dollar chips occupied the layout in front of him, about twenty thousand and ten more in a rack. I scooped up the deck and started to shuffle.

My floorman stepped up and said, "Hold it." Randy spread a fresh deck faceup over the felt in front of me. Turning away from the player, he whispered, "Get some hands out."

"Third deck they've changed," the player said. "Done 'em no good. I got 'em on the run."

Procedure and rules dictated my working life. Never vary; never gaze around the casino. Someone was filming every move. I nodded to the player, shuffled, and began dealing.

Ten minutes into my rotation, I was paying a bet when a cocktail waitress in the keno lounge shouted something. Her voice was all but drowned out by the rattling of dollar tokens and the ringing of slot machines. Then she screamed so loud the slot players stopped pulling handles. I looked up. A tuft of smoke spewed from the archway leading to Restaurant Alley and slithered snakelike across the ceiling. Players who wouldn't leave in the middle of a board if a pride of lions were let loose on them abandoned their keno chairs and dashed for the doors. Behind them the smoke darkened and blotted out the ceiling.

Unable to raise sound from my throat, I pointed toward the smoke.

The player on my table glanced over his shoulder and said, "Holy shit."

I found my voice and said, "Randy, fire in the keno lounge!"

Randy turned toward the smoke. The alarm sounded. Finally, I thought, *finally.*

"Fuck this," the player said and began stuffing chips in his pockets.

Randy leaned over the table. "Security will take care of it, sir. No need to panic."

The player palmed some more chips. "What will they do, toss a glass of water on it?" He glanced at me. "Man, if I was you, I'd get the hell out of here." Then he was gone, dashing toward the front exit, in his panic leaving a couple thousand in chips behind.

Randy, a slave to rules and procedure, failed to see any urgency. He told us to bring up the lids to our racks just as if closing a game on an ordinary day, then sit and count down the decks. Even as the wall leading to the restaurant burst into flame, he scratched down figures on a closure slip on the table behind me.

Harry, sitting at the table beside me, shouted what the rest of us were thinking, but didn't dare say, "You're an idiot, Randy!" He jumped to his feet and took off for the door.

"You'll be fired!" Randy shouted.

But Harry, who'd joined the stampede of players, was far beyond fearing threats. A few gamblers scurried toward the casino cage to cash in. Halfway, they ditched the idea and retreated. All of restaurant row was engulfed in smoke, and flames shot through the catwalk near the back end of the casino. The heat seemed to suck air out of the pit. A crap crew abandoned their table and ran, two bosses and a security guard following on their heels. I looked at the flames, then the doors, and back again where fire was swallowing slot machines and stools as it advanced toward the pit. Raining hot embers, portions of the false ceiling in the south pit crumbled. Crystal chandeliers, each costing more than six years of my income, slammed to the floor and shattered. The carpet flared up, and the fire began eating its way across the casino floor.

My voice cracked as I shouted at Randy, "Let's go. This is nuts."

I glanced at the rack of chips and the blank closure slip awaiting my signature. The predatory wall of flame, now seventy feet away, let loose an animal-like hiss. Buddy and Dan simultaneously broke into a run toward the front exit. Randy hollered, "Come back!" But like Harry, they would have no part of it. Still, I didn't budge.

Then I glanced at Edna, her face deathly pale, her lips quivering. For a fraction of a second we held each other's look. In that instant, the absurdity of everything struck me. She was terrified, but needed the job, and like me was as scared of being fired as she was of the fire itself. I looked at the fortune in chips in the rack, shoved my blackjack table over, and shouted for Edna to get moving. Then I reached down and grabbed the faux-leather table cover from the floor. I wheeled about, in the process slamming into Randy. The impact knocked both of us to the floor. As she leaped from her stool, Edna drove a spike heel into my hand and stumbled. She regained her balance, removed her heels, and ran.

A panel in the ceiling gave way. A flame shot out. I was cut off from the front entrance. I wrapped the table cover over my shoulders and, elbow to knee, began to crawl. I slithered blindly from table to table, knocking over stools in my path. A chandelier smashed to the floor as I neared the back end of the pit. I turned toward the aisle, glanced back, and saw Randy turning about in circles like a cartoon figure. He vanished for an instant in a wedge of flame that shot down from the ceiling, then lurched forward, tumbled over a stool, and collapsed. The air stank of burning nylon and charred wood. I dug my elbows and knees into the carpet.

I moved because motion was all that was left for me. Cinders spattered onto the carpet, some singeing my trouser legs. Progress was arduous and painful, elbow to knee, repeated over and over, lungs aching, blood pounding at my temples, throat burning. I thought of Anne alone at home watching television and seeing the casino burning, then of my boy being raised without a memory of me, and I trudged on, knowing that if I hesitated, the fire surely wouldn't. Gradually, as the instinct for survival took final hold of me, I came not to feel the pain.

Somehow I managed reaching the pit nearest the north exit. I knocked over two chairs and kicked each aside, then squirmed around them to the next table, then the next. Table to table, I advanced toward the north exit. Somewhere nearby a woman screamed for help. Her plea rose above the roar of the fire, then fell off, like the tables and chairs and carpet, consumed by flame. Even if I knew where she was, I couldn't help her, couldn't do anything for anyone, except what little I *could* do for myself. That was to continue crawling toward the exit.

I banged into a table stand, then a chair, and was blocked from advancing by what I quickly realized was a body. I maneuvered around it, assuring myself as I crawled by the corpse that if I kept my thoughts racing faster than the fire, I would live. I thought of Lucas, how I'd been warned of crib deaths, and on that first night from the hospital, I'd guarded over him until near dawn. I recalled the syrupy smell of breast milk when Anne handed him to me to burp. I thought of the car needing an oil change and my mother as she was before she'd left my father, young and pretty, then as she'd appeared when nearing death, her eyes vacant, her skin mottled and thin as wrapping paper. By fluke or internal compass, I managed to reach the aisle leading to the escalator and the lower rotunda. By then all but a small portion of the casino ceiling was burning. Above me I could feel the heat as ribbons of fire shot down like streamers strung up at a demon's prom.

I navigated in the dark by following a thin stream of what air blew up from the passage leading to the lower floor. Every few feet I stretched forward and reached out with my fingers, until finally the tips contacted the top apron of the escalator. It was as hot as a kiln. Passage down that route was impossible. A staircase was a few feet to the north. Provided the carpet wasn't yet on fire, I could use it. I rolled over and over in that direction until I reached the top side of the staircase. Flames were crawling down the wall nearby, but the carpet on the stairs was untouched.

Behind me the fire growled as it sucked in oxygen and consumed what still remained of the millions upon millions of dollars' worth of tables, slot machines, and luxurious extravagances. A string of flame raced across the carpet, and I felt its scorching heat on my ankle. I shed the table cover, turned sideways, wrapped my arms around my knees, and launched myself into the passageway. Bouncing from wall to stair to stair to wall, I rolled down, ricocheting off the walls like an underinflated ball until I came to a stop in the corner on the first landing. I sat on my haunches and slapped out a flame that was eating away my trouser cuff, then I stood and scrabbled down to the lower floor.

I opened my eyes. Though they stung from the noxious air and everything was hazed in smoke, it felt good to able to see again. That and the fact that I made it this far encouraged me. The vein at my temples throbbed. I examined my hands, the backs blackened and raw. Momentarily, I stared at them and wiggled my fingers as if that somehow confirmed my survival. I tried to take in a deep breath, but choked on the foul air. I glanced back. Beneath a billow of smoke, runnels of flame spread down the walls of the staircase and withdrew. The air burned my lungs. If I remained much longer, breathing the fumes would likely kill me before the fire did.

Light filtered into the rotunda from the glass doors where the north entrance was located. The exit lay no more than a hundred feet away. I cupped a hand over my nose, crouched, and headed toward the light. I was halfway to my goal when a man popped out from the doorway of the art gallery and pressed a painting against my chest. It was four feet wide and as tall as I was. Inexplicably, I opened my arms and received it as if it were the natural thing to do.

"Take it outside," he said, then he turned and charged back into the art gallery.

Painting in hand, I headed for the exit. It wasn't heavy, but it was awkward and caused me to walk sideways to see the path ahead. At one point I stumbled over a fallen stanchion and nearly fell. I thought to heave the painting away and even started to, but couldn't. Somehow it and the man who'd rushed back into the gallery had taken on an incomprehensible significance.

The sound of human voices ahead reinvigorated me. I picked up the pace. A few steps later I came upon a small anxious mob standing inside the double glass doors, which were sealed shut. I fell in at the rear of the group. One of the men ahead picked up a stanchion, intent on using it to break the glass. A man nearby cautioned him not to. On the other side of the exit the motor of a fire engine grumbled. Second by second smoke was thickening on the ceiling above us. We could hear the flames cracking as they advanced down the hallway toward us.

A man nearby shouted to the one with the stanchion, "Break the glass!"

Outside, firemen spilled off the truck's running boards. They wore gas masks and air tanks, heavy coats and boots and helmets and shiny yellow or black coats. One smashed the outer glass door with an ax, stepped in, signaled for the gathering to step back, then using the spiked end of his ax shattered the inner door with one blow. He lifted his mask and shouted for everyone to leave at once, that the air would draw flames.

A wall of fresh air rushed in as those closest the exit scrambled out.

Others followed on their heels. I stepped aside, making a path for the oncoming firemen. An instant later I was outside breathing a banquet of sweet air. For the first time since sighting smoke, I was aware of my heart thudding violently inside my chest. I stood motionless, waiting for it to slow, then I descended the concrete steps and skirted the fire engine to the sidewalk. I propped the painting against the retaining wall, slumped down beside it, and stared up numbly for a time at the clear sky to the north above the Maxim.

Sirens blared from every direction. Fire engines and police cars blocked the street from the Strip to the Maxim Hotel. Blue and red lights flashed. Across Flamingo Road a swell of people had gathered on the sidewalk. They stood gawking at the tendrils of dark smoke streaming out of the windows. Gradually, I became aware of all of this and of my needs. Water and a phone, I thought, those first. I had to get to a phone and assure Anne.

"Are you okay?" a paramedic asked.

I looked up blankly. The man repeated the question. I nodded.

"You look rough. There's an aid station." He pointed toward the Strip.

I nodded and when he walked away looked at the painting. It was a surrealistic oil of Prometheus, his neck and limbs chained to the parched earth. Its price written in black marker was on a tag affixed to the frame—an eight followed by four zeros. I propped the painting against the marble retaining wall and left it, then headed toward the back lot where I'd parked a few hours before when nothing of this magnitude seemed remotely possible. Along the sidewalk I passed dozens of people in all manner of uniforms as they scurried up and down doing the portentous work of men in uniform, laying hose, wheeling stretchers, shouting instructions. They moved with urgency, all of them overwhelmed. What they did was all about doing *anything* at all, because what needed to be done was really beyond them. I saw it in their eyes.

I walked rigidly. My neck seemed welded stiff. If I had to, I turned my entire body to see objects of any kind. Here and there, I stepped aside to clear a path for a cop or fireman or paramedic. One officer called to me, pointed in a general direction toward the front of the hotel, and said that employees were gathering for a head count. As soon as he passed by, I continued on. I wanted nothing but water and to find a phone, then start my car and hurry home.

I stood below the eastern wall of the hotel, the parking lot empty save for firefighters going about their business. The glare from the windows reflecting the morning sun was blinding. I craned my neck and looked toward the roof. Acres of dense smoke formed a canopy over the hotel and blotted out the sky. Black plumes spilled out of windows as if the hotel were bleeding india ink. Those trapped above shouted from windows for help, the panic in their screaming voices muted by the roaring fire and the chattering blades of two helicopters hovering just outside an umbrella of smoke.

I blinked, and in that instant, a man plummeted down the wall from a top floor. He careened off a ledge and tumbled downward to the convention-room roof on the second floor. Then, almost immediately, a second jumper followed, screaming as he descended. My insides went hollow. I looked away from the sun's blinding reflection in the windows and noted what a beautiful day it was, that it was almost cloudless and the air was cool.

That was the last thing I remembered until I found myself seated cross-legged on the carpet inside the Maxim, holding out a dollar bill as a change girl refused to give me change to make a phone call. Dumbfounded, I just stared at her.

"Casino rules," she said and walked away.

I remained seated, until a pair of shoes and trouser legs appeared. I looked up and extended the bill to a large black man in a guard's uniform. He was in his late thirties with the jowls and sad eyes of a much older man.

"You okay, man? You look a mess." He shook his head, then holding me gently by the biceps, helped me up. "Come with me," he said in a soft baritone and escorted me away.

"I need to call home. I'm fine. Really. I just . . ."

He led me across the casino floor, circling the craps pit, then up three stairs and into the men's room. I followed passively. Inside the lavatory two men washing their hands stopped and stared. The guard assured them everything was okay and pointed me to the sink. One shook his head and moved down a sink to give me room.

I turned on the faucet and looked at my reflection in the mirror. Only the stark gray eyes seemed familiar. They gazed out of their darkened caves as if repelled by the sight of me. My hair was singed, as were my eyebrows, and my skin from neck to hairline was the dull shade of a burlesque minstrel painted in blackface.

The guard handed me a fistful of paper towels and turned on the faucet. "I'll wait outside," he said.

I rinsed soot from my face and hands. My shirt was ruined, sleeves shredded at the elbow, studs gone, the front bloodstained. I ripped the sleeves off.

My arms were chaffed and bleeding. Wincing, I slowly washed the bleeding scrapes, then cupped some cold water in my hands and drank until water burst out of my nostrils and splashed into the sink along with a stream of blackened mucus.

The guard was waiting outside by the door. He guided me to the security office, where he pointed to a table and told me to sit. "First we put some stuff on them wounds," he said and lifted a first-aid kit from a cabinet shelf. He placed a topical on the abrasions and bandaged my arms one at a time. I clenched my teeth and let him do his business. He was gentle. If I winced, he stopped wrapping and told me to tell him if it was causing me pain. I saw no point in that. Finished, he looked his work over and asked if the gauze was too tight. He held up a pair of scissors and said, "Let's look at that," then he kneeled down and went to work on the trouser cuff, cutting through the cloth slowly and carefully.

I watched as he trimmed away the last of the shredded cuff. The skin all around my ankle was blackened and blistering and here and there ulcerating. Up to the moment it hadn't hurt, but the numbness quickly vanished, and I was aware of pain in most every part of my body. In an odd way I found it, too, assuring.

"Looks like a bad second-degree. Nothin' I can do with that. You need a doctor." He pointed to a phone on the desk and told me to dial 9 for an outside line. "Take your time."

Anne would be worried, I thought. No, in her current state not worried, panicked. I couldn't remember my home phone number. It got scrambled somewhere in my memory with my Social Security number and the work phone and my work card number and all the other numbers that go to form our social identities. The guard was calm and seemed ready to wait out eternity with me, and that too assured me. When at last I remembered, I dialed and waited through six rings until she picked up the receiver.

"Hello." She sounded angry, and I realized I'd awakened her.

"It's me."

"Jesus. I'm sleepy. The baby cried most of the night. I finally got him to sleep. Call later."

"There was a fire at work," I said.

"Baby, I'd love to hear about it, but later. I'm exhausted. I'm going back to sleep before Lucas starts again. Tell me about it when you come home, okay?" she said and hung up.

I cradled the receiver in my hand and looked at the guard. I sat for a moment with nothing to say that would fill the space that the dead line had created. Then as if involuntarily the words rose up in me. "I saw people leap to their death," I said. "Saw a boss burn up."

I'd obviously said more than my rescuer wanted to hear. He cupped his chin in his hand and looked at the floor in a manner similar to the way my father had when he pretended to listen to my mother. I gently replaced the receiver and rested my head on the desktop. Though I felt as if I could easily go to sleep and never wake up, I knew I had overstayed my welcome and it was time to leave. I lifted my head and looked at the guard, who nodded. I stood.

"Where you going, man? You need attention."

I moved in the direction of the door, then realizing I owed him more than just gratitude, I paused and offered a feeble, "Thank you."

The car wasn't mine, but the door was unlocked, so it was convenient. I needed it only for a short while. I sat on the driver's seat, my legs extended outside, feet planted on the pavement. I rubbed my hands up and down my thighs, kneading them as best I could to relax. I breathed the chemical air as my pulse throbbed in my temples. In time the morning swelled up inside me. I leaned forward and placed my head in my palms. How long I tried to purge the day with tears, I have no idea, but long enough to close my mind to the idea.

When I realized no tears would come, I climbed out of the car and walked slowly and unsurely as a blind man might in the direction of the still burning MGM. Although I couldn't articulate it then, I realized at that moment that ultimately life came down to the feel of fresh air entering the lungs and that the world I was reentering was populated with people who sought salvation in the next sealed sweepstakes flyer, and it had been so for a long while. Before today I had been just too involved with thinking I was living to be aware of it.

2 Resigned thereafter just to survive day to day, I'd walked out of an inferno that took eighty-five lives. For more than two decades I never spoke of the fire or what I saw inside or outside the casino, or of the terror that had gripped me. I avoided anything contentious. I punched a time clock, paid taxes and child support, and mowed my lawn. In the narrow world I occupied, I was Jude the Dealer, which in its essence was the same as being Jude the Banal or Jude the Invisible. I accepted this as my

lot in life, but all the while, without it surfacing, a mutinous passion to be Jude the Worthy simmered in me.

As I had before the fire, I earned a living performing the ten-fingered fandango in eight-hour increments on green felt, constantly in motion, eyes squinting under harsh, shadowless light, a cloud of cigarette smoke drifting around my face, an incessant clamor in the background. The ceaseless stimulus that flooded the casino floor and erased any sense of time dulled my mind to all but getting out the next hand. Shifts piled up like iron plates slapped on a barbell until the load was nearly too heavy to lift. But I accepted the work as my lot in life. Bent over the layout, I kept the cards moving and never complained.

Bosses called me a real clerk, meaning I was accurate and fast and followed procedure to a finite degree. I could grip six decks between my thumb and fingers, shuffle as efficiently as any machine, turn cards, total spots on six cards by sight alone, and pick and pay a table of bets smoothly without pause, no thought to any of it—every motion as effortless as breathing. If I didn't consider the stiff back and sore feet I left work with at the end of each shift. Year to year I made, on average for the house, a profit of about 60 percent of all the money that crossed my table. For my efforts I earned a tad more than minimum wage, and each working day an envelope containing tips in varying amounts awaited me at the casino cage.

That was me, the fixed course of my life, until a hot day in May 2003.

LAS VEGAS was still feeling some aftereffects of the 9/11 disaster, and the coming summer seemed bound to be a demon. Already business was more sluggish than the grim early '80s. June would start a season defined by bus-tour gamblers, coupon-waving tourists, and one-change-of-shirt conventioneers. In anticipation of a slowdown, a few joints had already fired workers. Layoff rumors ran rampant in the break room at the Monaco. Dealers grumbled about shrinking earnings and watched events unfold with a sense of surrender not unlike the condemned waiting for a cell-block door to open. It was a bad time to be on the bosses' watch list or late for work. And I was running late.

Flamingo Road was backed up with cars to the freeway. Any piecemeal progress of cars was measured by rising blood pressure. Even with air-conditioning blowing on high inside my Mustang, the car's temperature hovered around eighty. There was a time I spent summers in the sun. Now

I went from air-conditioned home to air-conditioned car to air-conditioned casino. As the thermometer measuring the outside heat bubbled toward a hundred, I wondered if Bugsy, the visionary who saw the Strip as a gambler's mecca, had his brainstorm in the winter. When he broke ground for the Flamingo, did he have an inkling how torrid Mojave summers could be? Did he consider how heat affected temperaments? Did he think he'd get shot for all his efforts? I figured the answers as no on all counts.

A pony-tailed blonde behind the wheel of a Chrysler in front of me applied brushstrokes to her eyelashes. To my left a man in a massive black four-door Dodge pickup swept his free hand dramatically as he gabbed over a cellular. Behind me a soccer-mom type in a black Mercedes SUV squeezed closer to my bumper as if in doing so she might make the lane of cars move. I sipped coffee and waited on the light to change.

Across the Strip sat Bally's, which before the fire had been the MGM and across from it the old Maxim, now remodeled as the Weston. The sight of Bally's invariably stirred up in me memories of that November day and the fire, but whenever I saw the casino that was once the Maxim, I recalled Christmas 1984, which for me was much like an Orwellian 1984, where Big Brother watched and waited for any act of nonconformity. Twenty-six of us in all had been fired without cause, our offense being that we were entitled to a three-week vacation and earned two dollars above minimum wage. So, the week before the holiday I arrived home with a termination slip in hand and announced that Christmas that year would be compliments of unemployment insurance. Though I was innocent, Anne, who chose to believe I had committed some infraction of the rules, never forgave me that.

Our marriage, the result of us getting high on some hash Anne had scored and both of us being too caught up in the moment to use protection against pregnancy, had a shaky beginning. She'd had a prior abortion and was determined to have the baby. For Lucas's sake we married, and for him and the subsequent birth of our daughter, Beth, we'd tried to make the marriage work. That layoff set the stage for the ensuing chain of arguments that doomed the marriage.

On the Bellagio side of the road two bikini-clad women, both tall and in their twenties, strolled the sidewalk on platform sandals en route to the walkover. As the women passed by, men craned their necks and looked back. The women, a pleasant diversion from what was otherwise traffic hell, chatted with one another, seemingly indifferent to the legion of stares they drew.

The light changed and traffic edged slowly forward. The taillights of the car in front of me lit up like a storefront. I brought the car to a stop and tapped the steering wheel with my fingers.

A voice blared over the radio. "Traffic Man here to save you a doctor's visit for high blood pressure! Avoid Charleston and the Strip, where a fender bender's clogging things up. Casino workers use D. I. Arterial or, as an alternative, get a tank. Traffic's backed up at I-15 exits to the Strip, especially Flamingo. That's it from your traffic reporter high above the Vegas skyline. Now a word from your favorite Ford dealer."

"Right," I said and switched off the radio.

The signal turned. I set my coffee in the dash holder and eased off the brake. The line of cars gradually gained momentum, and for an instant it appeared I might make the light. Then the woman ahead of me stabbed her brake pedal and screeched to a stop. Tires smoking, the SUV behind me came to a cockeyed stop just short of my bumper. My coffee spilled on the dash. Horns blared. A few drivers rolled down their windows and stuck their heads out. Her face bunched in an angry blister, the woman in the SUV behind me ranted. At me! I tilted the mirror so I didn't have to look at her.

Ahead a taxi driver, indifferent to the chaos he'd stirred, blocked off two lanes. Stuck again in this micro hell, I looked for the bikini-clad women, but they'd been swallowed by the throng of pedestrians riding the escalator up to the crossovers. Left to stare now at Bally's, I wiped a bead of sweat from my nose and thought, as I often did, of the two people I'd watched plummet to their deaths. What had they done that night? Had I dealt to either of them?

I PAUSED AT THE MIRROR in the hallway, strapped on my apron, and saw that I was developing a noticeable paunch. As a boy I'd been thin and ungainly, my ears too obtrusive, my legs too long, and my feet too large. I was no longer ungainly, hadn't been since putting on weight in my mid-twenties. I'd grown into myself, so to speak, but was still self-conscious about my feet. My ears troubled only my daughter, who was quick to say it was time to trim the wiry hairs that sprouted in them.

Either late or on the verge of it, I buttoned my collar, snapped the bow tie, and jogged down the hallway. On any given day three or four dealers strolled out late, the same few. Not today, not the day I was running behind. It occurred just then that I'd forgotten Lucas's present. My son, a college grad, receiving a diploma that night, and I'd forgotten the watch. Anne would insist my subconscious was acting on behalf of my conscious. I was subverting myself, again.

Self-subversion had become my ex-wife's mantra, one she'd adopted after attending a self-help seminar where people hugged one another and cried as they vowed to seek a life of self-empowerment. Self-subversion was her explanation for any whimsical package dropped in the mailbox of life. When she filed for divorce, I asked who was subverting whom.

I sprinted down the remainder of the hallway to the casino. If for no other reason than to prove I wasn't subverting myself, I slowed to open the swinging door and entered a wall of noise. Hurrying through stands of plastic palm trees and rows of blinking poker machines circled by glazed-eyed players, I nearly bumped into a woman in her sixties. She held up a twenty-dollar bill and asked for change.

I shook my head. "Ma'am. You want someone from the slot department. I'm a dealer."

"That's nothing to be proud of, young man."

"Right." I stepped out of her path and kept going.

I fell in behind Gus and Sandy at the rear of the line. The line moved methodically as dealers took assignments from Wrinkles, who was never in a hurry. He had that jaundiced look not uncommon to a longtime boss and seemed to have an aversion to moving. When watching a game, he appeared cemented in place. Gus glanced back and sighed.

"Just another day in paradise," he said.

"Paradise?"

"Is true, Jude. At sixteen I leave Cuba, the clothes on my back. Now I deal to five-hundred and thousand-dollar chips. I kiss the bosses' asses so my wife can kiss the feet of saints. I say, this gotta be paradise or hell. What'chu think?"

"Is paradise where God and Satan get together to fry up souls?"

Sandy glanced back and said something to me. I pointed to my ear to indicate I didn't hear. She repeated herself, but I still couldn't hear.

"She said your ex called," Gus said.

Gus and I had worked together for years, ate at the same table, played cards on breaks. I knew the story of his arrival on a boat that sank near Florida. He'd known but five words of English. Hungry and thirsty, he'd wandered a beach trying to surrender himself to anyone, but because he spoke no English, people merely turned him away. In desperation to be noticed, he'd kicked sand on a cop's shoes. I knew his favorite baseball team and his strategy in a game of pitch. It occurred to me I didn't know the name of his wife or kids, nothing of a personal nature.

I tapped his shoulder. "What's your wife's name?"

Gus's bushy eyebrows rose. "Why?"

"You always call her 'my wife.'"

"Tha's right, Jude. I do. She *is* my wife."

It was Sandy's turn at the podium. Wrinkles pointed to the high-limit pit where a table was reserved for Linus Berman. He'd been in the hotel for days, but hadn't yet sidled up to the game. Dealers were hopeful Mr. B, as he was known, would make a laydown soon. He wasn't a mere high roller. He was a whale, entitled to the Monaco's four-thousand-square-foot Platinum Suite, and a super George who tossed his winnings around when he caught a run.

In February we'd raked in $260 apiece from him on a Friday, that followed by $615 on Saturday, a record for tips. That particular evening I'd stood idle on a game and watched as Sandy dealt Mr. B only one losing hand through an entire shoe, the longest streak I'd ever witnessed and the biggest win I'd ever heard of in a single sitting—nearly a million and a half. Though she'd had no control over the outcome, we'd praised her for dealing him a run. She'd credited it to Gus, said he'd shuffled the shoe while she was on break. Berman's run came the week before shuffling machines were installed. It was also the last night I'd been assigned a table in the high-roller pit. Soon after, I had the feeling that I was under constant surveillance. I chalked it up to being paranoid, a normal state of mind for me ever since the fire at the MGM and my being fired from the Maxim. How could I be anything but paranoid? In a casino, someone is always watching.

"Go, make us some money, *Bonita*," Gus said to her.

Make us a thousand, I thought. I could use a grand—hell, even a couple of C-notes. But at the moment, I would gladly have given a C-note away to get to a toilet.

Wrinkles coughed. "If you two're through chitchattin', Gus, take a break, and when you come back, go to wheel 1."

Gus nodded and strolled off toward the hall to the break room.

"Jude, you're last. Never saw that before."

"I'm a man of surprises."

"No, you're not. Did you forget where you worked?"

"No, I forgot my boy's present. He's graduating tonight," I said. "The university."

"Really? Hell, I didn't know you had a son."

"You never asked." I squirmed. "Jesus, I gotta pee, Gus."

He stared at me a couple of seconds, having his fun. "If there's one thing I can't stand, it's the smell of piss in the pit. Go."

As I neared the staircase, I had a passing thought that I was being watched. I looked at the mezzanine rail, but saw no one. I shrugged it off. Finding a urinal was far too important.

I ducked into the casino restroom, a violation of house rules. At the moment I didn't care. A prolonged sniffing sound surged from behind the closed door of a stall. I'd worked in joints long enough to know the sound had nothing to do with allergies. I was washing my hands when the stall door flew open, and Buddy, a bartender at the service bar, sauntered out, adjusting his black vest. I glanced up as he passed by.

I said, "Hey, Buddy. You might want to wipe your nose."

He stopped at the next mirror, tilted his head back to examine his nostrils, then turned on the faucet and flushed his nose. He dried his hands and said, "Thanks, Jude. Have a nice day."

I hurried to a pay phone outside the break room and called Anne.

As I waited for the phone to ring through, I thought about the Afghan hound. Over coffee at breakfast, I'd decided to put a stop to matters. I endured enough rudeness when manning a blackjack table. I didn't have to suffer it elsewhere. I made it a habit to respect other people's property and did my best not to inconvenience others or infringe on their rights. I was rarely rude. And I *never* crapped on anyone's lawn.

Anne answered. I asked what she wanted.

"Just want you to remember Lucas's graduation."

"I remember."

"I'm just making sure."

It was at times hard to imagine that I'd stayed married to her for eight years and that we'd had a son and then a daughter together. Beth, just as Lucas had, came unexpectedly. "Anne, why do you talk to me like I'm a kid?"

"You do forget your daughter's child support."

"I've been late twice in seven years. And right now I'm ahead by three weeks. That hardly constitutes forgetting."

"You're not ahead. Anyhow, you can sit with us. We'll save a seat."

"I am ahead, Anne, and I don't think I'll be there in time to find you. I got to work too late, and I'm stuck up to the last minute. I'll be lucky to get there on time."

"There you go subverting yourself."

The weight of the day—the owner of the Afghan, the woman cussing me out for stopping, the idiots who didn't know how to drive, the spiraling cost of gasoline and coffee to go, Anne's petty sins and gross omissions, and the clusters of similar nightmares that kept me pacing the floor—pressed against my forehead. My temples throbbed.

"I'll be there. 'Bye." I hung up and went into the break room for a quick drink of water.

As I hurried back to the pit, I mapped out a strategy, understanding that if I arrived at the Thomas and Mack later than seven thirty, I'd have to fight a thousand cars for one space. My plan was uncomplicated. Run to my car, rip rubber out of the parking lot, and if need be blow every red light to make Lucas's graduation ceremony, park a half mile away in the shopping center on Maryland Parkway, and run to the arena. That might change if I found a sympathetic dealer who'd trade breaks, or if business was so slow the pit boss would ask me to clock out early. I couldn't count on either, but I hoped there might be a chance, a slim one, some dealer would trade breaks and give me an early out. Then I reminded myself that I worked in a casino, and dealers hold on to the last break like death-row inmates clinging onto a last appeal. Stick to plan A, I thought. Drive like an ambulance driver on crystal meth, park in a shopping center on Maryland Parkway, run a half mile to the arena, and see my son cross the stage.

Entering the casino, I suddenly did what I sometimes couldn't help doing—imagined the smell of smoke. It seemed always lurking in a ceiling above the hall or behind some closed door. Because of this I knew the quickest path to every exit in the hotel. As I neared the tables, a thin, swarthy man about thirty dressed in faded denims and a body-tight T-shirt backed away from a roulette game and bolted for the door. Cam Anderson, the boss in the section, shouted for security. Players craned their necks to see what the disturbance was about. The man rounded the blackjack pit and headed up the aisle toward the front of the casino. Startled customers cleared a path for him. He dodged an elderly couple and came straight at me. I stepped aside and watched him zip by. A second later he took the three marble steps at the casino entrance in one leap, shoved open the glass doors that led to the Strip, and vanished into the throng of tourists on the sidewalk.

When I entered the pit, Wrinkles, who'd nonchalantly watched the incident from the podium, grinned. "You're going to hear about that."

Several guards, keys jingling, hurried toward the exit. One, perhaps twenty-five, dashed by. The others, aging and overweight, huffed their way up the stairs and stood outside the glass door, their chests heaving as they looked up and down the sidewalk.

"They couldn't catch the clap in Tijuana if they spent a handful of C-notes," Wrinkles said.

"What table am I on?"

"Jude, you have no appreciation of this pageant."

"None whatsoever. It's a payday."

I went to my assigned table—in Anderson's section.

Anderson, petty, smug, unimaginative, ambitious, a casino version of a dungeon master, was in his midthirties. He fancied himself an intellectual in the tradition of Ayn Rand and divided his workday between preaching something he called radical libertarianism, writing up dealers for minor infractions, and groveling before the casino manager or whatever other boss happened to stroll into the pit. As did most dealers, I avoided him whenever possible. He sidled up to my table after I relieved the dealer and asked why I'd made no effort to stop the past poster. I was paid to smile mindlessly as I dealt out cards, paid winners, and raked in losers. Catching someone who laid down a bet after the roulette ball dropped wasn't listed in my job description.

I shrugged. "They pay me forty dollars a day to deal and nothing to chase people."

"You could'a tripped him."

"He falls, breaks his nose, sues, and I'm fired. No, I'm holding out for an Afghan who's been shitting on my lawn."

"Afghan? Like an Arab?"

"No. Like a hound."

"What kind of weird excuse is that?"

"Best I've got. Say, aren't you the defender of free choice?"

"What?"

"You know, deciding on your own what action to take."

"Here's your choice. You work here. Get some hands out," he said and walked away.

I exchanged the fanned-out deck with one waiting in the automatic shuffler. I felt myself as much of a machine as the shuffler. Dealers once got a break from pumping out hands when we shuffled cards. Now a machine drove me like a straw boss to keep the hands moving over the layout at a ceaseless pace. I offered the deck to the player on first base to cut.

"You think maybe I'm lucky?" the man asked.

"Can't be sure. I haven't seen your wife," I said.

"That's an old saw. How long you been dealing?"

"I dealt to the disciples at the Last Supper."

The man nodded as he placed his last two chips in the betting circle. "Me, I been losing longer than that."

TOWARD THE END OF THE WORKDAY, that period when a dealer's attention shifted from the layout to the wristwatch, a large woman wearing a Mae West outfit, including a full-brimmed hat with a feather, sat down with a single five-dollar chip. I scooped the deck off the layout and took a fresh one out of the shuffler. She placed her single chip in the center circle, then cut the deck.

She went on a twelve-hand streak and refused payment in anything but red chips. She had a sense of theatrics about her, didn't talk, didn't want me to talk, just played one to three hands at all times, asking for hits or staying with grand sweeping motions of her hand and issuing pleased sighs when she made a hand. I kept my head down and dealt. Anderson, a step away, paced and sweated like a dervish in a steam bath. As the end of the shoe neared, the woman had won all but three bets and parlayed her five-dollar chip into more than eight hundred dollars. She lost two bets before the cut card showed, shrugged, and said, "I quit. Not likely to have another streak like that one." She asked me to convert her chips to hundreds. I counted them down—$835. I gave her eight black chips, one green, and two reds. She tossed a single five on the layout.

"For you," she said. "You were good to me."

I looked at the red chip and said, "Thanks, ma'am, for your largesse."

She left in a huff.

The last minutes of the shift, I was tapped off a game early and sent to the security office where two guards and a Metro detective waited. The officer introduced himself, said he was from the Intelligence Detail, and explained that the man who'd fled had past-posted the roulette table and was part of a cheating ring. He showed several mug shots to see if I recognized any of them. I didn't, but then I hadn't paid attention to the man's face. The cop said he had some questions.

"Will this take long?"

"Depends," the detective said. "You in a hurry?"

"My kid graduates tonight."

One of the fat guards who'd earlier stood on the sidewalk looking at the crowd sat down at the desk. He said, "Don't worry. You're on the payroll. I cleared you for overtime."

I earned forty-five dollars an hour in wages. I gave him a blank look. "How can I thank you?"

By the time I completed my statement, it was eight forty-five. Commencement would be over in fifteen minutes, about the amount of time it would take me just to find an open parking spot. I drove home, undressed, and stood in the shower until the last vestiges of the casino were washed away, then I called Anne's and left a message on the machine apologizing. I knew it would do no good to explain what had happened. I only hoped Lucas would understand.

AT TEN THAT NIGHT I put on jogging shoes and selected a plastic grocery bag from a kitchen drawer. I went to the garage for a shovel, turned off the inside lights, and sat on the couch in the front room. I cracked the drapes enough to see a sliver of my yard lit by a quarter-moon. Since the fire, I largely avoided confrontation, a characteristic that during the latter stages of our marriage upset Anne, who got angry because I would quit in the middle of an argument. During a heated one, shortly after I was laid off from the Maxim, Anne called me "cravenly." I asked if she'd found the word in the dictionary.

"Yes," she'd said. "I looked it up."

"Well," I'd said, "next time look up *bitch*."

She'd said, "This bitch wants a divorce."

Despite that argument, we stuck the marriage out for several more years until after Beth had turned one. Then Anne said that she lost all hope of the marriage working and wanted out. She said that it was only fair that she keep the house because she would get the children. She got both. In the end, I got a six-year-old Dodge, child support, and liability for half the outstanding bills. Recalling that finale to the marriage primed me for what I had to do. I thought of other things she did that aggravated me, her analyzing my nightmares as if she were an authority on dreams. She claimed dreams carried a message, but my mind was too blocked to hear it. That I was too uptight, too consumed with being punctual and accurate, had too many fears. I told her nightmares result from electrical stimulation in the amygdala. It wasn't like I came home, locked the front door, and hid in a closet. So I had nightmares. So what? I had real fears too. Who doesn't?

Over the years there were vacations, starting the spring following our divorce. She went to both Hawaii and Jamaica, taking along her boyfriend. My child support payments had been absorbed into her household, so in a sense, they'd flown on tickets I'd subsidized. She went. I stayed and kept the kids for a month—and paid support. Inequity was built into the system, but court orders were just that. Orders. After her vacations when I returned the kids, I often sniped at Anne, remarking about how good she looked with her island tan or how fancy the silk shirt was that she'd bought for her latest boyfriend.

The digital clock snapped off seconds, then minutes. I waited, never wavering from my post and building up a good store of anger. In a half hour the man arrived, thin, in his late forties, stooped at the shoulders. He didn't bother to check before he walked the dog into the middle of my yard. He casually lit a cigarette and puffed it to life. The shaggy Afghan curved its back and defecated. The owner looked away and blew smoke toward the moon. The dog's business done, he pulled on the leash and trekked west, his cigarette propped in his lips.

I counted off five seconds before going outside. By then he was trudging up the sidewalk, unaware of anything but his cigarette and his dog. I scooped up the droppings with a shovel, dumped them in the plastic bag, and left the shovel propped by the garage door. I thought to use my car, but instead followed on foot about 150 feet behind. Neither the man nor the dog seemed to take notice.

At the end of the block he turned left, then right, traversing two streets before he took another right on Aberdeen. The dog stopped occasionally to sniff the air. Gradually, I gained on them. Halfway up the block, the dog walker turned at a driveway. I held back until he opened the screen and unlocked the door, then stepped up as the dog ran inside. The screen door slammed.

"Excuse me." I smiled so as not to alarm him.

"What do you want?" He stood illuminated in the bare light. He was gaunt, younger than I had thought, perhaps only forty. His eyes narrowed. "Do I know you?"

"Not exactly." I held the bag at my side and inched closer. "I live two streets over."

He noticed the bag. "What's that?"

"Something you forgot. I thought you should have it." An arm's length away now, I offered the plastic bag. At the moment, I intended only to hand it to him and leave. "For you."

Making no effort to take it, he stared at the bag. It forced me to improvise. I held the bag at chest level, turned it inside out, and dumped the ripe turds on his shoes. Behind the screen door, the Afghan whined.

He looked down. "Christ! What the hell you do that for? You're crazy," he said, his face alight with indignation and fear.

"That's the truth. Let's don't have a next time, asshole."

When I got home, I went straight to the bedroom. I fluffed my pillow, threw back the covers, and rubbed a palm across the sheet. Though many years had passed and I didn't miss Anne, I sometimes missed the warmth of her body on the sheet and the feeling of having a heart beating beside me. I slapped the pillow again. The opposite of craven, I thought. I crawled into bed.

The day had been interesting in a strange way because of the cumulation of events. I'd been late for work for the first time ever, let a thief escape, missed my son's graduation, and gave a lesson in courtesy to an ill-mannered neighbor. For a moment I lamented that it was over. Then as I turned the day's events over in my head, I caught a momentary glimpse of who I'd become, and I wondered, is this what's left for me? Is this my life? Surely not.

I turned my thoughts to the kids, coming for the weekend. Although the court-mandated visitation days for Lucas had long ago lapsed and he now shared an apartment with a friend, he came over on weekends just as he had on court-ordered visitation days. He didn't do it out of a sense of obligation, but because—though he'd be hard-pressed to admit it—Lucas loved his sister. Whenever the two of them got together, he forgot that he was a man now, a college grad, and reverted to his boyish ways, teasing her and playing dumb to get her goat.

The one consistent joy in my life was being a father. When they were young, I took delight in their excitement at the smallest of things. Now that they were older and at ease around me, they teased me as much or more than they did each other, and in ways that they never would with their mother. And I enjoyed their company more than I'd ever imagined possible. I would apologize for missing the ceremony and hand him his graduation watch. I figured he would make some joke about it and we'd laugh it off.

I stared at the shadowed ceiling and sighed. "Kids," I said, meaning so much more. Then I rode to sleep on the image of them seated in the kitchen while I cooked, the three of us laughing as I explained why I missed the graduation ceremony. I hoped the recurring nightmares of being trapped in a fire would abate for one night, but they didn't. Heart racing, I awoke around three o'clock to the smell of smoke in the air and walked the entire house until assured there was no fire. I'd forgotten completely about the woman who dressed like Mae West.

3 Patty Lane reached across a blackjack table to gather up glasses. House rules dictated that she was to serve customers from the aisle outside the pit. She, however, was above normal edicts. She waited on players from inside or outside or from wherever she pleased. Her personal life, though unknown, generated a steady flow of speculation and gossip among women who worked in the casino. Rather than spread rumors about her, men fantasized from afar and salivated over Patty Lane. She was their Vegas ideal, a long-legged, bleached-blonde package of anorexia and augmented breasts. They distinguished her from all the other Patties they had ever known by using her Christian and surname as one, said quickly and reverently, Pattylane, as if she were a street in an exclusive Boston or London neighborhood.

Patty Lane rarely fraternized with women, and, with the exception of the pit bosses with whom she freely flirted, she largely ignored men, especially any who paid her attention. Tips from her serving cocktails earned her well over a hundred grand a year, but not enough to support her lavish lifestyle. She was decidedly well kept, but no one knew her sugar daddy's name. What was known was that she drove a new black Mercedes, lived in Spanish Trail, and vacationed at least twice a year, usually in Europe, Hawaii, or the Caribbean. Once she'd visited the Great Wall, as one chagrined dealer had said, "only to be disappointed that it didn't offer four-star dining."

I kept a respectable six feet between us as I entered the pit. While others drooled at the sight of her, she made my mouth go dry ever since the year before, when in response to someone whistling at her, she'd grabbed the base of her three-and-a-half-foot braid and wheeled about from a table. I was passing behind on my way out of the pit when the whipping rope of hair neared its full momentum. The knotted tip, whizzing over her shoulder like an unmoored centrifuge, caught my eye full force. The impact sent me to the carpet. Patty Lane, unaware of what she'd done, sashayed to the next table and asked for drink orders. I wore a patch for two weeks, and for nearly a month the world in front of me appeared as distorted as a static snowstorm on a television screen. When I returned to work, after four days off without pay, she apologized and said that she didn't remember doing it, then asked how long I'd been working at the Monaco. I told her since opening day. "Really?" Sincerely baffled, she'd said, "Then why haven't I ever seen you before?"

Wrinkles leaned over the podium and jotted some figures on an evaluation slip. He dropped the slip in a slot on the side of the podium. I started to ask what he wanted.

"Hold on," he said, his attention on Patty Lane, who was nearing the podium. "She dumped her boyfriend."

"Wrinkles, don't listen to rumors."

According to the latest talk in the casino scandal mill, Patty Lane had broken up with the man who'd committed a small fortune to her plastic surgeries—some two hundred thousand. At least, that was the figure the scandalmongers tossed around. No one knew the precise amount, and Patty Lane wouldn't even admit to having had any surgery, much less to volunteering the cost.

"Wrinkles, why was I taken off my game early?"

He was too engrossed with Patty Lane to answer. I waved my hand in front of his eyes.

He blinked and said, "Ain't she *it*?"

"The product of a scalpel, Dow Chemical, and peroxide."

He looked at me with his spaniel eyes. "You have no appreciation for beauty."

Patty Lane stepped up to the podium. She had a direct, seductive way of looking at a man to hold his attention. She gazed into Wrinkles's eyes. "Coffee or water, handsome?"

For an instant it appeared he'd wilted, but he recovered and winked slyly at her. "Water."

"Wrinkles, why am I here?" I asked.

"She wants me," he whispered.

"She wants you thirty years younger with movie-star looks, a full head of hair, and a seven-figure bank account," I said. "Besides, you got a wife."

Patty scooped up two glasses from a nearby blackjack table, smiled over her shoulder, and walked off as if she'd just received an Oscar.

Wrinkles cut an eye at me. "I could get rid of the wife. That's a start."

"Wouldn't help."

"Okay, wiseass. Hefty wants to see you in the casino office."

I felt a jolt in my guts. "Why?"

Getting called up to the casino manager's office was unusual. Hefty and I had broken in at the Mint more than twenty years ago, but since he'd come to the Monaco, he offered only a nod and a cold "Hello" in passing, which suited me. In fact, I preferred it.

Wrinkles shrugged. "How should I know why? I'm just a flunky. But maybe you should'a tackled that guy yesterday."

"Is it going to take my whole break to get chewed out for not being a comic-book hero?"

"Hero?" Wrinkles said. "Track the play of thirty players and run a table schedule like I do? Now, that's a hero, if you ask me."

I looked toward the mezzanine. "It's not like you have to disarm some outraged customer who's waving a gun."

"Go on, get outta here."

No one trusted Hefty. He *was* slippery and ambitious and shrewd enough to waylay any competition in his way to advancing to the top. He'd sabotaged the former casino manager, Walt Silverman, and moved into Walt's office after Walt resigned, settling in while the desk chair was still warm. For all his ambition, what had Hefty accomplished? Mostly he'd fomented paranoia. From pit boss to porter, workers feared and resented him. Those who curried favor, such as Anderson, advanced, while those who knew the score left for other jobs or simply capitulated. Supervisors now zealously enforced petty rules that in the past had been mostly disregarded.

On the way to the mezzanine offices, I considered whether Wrinkles was right about the previous day's incident. What if the fleeing man had been an irate customer, whose offense was merely arguing with a boss? How could I know what he'd done? No matter how I spun it, I saw no obligation to get involved, nothing that merited a reprimand. But then, a safe maxim when working in a casino is hope for the worst but expect something even worse.

I should have been sitting in the break room, coffee in hand, listening to dealers bitch about yesterday's tokes, or watching a soap opera with the zombie-eyed waitresses who worked in the Rose Room. Irritated at the intrusion into my break time, I reached the mezzanine and neared the executive offices. Hefty stood in the reception area dictating a memo, his chin just above the secretary's shoulder. His flat face reminded me of a catcher's mitt. The secretary, an attractive brunette in her midtwenties, had the top two buttons of her blouse unbuttoned, and Hefty appeared more occupied with the content in her bra than the content of the letter. He glanced up, signaled for me to sit, and returned to the memo. He dictated. She pecked. I sat in the corner and thumbed through a magazine, as the clock ticked my break away.

"Don't forget to spell-check." Hefty let his hand linger a moment on her shoulder, then walked by without looking at me and pointed at his office door. "Come in."

I stood and followed.

"Shut the door."

I closed the door and took in the room—Monet reproductions on the wall and a plaque given him by the corporate CEO for good employee relations.

He said, "Sit down," but himself kept standing.

I sat. He shuffled a few papers about, settling on one he held up to the light before placing it in an out basket. I pictured him as he'd been at the Mint, a plump, humorless drone. He'd lost weight since then and picked up a golf tan. Rumors claimed he was a casino Casanova—cocktail waitresses, front-desk clerks, female dealers. Margaret, a crap dealer on graveyard, claimed that he kept the names of all those he'd had sex with in a log locked away in his desk. How she came by that information, I never asked.

I decided to treat all of this casually. I smiled and said, "So, what's up?"

He looked toward me, but not at me. He seemed half-amused.

I thought that maybe he'd gained some sense of humor over the years. "Ever think about the Mint, the old . . ."

I didn't finish my question because his face went blank. For several seconds, the sound of the air-conditioning coming from the vent filled the room. Then as if recalling a private joke, he grinned. He glanced again at the papers on his desk, then the wall to his left, then the floor. He sank into his leather chair, leaned back, and gazed in the direction of his secretary.

His eyes still on her, he broke the silence. "I'll get to the point. We're letting you go."

I'd worked at the Monaco long enough to be a fixture, no warning slips, no customer complaints, no unexcused absences. "What?"

"We're letting you go. Laying you off."

My pulse pounded in my ears. My mouth went dry. My cheeks burned. The Monaco had no history of random firings, like those at the Maxim. The Monet prints, brass lamps, and the very walls seemed to shrink away. I sat speechless as I gathered my thoughts. Was I targeted specifically to be fired? If so, for what reason? Or was I just hit by random debris from another casino weed-whacker management decision? I found my wits, and I remembered that the human resources employee handbook outlined a "for good reason" clause for termination policy.

"You're joking. You have to have a reason."

"I don't joke or tell jokes. That way no one laughs at me."

There had to be something I wasn't seeing, some act or action I could defend. "Is it about that past poster?"

For an instant he looked confused, then said, "A past poster? Someone past-posted you?"

"No." That he wasn't even aware of the incident took me by surprise. "If not that, what?"

"You were late."

"What? Two minutes in seventeen years."

"I'll take your word on that. However, you did tell a lady she had a large ass. She complained."

"I never."

"There's a witness."

I thought a moment. The incident flashed through my mind, the woman with the hat, the five-dollar tip, Anderson watching, his sweat glands on overdrive. "I thanked her for her largesse, not her large ass."

"There's a witness."

"He's lying."

"He said that's what he heard."

"Jesus, Anderson's got the brain of a pup fish. And—"

"I don't care to argue it. Besides, you well knew what you were implying. That may as well have been French for 'fat ass.' Your termination will read 'seasonal layoff without cause.'"

I saw my one opening. "I'll appeal it to a personnel board."

"Can't. You have to be fired for cause to appeal. It's a layoff."

Did that mean I'd been hit by flying debris? Were more to come? Were they downsizing the casino staff over the slow summer to save employee costs? If so, the management had to follow the protocol and lay employees off by seniority. "Are you laying off others?"

"I'm not at liberty to say." He looked in the direction of the outer office, nodded, and then picked up the phone and looked directly at me. "We're not going to have problems, are we?"

My cheeks burned. I wanted nothing more than to reach over the desk and grab his throat. Instead, I said, "You're firing me for no reason. That's a problem."

His gaze again strayed to the outer office. "Don't make me call security."

Gutless scum, I thought. I half-wished he *would* call security. I'd give them a reason to be there, then I thought of Lucas and Beth and weighed my position. He could block my being hired elsewhere. Still, I had to speak up or explode. "Guess if I tell you to go fuck yourself, I'll get a bum rap when I look for another job."

"Is that what you want to say?"

I stood. "No. Right now, I want to bash your head in. But I won't. I'll just hope someone else does."

He leaned back in his chair and stared as if he'd come to some unexpected but pleasantly surprising revelation. "That's fair." He smiled. "Use my name for a reference."

"How far will that get me with all the people out there you've fucked over?"

He told me to turn in my shirts and tie and apron at the uniform shop, said I'd have termination forms and a check with vacation pay waiting for me at the time office day after tomorrow. "Get all the required signatures. Your tips will be added to the last payroll check."

"If I miss a signature, what will happen?"

"We hold your last check." He opened a side drawer and began to rummage in it. "Oh, and except to turn in your uniform shirts and pick up your last paycheck, you're not allowed in the casino for ninety days. If you come in, security will escort you out."

I lingered at the door.

"What now?" Hefty said.

"The guy whose job you stole? Walt?"

"Inherited," Hefty corrected.

"He was ten times the man you are."

"Do I have to call security to get you moving?"

I walked through the casino where dealers pitched cards mechanically and supervisors looked up over reading glasses with seeming disdain as they tracked play on log sheets. After seventeen years working here, I felt I knew no one well enough to bother with a good-bye, and they didn't know me well enough to care whether I did. I would be a rabbit pellet of gossip in conversations for a day or two, then quickly drop from their collective memory, one more faceless name they'd once worked with. We were strangers, among ourselves and to ourselves. Welcome to Loony Land—one day you have a job, the next you're a candidate to become a rag picker.

Once outside, I sat staring numbly at the windshield in my Mustang. A stomach-curdling anger gradually replaced the numbness. When I was fired from the Maxim, I'd felt betrayed and angry, but not to this degree. I wondered why I hadn't been more incensed at the time. Back then, I figured I'd just go find a new job. Under present circumstances, the usual slow summer season and shortage of conventions, I had scant hope of getting a new dealing gig. It might even be impossible. I gripped the steering wheel until my knuckles turned white. I imagined Hefty's frog eyes bulging as I dug my fingers into the soft flesh of his throat. I fired the ignition, leaned back, and took several slow breaths until by degrees my anger subsided.

I flipped the air-conditioning on high and put the Mustang in drive. Leaving the lot, I burned rubber. I noticed that the gas gauge was near empty. I had eleven dollars in cash. I'd have to use a credit card and figured I'd best get used to it. Fortunately, my bills, including child support for Beth, despite Anne's claims otherwise, were paid, and the $350 a month I was obligated to pay for Lucas's education terminated when he walked across the stage at Thomas and Mack and accepted his diploma.

With a week's vacation pay and tips coming, I could skate through to July. Then what? Unemployment checks? Hardly enough to pay the bills. I needed a job, and summer was the worst time for finding one. My anger leveled off to the helpless can't-change-the-world rage one feels when a terrorist kills a busload of children or when a CEO screws investors out of their retirement funds. I consoled myself as I pulled out that at least the day held no more surprises.

Afternoon rush madness was two hours away. Traffic on the freeway was thin. I pressed the accelerator, took the car up to sixty-five, slipped into the middle lane, and relaxed. I thought about my break-in days at the Mint, the few good times in the business—male and female dealers working together, all of it unprecedented in those free-for-all pre-AIDS days, everyone fucking everyone. Nights rolled into daylight, then nighttime again. The party seemingly never ended. Weed, LA cross tops, Quaaludes. Other than an occasional hit from a roach, I hadn't fallen into the drug scene, but had hopped in and out of a few beds. Where had Hefty fit in when the party was in full swing? I recalled an innocuous shape filling space behind a twenty-one table, except when a boss came around. Then syrup had oozed from the corners of Hefty's mouth.

On Monday I'd look for a job, anything. Hell, McDonald's. Or just maybe I'd go to the Monaco and perform brain surgery on Hefty with a hammer. I turned on the radio. The Eagles sang "Desperado." I cranked up the volume and sang along. Hell, I thought, that's me, the desperado, the Dog Shit Vigilante, a dangerous guy. My picture's on wanted posters. I deliver the goods. In plastic shopping bags. But I don't tell women with fat butts that they have large asses.

I flipped on the turn signal and looked in the side mirror. The lane was clear. A horn blared. I felt the crunch of metal slamming into metal. The world went topsy-turvy. My hands were ripped off the steering wheel.

As if in a dream, I heard talking nearby, heard the whoosh of traffic. I tried to move and discovered I was pinned upside down to my seat by an air bag. The interior of my dream car was filled with dust. I saw out of only my right eye. Blood dripped from somewhere on me onto the head liner. My body felt dulled from the shoulders down.

"Can you hear?" a man asked.

Two ambulance attendants and a Metro officer stared at me through the window. The air smelled of gasoline and dust. The inflated bag pressing against my chest made breathing difficult and speaking nearly impossible.

I managed a weak "Yes."

"Your car's leaking gas. Hold on. We'll cut you out in a bit."

"Lucky fucker," an attendant said.

The cop motioned the medics aside, bent down, and said, "We can't puncture the bag till you're ready to come out. Can't take a chance. Do you understand?"

I nodded, thinking how ironic it would be if I died in flames. A siren burped to a halt nearby, and within seconds, my car was engulfed in foam. Then a team of firemen began cutting away at the door.

"Okay in there, buddy?" a fireman asked.

I nodded.

A fireman stuck his head inside the passenger side and said, "Okay, we're going to pry the door open. Before we deflate the bag, we need to know if your seatbelt's fastened."

"Yeah."

"Good, that'll make it easier. See if you can move your toes."

I tried and was relieved to realize I could. I nodded.

The car trembled as the men put their weight to the task. Finally, the door broke away. Four hands reached in at once and grabbed me. Then another man reached in and cut the seatbelt. They were careful and efficient. One asked where I hurt or if this or that caused any discomfort.

"Okay, here goes the bag."

An instant later they simultaneously pulled and pushed me out. One slipped, and the edge of the door banged me on the bridge of the nose. The fireman apologized.

For some unfathomable reason, I said, "I was just fired."

"Bad day, huh?" my rescuer said.

"I've had worse."

"Hard to believe," his partner said as they laid me on a stretcher.

They strapped me down with my head and neck secured by an inflated brace. As they wheeled me away, a paramedic looped a blood-pressure strap on my arm and pumped it up. Another attendant said to a cop who was standing by the wreck, "No alcohol on his breath."

I caught a glance of the mangled Mustang as they lifted me onto the ambulance. Lucky, I thought, on the second most unlucky day of my life.

4 I'd survived three rollovers and came out of the accident with no broken bones or concussion. The doctor insisted I was fortunate, a view I found difficult to share, considering my overall condition. He sewed seven stitches into my brow and told me to stay off my feet for a while, that I'd have a couple of black eyes and healing was a matter of my giving the body rest. In addition to stitches over my left eye, I had a minor cut on my nose, a dislocated thumb, a bruised shoulder, and a sprained ankle. The only parts of my body that didn't ache were my hair follicles and toenails. And the Mustang, my dream car, was a steel accordion in a salvage yard awaiting a verdict from an insurance adjuster.

After an overnight stay, I checked out of the hospital and took a taxi to Rent-a-Clunker, where I rented the most affordable car on the lot and drove home to an empty house and a near-empty refrigerator. I hobbled back out to the car and drove to the neighborhood Von's. The shopping cart I picked had three wheels that wanted to go straight. Another insisted on going left. I gathered up enough for a few days, easy-to-prepare food—powered soup, oatmeal, pasta, pasta sauce, bread, and hamburger. I limped to the checkout. Five registers were open. All had lines backed up. Although I had thirteen items, I fell in at the rear of the line at the quick-check register.

A man dressed as if in training for the Tour de France stood in front of me, and two women were ahead of him. The guy, pushing fifty, wore a baseball cap backward and fidgeted like a high school kid counting off seconds on a classroom clock. A band of flab protruded where his red Spandex shirt tucked into his matching black and red shorts. At his side he held a packet of chocolate energy bars. The woman at the register completed her purchase and swooped up her sacks. The next in line stepped up. The bicycler heaved a sigh of exasperation, dropped his bars on the conveyor, and looked about as the checker began scanning the woman's groceries. The man's cheeks reddened and his lips trembled as he tried to speak. Too upset to muster a word, he huffed and waved his index finger at the woman's groceries to get the cashier's attention.

"What is it, sir?" the cashier asked.

He finally found his voice. "She's got fifteen items. Fifteen. Count them." He pointed to a sign above the register. "Twelve items, no more."

"Sir, I've already started. It'd take more time to reverse this and send her to another line."

"Stop checking her food," the man said. "I want a manager." He turned to me. "You're my witness. Fifteen."

Twelve items, fifteen, it didn't matter. I said, "I just came here for groceries."

The clerk scanned the next item. "Sir, I'm almost finished. Won't take a minute."

"Miss, I told you to stop," he said.

The woman customer glared at him. She was in her fifties, had a nononsense face, and sported a plain wedding band. "If my husband was here," she said, "you'd be bleeding words right now."

"She's threatening me, miss. You heard her."

"Asshole," the woman said.

"What did you call me?" he said, loud enough to be heard several registers away. "I'll sue the store."

The clerk's face flushed. People nearby stared in our direction.

He seemed compelled to spread his misery around and turned his attention to me. "She was doing it to you too, friend. People like her take advantage."

Undaunted, the woman said, "You're rude and you *are* an asshole."

"You'll be my witness, right?"

I pointed to my eye, swollen nearly shut. "Do you think I care? Besides, she's right."

His eyes narrowed. "What do you mean, *right?*"

"I mean, you seem to be an asshole."

He folded his arms across his chest and asked when the manager was going to arrive. The checker had finished and the woman was receiving change. The lady dropped the change in her purse and wheeled her shopping cart off without looking back.

"Some people," the man said.

The clerk began scanning the bars. I caught her eye and offered a supportive smile.

"What happened to you?" the bicycler asked, his voice calm now as if the disturbance he'd caused never occurred.

I fingered the gauze covering my stitches. "It's a long story."

He said, "This isn't really a quick-check counter. We got time."

"I don't," I said.

He shrugged, looked at the clerk, and said, "What is it with people?" He gathered up his plastic bag and waddled off, his bicycler shoes clicking on the shiny linoleum.

I smiled at the clerk and said, "I've got thirteen items."

She grinned and scanned the first can of soup.

THE RENT-A-CLUNKER, a 1991 Chevrolet Corsair with a dented left fender, leaked oil, so I parked at the curb in front of my house instead of in the driveway. The engine sputtered as I turned it off. Inside, I set the groceries on the countertop and checked my phone messages, seven in all, three from Anne, one asking why I missed Lucas's ceremony, another making sure I would be on time with my child support for Beth, the last informing me she'd heard about the accident and hoped I wasn't injured too badly.

Among the messages were some from dealers asking why I'd been fired, their curiosity prompted most likely by their own concerns about being fired themselves. My history with them suggested they didn't really care if I dived off Hoover Dam. When an appendectomy had landed me in the hospital for three days and kept me from work for an additional five, no one at work had called to check on my well-being. The same occurred when Patty Lane's braid put me out of commission for four days. I didn't return any of their calls.

The last message was from Lucas, asking if I was okay. I sat on the stool at the counter and picked up the photo of him in his high school graduation gown. I wished the two of us were closer. After the divorce, we'd stopped the usual father-and-son activities, no camping or fishing. He'd quit Little League and had forgone playing sports in school. Since turning fourteen, he'd bused and waited tables at the same restaurant and saved money enough to pay for scuba-diving school and a two-year-old Honda, black with custom exhausts. He was serious and mature about most of his decisions, but he often turned adolescent when around his little sister. It was a game that he enjoyed and she too often encouraged. When Lucas enrolled at the university, I helped with books and tuition as was required by the divorce, but he'd borne some of the cost himself and earned two small scholarships. I would have gladly helped without its being required.

I set the picture aside, took the phone to the couch, and dialed.

Anne picked up the receiver on the second ring. I said hello.

"How are you doing, Jude?"

"Sore."

"Your neighbor Mel Clemmens saw your car on the late news and said it was totaled."

"Yep. I was lucky."

"Whose fault?"

"Like I said, I was lucky. Just as I started to go right, she drifted into my lane. She was inside the lane marker two feet when we collided. She came out of it okay. The cop who came to the hospital to get my statement said she's got insurance."

"They put you in the hospital?"

"Overnight to make sure I didn't have a concussion. Anne?"

"What?"

"I got fired."

"Why?"

"I don't know. Hefty fired me just before the accident."

"The fat brownnoser we worked with at the Mint?"

"Forty pounds lighter, but otherwise the same."

"Fired? What did you do?"

I looked out the window. A gust of wind whipped the branches of the paloverde. "I didn't tackle some guy who past-posted roulette. I thanked a woman for her largesse."

"For her what?"

"Largesse, her generosity. You're the one who goes to France, for Christ's sake . . ." Don't, I thought, be cool, give her a chance.

"I remember when they fired you from the Maxim. It was terrible."

Terrible, I thought, and disheartening. The termination was a literal decimation, 10 percent of the blackjack dealers dismissed in one day. Then adding insult to injury, the casino had hired a Santa Claus who'd been fired at the Boulevard Mall for drunkenness on the job. The Santa, in faux white beard and red flannel suit, walked the casino floor, handing out key chains from a gift bag.

"You must be angry."

I was too sore at the moment to be angry. "Mostly frustrated."

"You have to put the right message out to the universe. Good will come. Money, even."

At least she hadn't accused me of subverting myself. The universe? But why go small when messages to the universe are such a bargain? Make me a millionaire. No. A billionaire.

"I'm sorry you got fired. The business sucks. But the universe is teaching you a lesson."

Now the lecture, I thought, from a woman who'd spent a fortune on tarot-card readings and dream-interpretation counseling, as well as a dozen New Age workshops. A fortune, to sit cross-legged in a circle with a group of yuppies holding hands and chanting to connect with an inner voice, then go home to sleep under a pyramid? Is that why she'd taken on a succession of lovers since the divorce, each younger than his predecessor? At forty-six, Anne was nearly two years younger than I was. If I'd taken up with younger women, she would have accused me of self-subversion. Was her inner voice guiding her? Why didn't her inner voice ever ask her why her children resented her?

"Anne, I don't think the universe is interested in me."

"How can you know? I'm not going to bitch about child support, but I've got concerns."

"Concerns? You push cocktails at the Mirage. You make what? Twice what I do?"

"Three-fifty per kid," she said. "You had it easy, and I never took you to court for more."

"Lucas graduated. I agreed to pay for his expenses until he earned a degree. No more after college."

"Then next month you'll be down to three-fifty."

"You just got child support, but I may be late next month. Is Beth there?"

"No."

"I'm still a mess, can't take her this week, but I want her next weekend."

"Can you pick her up?"

I looked out the front window at the rented clunker, a dinged-up hundred-thousand-miler. There had been a dearth of things to be grateful for lately. I took the car getting me home as one. I didn't share my ex-wife's believe in pyramid power, extraterrestrials, or tarot cards, but I could put a modicum of faith in a piece of six-cylinder junk. "Yeah. I'll be able to."

"Really, Jude. Take all this as a lesson from the universe."

"Sure, but you'd think occasionally it would teach me a lesson in an easy manner." I changed the conversation. "Anne, do you remember anything happening at the Mint that might have prompted Hefty to fire me?"

"Jesus. So long ago. Let me think." There was a pause, then she said, "Everybody made fun of him. He was a twerp. Anyhow, I'm planning a trip to Italy late this summer. Can you take Beth for three weeks? She's starting the boy thing and is just too much for Lucas to handle."

Italy? I felt a stab of pain in my ankle. When it passed, I said, "Sure. I'll take her."

"Jude, I know you don't believe in such things, but Hefty may be acting on behalf of fate. Or maybe you're just subverting yourself?"

"Anne?"

"Yeah."

"Spare me."

I SAT ACROSS FROM A MAN who snapped his newspaper and mouthed the words he read. Every once in a while the receptionist looked in my direction and smiled. The court, I'd been advised by the lawyer's secretary, was the villain. Can't ever tell how long a hearing will take. Judges, she said, determine everything, and the defense will delay a settlement as long as possible. I looked at the questionnaire, two and a half pages of personal history about everything but my sex life. State the nature of your injuries. Describe the accident. Have you ever sued anyone? If so, what was the outcome? Have you ever been on workman's compensation? Disability? Ever been sued? Any felony convictions? I began writing.

The man snapped his paper and looked at me. "You'd think they'd have a secretary fill those out. One-third they get. Hell, a little help with the form is in line, right?"

I was reminded of the jerk in the grocery line. The man snapped his paper again. I came to the question about being sued and asked the receptionist if divorces counted as suits. She winked as if we were conspirators in some scheme and said she didn't know. I left the answer blank.

The man with the newspaper folded it and leaned forward. "Been at this three years trying to get what's due me for a busted knee. Doctors, insurance companies, lawyers, three years of it and we got another hearing. I heard some cases take five, six years. You took a nasty hit, I see."

I nodded. I just wanted a car comparable to the Mustang. The woman's insurance agent had called and offered two thousand for pain and suffering. Two grand wouldn't cover a down payment on a Mustang. My company was handling the comprehensive, but that settlement would be only enough to pay off the loan and a portion of the Rent-a-Clunker.

"Three years," the man repeated, snapped his paper, and returned to reading.

I completed the forms and handed them to the receptionist. She scanned the papers and said, "Thank you, Mr. Helms. Have a seat. We'll call you in a few minutes."

I looked around the reception room, floor tiled with tumbled marble, on the walls terra-cotta reliefs of faceless postmodern archangels playing trumpets, an oak door. Thirty percent put to use, I thought, and picked up a copy of *Time* that named the ten most powerful people in the world. Five minutes later, the phone rang.

The receptionist informed me that Mr. Friece would talk to me now. A secretary in the inner office led me to the attorney's door. Abraham Friece stood up from his desk and gave me a stiff handshake. He told his secretary to hold calls. "Still in pain? Can I call you Jude?"

"Jude. Yes. Ankle hurts."

"Too bad it's not a back. Are you seeing a doctor?"

"Just the ones at the hospital."

"Not a private physician?"

"Not yet."

"We have a list of clinics that might work with you. I assume you have insurance."

"I think I do. Yeah, I have some. They call it COBRA or something."

Friece smiled. "Well, that's the first priority. Have a seat." He walked around his desk and seated himself. "Tell me what happened." He flipped on a tape recorder and motioned with his hand for me to begin.

I related details of the accident. Occasionally, the attorney jotted something down with a pen, but mostly listened. When I finished, he leaned back and swiveled in his chair, then grinned. "Here's the thing. It looks cut-and-dried, but insurance attorneys check everything, like if you've ever sued anyone before. Divorce doesn't count. They'll look at your whole medical history. By the way, if you start having neck pain or headaches, note that."

"Headaches or neck pain?"

"Yes. Sometimes the symptoms don't appear at first because of other traumas. Kind of like a delayed reaction. You understand."

The point was obvious. "Yes."

"I can't be surprised by any health issues or questions about credibility. Have you ever been convicted of a felony?"

"No."

"Ever been denied an insurance claim?"

His question were identical to those on the form. "Never made one."

He jotted something down, then asked, "How many days of work have you missed?"

"None."

The attorney sat upright. "None? You went back to work?"

"No, I was fired just before the accident happened."

Friece leaned back and nodded. "Too bad. They have to compensate for lost wages." He interlocked his hands behind his head. "Well, it's a mixed bag. After all, you can't find another job in your current condition. Could go either way, but we'll work it in. Bad day, huh?"

"Not the worst."

"Why were you fired?"

I shook my head and looked outside the office window at the beds of zinnias and roses all in bloom, not a dead flower or brown leaf anywhere. "I don't know."

Friece narrowed his gaze. "I can't have surprises. What's your work history?"

I met his gaze. "I was fired for no cause. It happens. Once before I was fired for no reason and replaced by a Santa Claus. And another time I lost a job because I crawled out of a fire instead of getting burned to death. That sort of sums up my work history."

THE DOCTOR TOLD ME TO DRESS. He was soft-spoken and his cherubic manner ideal for telling a patient he had a terminal disease. "You're coming along. Lucky it wasn't worse."

I buttoned my shirt. The bruises had faded. Although it still hurt, my ankle was sturdy enough to support my weight. The cut would leave only a slight scar. Everybody agreed I was lucky, except for Friece, who might say that my condition, being good, was unfortunate.

"Doc, I've been having headaches, and my neck stiffens up overnight. I feel like I'm made out of spare parts," I said. It was a lie, but I didn't create the system. What choice did I have? I needed to replace a car. A mortgage hung over me. Doctors, attorneys, drug companies were going to make a dollar. How could I resist being cynical to turn a buck?

The doctor jotted something in the file. "I'm not surprised. Air bags save lives and minimize injury, but trauma is trauma." Setting the paperwork aside, he shined a light in my eyes and told me to look away, then look straight ahead. Finished, he said, "We'll set you up with therapy starting next week. In the meantime, hot and cold packs on the neck will help. I prescribe Darvon with codeine. It'll help with the ankle and the headaches. Use only the prescribed amount, and stay off the leg as much as possible, and elevate it. Stitches come out in a week."

"Doc, I need a job. What I do requires standing."

He wrote a prescription and handed it to me. "The body's an amazing thing if you give it a chance to work for you."

"I've got no income."

He waved off my comment. "The way you look right now won't help you land a job."

I didn't want to think how I looked.

"Elevate the ankle and apply heat. In a week I'll have a better idea of what we're dealing with. I'll check the X-rays. If needed, I may schedule an MRI."

I grimaced as I slipped into my loafers. "Thanks."

The doctor nodded. "We'll forward copies of your records to your attorney."

I STOOD BY THE TIMEKEEPER'S OFFICE. The guard nodded and lowered the receiver. "You're short a shirt, an apron, and a tie. They have to deduct it and cut a new check. A week or so."

"I was in an accident. The shirt was ruined. The tie and apron are probably going to be crushed along with my car for scrap."

He shrugged. "I don't make the rules."

Who does? I thought. That's the son of a bitch I want to meet.

The evening made a person want to live forever. A light breeze blew in from the west where the Spring Mountains stood in jagged relief before a silver sunset. The air smelled of new-mown grass, blooming desert-willows, and hamburger sizzling on the grill. I stared off from my patio, spatula in one hand, spray bottle in the other. The kids sat inside watching television. I'd tried to coax them outside, but they'd said barbecuing was for old men. So, old man, I thought, what next? Lose the house?

I stood transfixed a moment, my gaze on the horizon, as if something in the evening sky might provide an answer. My options came to cashing in a paltry retirement account and paying penalties, going on unemployment and losing the house, or finding a job. Soon. Anything. Hell, rather than wait on unemployment, I could stand on a bad ankle and turn burgers for minimum wage to make the mortgage.

In a sense, the house had become my identity. After the divorce, I'd saved twenty-five dollars a day, gone without amusement for fourteen months, and bought it as a fixer-up. It was thirty years old, but I'd made it new, planted lawn and garden, laid tile throughout, painted walls, refinished cabinets, built a block-wall courtyard, and poured five yards of cement for the patio. I'd lost feeling in my fingers after laying the tile for six weeks one summer. For a few months, I'd dealt cards with almost no sensation in the fingertips. It was worth it.

The barbecue flamed up. I sprayed the coals with water and turned the patties. Since getting the ax at the Monaco, the anger came and went. I'd struggled to sleep. In part, the problem was I didn't know who to be angry with and who to blame. Hefty? Yes. But he was just a puppet talking to the audience. Behind him was the puppet master, the corporation that owned the Monaco and four other casinos. Ultimately, I took blame myself for never following up on my plan to leave the casino business. Anger and blame aside, my money was dwindling, I was unemployed, and a settlement for the accident could take two or more years.

The neighbors' sliding door opened. Towel hanging from her forearm, Gay stepped out. She wore a white bikini, her normal summer garb since getting breast implants two years ago. She owned a dozen suits, all similar, white or flesh colored and sheer as tissue paper. Her nipples protruded. She made no effort to conceal anything as she waved.

"Jude, what're you barbecuing?"

"A casino manager."

"Funny. Now, really, what are you cooking?"

"Hamburger."

"Smells good." She crossed the lawn to her spa, where she turned on the jets.

Mel and Gay were vegetarians. His idea. I figured Gay snuck into a Burger King or Wendy's now and then and maybe cheated in other ways as well. Mel worked as a floorman at the Horseshoe. They followed a pattern: he'd soon join her in the spa, and later they would cavort naked in the spa and probably spread a towel on the lawn and make love. I'd watched them from the window of a corner bedroom upstairs. I suspected they knew and wanted it that way.

I hoped to spare my kids the sight of Mel's pale butt humping away under a full moon. It wasn't as if they weren't exposed to that stuff elsewhere, Anne having a string of men over the past seven years. Lucas told me of coming home early from school once to find her on the couch as a guy Lucas called Stripper Boy gave her oral sex. Well, she was human, and after all Lucas was supposed to be in school. Disturbing as it was to Lucas, it wasn't something she'd intentionally exposed her son to. It was life and kids grow up fast now. Still, I figured, Gay and Mel fucking on a wet lawn was a bit much, even for sophisticated kids.

"Kids are over for the weekend," I said, sending a hint.

"That's nice," she said. "They're good kids."

Her bikini bottom lay out on the tile edge. Her top would be next. She turned her back and struck a match. A few seconds later the smell of burning marijuana, her vegetable of choice, drifted over the fence. I was glad the kids were inside watching TV. Vegas has always been tough on kids. I'd witnessed some remarkable human deterioration from gambling, drugs, or alcohol—or the combination of all three. A few popular girls from Vegas High were now middle-aged and fried hard from booze and gambling and grinding out eight-hour shifts on their feet in dead-end casino jobs. I didn't want Beth ending up like them. Some boys I'd gone to school with had done hard time in Carson City for burglary and drugs. In the kid department, I'd been lucky. Mine were good, steady students. I was certain neither used. I'd seen enough drug abuse to recognize the signs, but can a parent ever be sure? I turned the patties again and laid the buns on the grill. The patio door next door slid open. When I looked up from the grill, Mel was staring at me over the wall.

"Meat? Burgers?" He wrinkled his nose.

"Hello, Mel."

"Heard you're outta work, Jude."

"That's true."

"Nice black and blue around the stitches, good buddy. You've looked better."

"I've felt better."

He sniffed the air. "Didn't your father die of a heart attack? Stuff'll clog your pipes faster than wood glue."

"Mel, you ever try to eat barbecued glue?"

"Can't say I have. How'd you like to work at the Shoe?"

I hadn't considered downtown casinos. Fremont Street was hurting. Resorts on the Strip had taken the lion's share of business. Still, a downtown gig was better than unemployment.

I said. "The Horseshoe needs dealers?"

"Dealing?" Mel chuckled. "They wouldn't let you deal downtown. You'd be on the floor. I just got a backup pit-boss job. I got some juice. You got the experience behind you to watch games. What I'm saying is, think about it. You can't deal forever."

The floor? Downtown? That prospect discouraged me nearly as much as having no job. Forty-seven and a half and already a sympathy case. The last thing I wanted to become was another Vegas woe-is-me story. Feeling sorry for myself was one thing. A dope-smoking, exhibitionist vegetarian feeling sorry for me was quite another. "Thanks. I'll think about it."

"You know the story. They want fresh, smiley faces, not real dealers. The old days are gone, and you're part of the old days. Aren't you afraid of cholesterol?"

"I will be after the first heart attack."

"That dog still shittin' in your yard?"

I shook my head. "Sometimes good things happen."

"The lady awaits." Mel smiled and disappeared.

I carried dinner into the house. The kids sat in the kitchen, Lucas leaning back on his stool. Pain shot through my arm from my thumb, and I nearly lost control of the platter as I laid the patties down on the counter. The platter rattled. I massaged the joint.

"Dad," Beth said, "when did you get clumsy?"

"I guess when my thumb didn't survive the accident. And don't lean back on the stool, Lucas. I've been telling you since you were three not to."

"Dad, have I cracked my head? Am I the one with stitches, a sore thumb, and a busted ankle?"

"No, you're the one leaning back on the stool."

"Right." He leaned forward, his long legs crossed at the ankles. Like me, he'd been gangly, but was finally shedding that stage of boyish awkwardness. I knew that underneath his boyish behavior was a young man who was quite responsible. He'd worked full-time and attended classes full-time for four years.

Beth stood facing the kitchen counter, mixing salad. She was modest and particularly self-conscious about her boyish hips and had a habit of crossing her arms over her chest when talking, as if to hide herself. "Dad, are we having potato chips?"

"Dad, why haven't you learned to make french fries?" Lucas asked.

"No need. Potato chips are fine with a hamburger."

"What kind of answer is that?"

"Am I on the witness stand?"

Most days I felt secure about my relationship with my children. Early in my parenting, I'd worried they might slip away from me and at times felt I was not a good example. One thing I never questioned was my feelings for them, the pleasure I took in being around them, hearing their voices, and seeing their animated faces.

Beth looked over her shoulder. "Don't pay attention to him, Dad. I'd rather eat what you fix than what Mom cooks. When she does, she makes that tuna dish that tastes like cat food."

Lucas asked, "You been eating cat food?"

"Don't have to, Mr. Just-Graduated-College-but-Knows-Nothing. Taste is influenced by a sense of smell. Men have an inferior sense of smell, just like they're inferior in most ways, so you probably can't understand the concept."

Lucas rolled his eyes. "Good thing we've got a genius in the family."

"You got her started," I said. I knew their game. The more mature Beth acted, the more immature Lucas pretended to be.

"Dad, I don't want to hurt your feelings, but you look like shit," he said.

Their outspokenness suggested confidence, something I admired because since the fire I'd lost some of mine. "Could you be a little diplomatic?"

"Diplomacy isn't genetically entrenched in this family," he said.

Beth raised her foot to examine it. "Think Mel and Gay will do it on the lawn tonight?"

I set the hamburgers on the table. "If they do, don't watch them."

"If they do it in the Jacuzzi, is it okay if I watch?" Lucas asked. "As a college grad, I'm thinking of taking an advanced degree. Maybe human sexual behavior."

Ignoring him, I asked Beth if the salad was ready.

She dropped her foot and smiled proudly.

"Okay," I said, "chow's on."

I ate a fork full of diced carrots, a potato chip, then bit into the hamburger and chewed slowly. The kids talked as they ate and occasionally tried to draw me into their conversation. When they did, I nodded and offered some benign answer. I felt another bout of anger festering in me and struggled to suppress it. I didn't want to misdirect it at them.

"Dad! You weren't listening!" Beth scolded.

I took a deep breath and exhaled. "I'm sorry. Did I miss something?"

"Dad. I mean, really, should we like shout?" she said, her voice rising with enthusiasm. "I was saying that Tiffany's mother is throwing a party at Jitters. They're going to do karaoke. I told her we'd go."

"I hear fine. You don't have to *like* shout," I said.

"Anyhow, we should all go do karaoke," she said in her normal voice.

"We?" I said. "You mean me?"

"Hey, don't include me," Lucas said. "I've got plans with Heather tomorrow. You and all those girls singing?" He placed his palms over his ears and shook his head.

Beth said, "I sing better than Miss Heather Elaine Romano."

"Karaoke?" I looked at my half-eaten dinner. I'd lost whatever remaining appetite I had.

"Yes, Dad. And we don't need Lucas coming along." Beth's expression gradually changed. She laid her fork on her plate, looked at Lucas, then me. "Dad, I have almost four hundred dollars saved up."

"Are you offering me money?"

"I've got more than that, Dad," Lucas said. "It's yours."

I looked from one to the next. They nodded. Where'd they get the idea of saving money? Not from their parents. I wondered how these two sprang out of my union with Anne. How did they get to be who they were? My throat constricted. I sipped some water, waited for it to settle, and said, "Thanks, but I'll be okay."

Lucas grinned. "What a relief! I sure hated the idea of giving up my money."

"Well, it would have just been a loan," Beth said. "At current interest rates."

"I've got enough in savings to afford ice cream," I said. "Who wants to go?"

"My treat," Beth said. "I feel like I just won four hundred dollars."

I wondered why I hadn't been more frugal. Why I hadn't kept saving to start a business. I remembered after the fire I couldn't find a job, was told flatly by some bosses to invest in silicon breasts, that to fill quotas only women were being hired as blackjack dealers. Anne had found a job right away serving cocktails at the Stardust, but for two months I'd been a stay-at-home dad and watched bills swallow the savings for the business.

"No," I said. "I'll buy tonight. Save your money for when I'm too old to work."

SLEEP THAT NIGHT was shortened by a nightmare—the choking smell of synthetic carpet charred black, me crawling a desperate path over it, a shower of hot cinders falling from a crumbling ceiling, a body plummeting down from an open window. I sat up from the dream in which flames had engulfed me, then stood and limped to the bathroom. My heart was a jackhammer. I'd not had a nightmare about fire in days. The night promised to be a long one. I lay for a while wondering what other too familiar terrors would invade my sleep.

I drank a glass of water and began pacing. The old days when knowing someone ensured a dealer of an audition had long passed. Now I didn't know a dozen people in casinos other than the Monaco. The city had grown, and the casino hiring system had changed. I hadn't thought of myself as old, but in the eyes of the new casino business, I was. I would be competing for a job with younger people, attractive women, minorities, dealers with connections.

Thinking came easier so long as I moved. I considered the paltry check I was given a year after the fire—$2,812.19, the arbitrary amount an insurance company and a conference table full of attorneys decided a burned ankle merited. It didn't replace the savings I'd spent or put a dent in the bills that had accumulated during weeks of unemployment. I realized I'd not listed the MGM insurance settlement on the form at Friece's office and worried that it might be considered a lawsuit, a fresh trouble to walk off in the next round of pacing.

6 I was as out of place as a ballerina in a prison yard. In an audience largely of women wearing bullet-size diamonds on their fingers, I sat alone at a corner table in Jitters, a coffeehouse that specialized in designer blends, whatever that meant. Most of the others were mothers in their forties and dressed like their daughters—designer jeans and

tank tops, both too tight. I recognized the type from dealing, women who tanned year-round and measured each other by the carat weight of their jewelry, the success of their cosmetic surgery, and their husbands' positions and incomes. Occasionally, one or another among them glanced my way with an expression suggesting I probably looked much the way I felt.

One among them stood out and not just because of her auburn hair and pale complexion. She wore gym shorts and a gray cotton blouse and no jewelry or makeup other than lipstick. She was in her late thirties, I guessed, not the kind Lucas might call smokin' hot, but the type who invites a second look wherever she goes. She seemed amused by the spectacle. Whenever I glanced in her direction, she invariably caught me and smiled. I imagined her being merely fascinated with the grotesque. With two black eyes and a bandage on my brow, I looked like burlap bags stitched together.

The girls, Beth among them, sang the final chorus of "Wind Beneath My Wings" as if volume alone created music. Two helicopter mothers captured each missed note and bungled lyric on video as another narrated the event blow-by-blow over a cell phone to whomever was on the other end. The girls' voices crescendoed, the mothers applauded and nodded to one another, and the lone woman caught me looking again. This time she held eye contact and I smiled, after which I kept my eyes trained on the girls as they went through a dance routine.

"By next week," a self-appointed mother-in-charge said, "we'll get it right."

As painful as the singing was, I was glad Beth was still a girl and not nearly as cynical and mature as she sometimes acted. Her hair, in a ponytail the way she'd worn it at six and seven, reminded me of how she'd light up on my visitation days. Unlike the others, my daughter wore no lipstick. She stood in the gathering in the far corner, whispering to a friend. Then suddenly, leading a thin, dark-haired girl by the hand, she broke out of the tittering pack.

She stood in front of me, smiling. "Dad, this is Katie, my friend."

I pulled myself to my feet and offered her a handshake. "Hello."

The girl shyly shook my hand. "Pleased to meet you, sir." She was slim with brown hair and dark brown eyes and a small upturned nose that made her look younger than Beth by years.

"Her mother's Audie. She's the one sitting over there." Beth held her hand so that only I could see it and pointed to the lone woman I'd notice.

I was surprised who her mother was, their coloring, except for the brown eyes, being so much different. Like her mother, Katie was pretty. I looked for other similarities, but saw only a vague resemblance. "Oh, yeah," I said. "The one that's alone. You look like her."

Her mother stood from her seat, brushed her hand down her lap as if ridding it of crumbs, then walked to the door.

"My grandmother says I look just like my dad."

"Oh. Well, I've never seen him," I said.

"Me either. Just pictures. He's got black hair or maybe just really dark brown."

"I see."

Beth turned to her friend. "I'll call. We gotta go now."

Hearing that, Katie smiled and skipped off to the door, where her mother waited.

Beth sounded better singing softly along with the radio. If she didn't scream, she could actually carry a tune. Hearing her kept my mind occupied. She stopped singing and rolled down the window. A gush of hot air rushed in.

"Hey," I said, "the air conditioner doesn't work so good, but it doesn't blow hot air."

"This car stinks. Are you going to get a real one?"

"I'll look this week." I glanced over at her. She was staring out the window.

"No, you won't, 'cause you don't have a job."

"I'll get one."

She fired three questions at me at once. Why was I alone, was it because I still loved her mother, and when was I going to find a girlfriend?

"Don't know, no, and someday maybe," I said.

"Well, you better get a good job if you intend to date Katie's mom."

"Who said anything about dating?"

"I saw you in there."

"Just roll up the window," I said in my Dad's-in-charge voice.

She sneered, but did as told. "I saw you. Looking at her like she's an ice-cream cone."

"I didn't either." I stopped for a red light, reached over, and brushed back a strand of her hair. "I'll get a better car. First I need a job."

Beth looked out the window again. "She's been in prison."

"Who?"

"Katie's mom, Audie, the one you were drooling over."

"She hardly looks like a convict. And I wasn't drooling."

She smiled smugly. "You were too."

"If you say so. Prison? Really? Are you making that up?" Beth didn't lie. If what she said was a lie, she wasn't the one who'd fabricated it, just the one repeating it.

She shook her head. "That's what Katie said once. She's Katie's mom. Her name's Audra Moser. Sounds like an actress, huh?"

Prison? I pictured her watching the girls sing, amused and smiling. Impossible to imagine in prison garb. Easy to imagine in other ways. Kids lie to impress each other. Maybe Katie made it up. No matter, Katie's mom was beyond my current means and probably me, an unemployed, washed-up dealer average in looks at best.

Beth slapped the back of the seat and said, "Dad! You really have to get a hearing aid. I said the light . . ."

The driver behind us pressed his horn. I hit the accelerator too fast, and the clunker stalled. I cranked the ignition and pumped the gas pedal. The light turned red before the car started. The driver leaned on his horn and cursed me. I looked at his red face through the rear-view mirror. In his midthirties, he was shouting and banging his palms on his steering wheel. When the light turned green, I pulled into the intersection. The driver passed on the right and flipped me a finger.

"Hey, asshole!" I shouted. "I've got my daughter in the car."

"Dad, I would have flipped you off too."

We didn't speak for a time. Beth hummed to music on the radio. I couldn't stop thinking of Katie's mom, wondered if she'd truly been to prison. If so, what was her crime? Killing a husband? Injuring someone in a traffic accident? Was it jail or prison or a child's imagination?

"Dad?"

"Yes?"

"Thanks for taking me. Mom wouldn't. She went once and says the mothers are all silly."

"Honey, they just want to be part of their daughters' lives. That's all."

"And Mom doesn't."

"That's not what I said. And don't go telling your mother I said that."

She took a moment to digest what I'd said, then smiled. "Mom's right. The way those mothers are is kind of silly. But we have fun. Did you?"

"It was just short of enchanting."

"Liar."

"That's me."

7 The clerk in the MGM looked at my application, making notes as she read the information. Near as I could determine, she was no more than twenty. I wondered how someone so young could make a valid assessment of an applicant—specifically, me.

She smiled perfunctorily and cleared her throat. "How do you deal with a bad day?"

I thought, I'm the Dog Shit Vigilante. I get an Uzi and wipe out the neighborhood, twice, three times if I'm really pissed.

"What kind of bad day?" I asked. "One when your wife tells you she wants a divorce?"

"A typical bad day," she said without cracking a smile.

"Oh, a typical bad day. I listen to music." That seemed like something that would satisfy the question. "You know, classic rock and roll."

She made no notations on her form. "No. What I mean is, how do you handle people?"

"Of course, people." I cook my kids. I chase down priests and blaspheme the saints. "I'm polite no matter my circumstances."

She started writing. I tried to peek. She blocked my view with her forearm. I leaned back and thought of her, Audie or Audra, or was she just Katie's mom? I wondered what she might look like in one of Gay's thin bikinis and how easily she might slip out of it. As the clerk finished her notation, I gazed around at the sterile room, walls a soft rose color, tile bland gray. Impersonal. Isn't human resources by design impersonal? And who the hell coined that term? When were humans reduced to resources like coal and oil and copper?

"You were laid off from the Maxim Hotel in December 1984."

"Yes."

"Why?"

To make room on the payroll for an alcoholic Santa Claus. "It was a mass layoff, more than twenty dealers in one day." They replaced us with cheaper help, so management could ensure their bonuses. "No one told us why. 'You're terminated; pick up your last check on payday.' That was all."

She looked up from the paper she was making notes on. "That's terrible."

"Happened a lot back then."

"Well, this company doesn't operate like that."

How does it operate? Scalpels? "I'm sure those days are gone. Especially at places like the Mirage and the MGM."

"So, why were you released from the Monaco?"

I smiled. "I guess because those days aren't really gone."

The interview continued another five minutes before the clerk informed me there were no current openings. She said that my application would be held on file for six months and I should check back from time to time. I thanked her and limped out of the office. It was past four, too late to apply elsewhere. So far, I'd been to human resources at eleven Strip casinos. My prospects with them were no better than they would be with number twelve. I decided to have a drink.

I PULLED TO A STOP at Sahara and the Strip. Only then did it occur to me to go downtown. I'd not even seen the Fremont Street Experience. I well remembered my own Fremont Street experience, warm nights cruising in cars from Five Points east up Fremont to the Union Pacific, cops in powder-blue uniforms strolling sidewalks, vendors calling out, young women in white shorts and sequined T-shirts passing out pamphlets. Rudy Smelich and I had once mooned cops from Ira Nordhaggen's '70 Malibu. Ira gunned the engine and blew a red light to escape, but a patrol car intercepted us two blocks away.

I ended up taking the Fourth Street turnoff and three minutes later passed Fremont, barricaded to keep out automobiles. I looked up at the steel-mesh canopy that barred the skyline. Though I couldn't say why, seeing it bothered me. I parked on the third floor of the Horseshoe garage. As a teenager, I'd gotten drunk here and puked in the parking lot.

Business in the Horseshoe was slow. I ordered a draft beer and asked the bartender to run a tab. I sipped from the glass and looked around. The taste of beer didn't do anything to wash away the day. I downed the glass, stood, and reached for my wallet.

"Say, pal. Glad to see you." A hand came down firmly on my shoulder.

I turned and looked in Mel's face. "You too, Mel. Haven't been downtown in years. It's changed."

"You see the metal fishnet over the street?"

I opened my wallet. "I saw it. It's ugly."

Mel held up a palm. "Let the joint pay for that." He motioned for the bartender. "This guy's a friend."

Mel signed for the check, and I laid down a dollar for the bartender.

"Remember when beer was, what, fifty cents anywhere?" Mel asked.

"Next week we'll have to drop in two quarters to use the shitter. I'm surprised the corporations haven't charged for air. You come down to apply for a job? I can get you on the floor tomorrow."

I glanced at the bosses in the pit, noted the dead-end stares in their eyes. Standing and watching wasn't for me, not yet. "How about just dealing? I'm not ready to track players' bets and sweat five-dollar double downs."

"Cynical, cynical. I imagine you're as good a clerk as we could get for what you'd make, but you got those Strip habits. The joint's changed since the old man died, and Jack gone, and Teddy's dead now, but you knew that."

"Before the Horseshoe bought and tore down the walls, I worked on the other half when it was the Mint," I said. "Crazy times. Only fun I ever had in the business."

"I remember." Mel looked away a moment. "Say, I do know a guy at the New Laredo. You won't make Strip tokes, but you can grind out a buck. Guy runs it is from Montana, old school. Puts his dime on the line. Interested?"

I could make do with a small gig until Strip hiring opened in September. And maybe, like some other old-timers in the business, he knew my father? "Sure."

"Have another drink. I'll give him a call." Mel patted my shoulder.

I ordered a Coke. The bartender asked if I'd be needing a taxi to get home. I chuckled, laid another dollar down, and said, "Thanks for asking."

Mel returned and took a seat. "It's slow. He'll put you on the extra board. Even little joints run extra boards these days."

I hadn't been on an extra board for fifteen years. I didn't like the idea of hanging around my house waiting for a call to come work, but what else did I have to do? And there was child support, a mortgage to consider. I would do it. "Thanks. I appreciate the help."

"Probably no audition. Show up tomorrow at noon," Mel said. "They provide a cowboy shirt and scarf, but you have to wear black pants in case he puts you to work right away."

"Tomorrow?"

Mel nodded.

The New Laredo was a barnlike building with a four-acre wooden floor and open beams. Above the main floor was a loft with a coffee shop and a two-foot sign that read "Gambler's Special, Eight-Ounce New York Steak and Eggs and Toast for $4.98." The gaming tables, six blackjack games and one crap table, sat in the center of four concentric circles of slot machines.

I limped over to the pit and caught the attention of the pit boss, a craggy-faced man of indeterminate age, somewhere between sixty-five and eighty. "Excuse me, sir."

He turned his head slowly, as if storing up energy for something more important, and lumbered over to me. "Can I help you?"

I extended my hand. "Name's Jude. I'm here to see Danny Forrester."

"I'm him." A buzzer went off in the slots. He looked in that direction.

"Mel sent me about a job."

"Oh, guy got canned from the Monaco." He shook my hand and looked me over. "That manager there is an asshole. Worked with him back at the Stardust. Didn't know shit, but was a master ass kisser. Him firin' you's the same as a testimonial from Christ his self."

"I broke in with him at the Mint."

"There. See? That's how the business has changed. No loyalty. My ol' man ran joints in Butte that were flat as a boxer's nose. Flat dice, deuce dealers, rigged slots. Took chumps for whatever he could, but never fired a loyal employee. Ain't been like that for decades."

"Do you want me to audition?"

"You been at it twenty years. You don't know how to deal yet, I'll fire you. Question is—are you going to steal from me?"

I'd never stolen a penny from a casino, never even considered it. I'd been approached by a boss at the Maxim to join a scam involving phony payoffs of markers, but had turned him down. I'd wondered, after that fateful day, if that had been the reason I was fired. Were others dumped out on the street because they too had turned down a proposition to cheat the joint?

"Any chance of getting away with it?"

Danny offered a half-amused smile. "No."

"Then I won't."

The dealer on the empty blackjack game, a woman with a look that said she'd been on the merry-go-round long enough to know there was no brass ring and no getting off, said, "He asked his mother the same question."

Danny winked. "She was honest enough, but couldn't count past twenty-one. Didn't put her to work. When can you start?"

The informal atmosphere reminded me of the way it had once been at the Monaco.

"Anytime."

"Go on upstairs. I'll meet you in the coffee shop at the executives' table."

THE HOSTESS SEATED ME in the bosses' booth and asked if I wanted coffee. I thanked her and took a seat. Four or five minutes passed before Danny ambled over and slipped into the booth, facing me across the table. He handed me an application and a pen.

"We ain't got a fancy human resources office. I do the interview and tell 'em to put you to work."

I began filling in the blanks.

"You'll start day after tomorrow. Graveyard shift. You used to graveyard?"

"I'm up to it, though I haven't worked those hours since the MGM." My nose seemed to fill with the odor of plastic fumes.

"When were you there?"

"Eighty."

"The fire?"

I shook my head. That day was nothing I ever discussed. "I was off that day."

"Lucky you. We'll get the other paperwork goin' when the pit boss gets back from his break. We run short on help here and do little things those big joints don't to keep employees happy. Still, it won't make up for the shitty buck you'll make. Tokes are split shift for shift."

I paused long enough to nod, then returned to filling in blanks.

9 The morning of my fifth shift, I was on break with Celia, a transplant from Atlantic City. On the way to the pit she forecast tips would be a record. I'd asked how much the record was. Smiling, she said, "I mean the low end. We're down to bus tours, grandmas from Oswego, and Vietnamese from Orange County. Instead of tips, we'll get IOUs."

The graveyard boss, Norm, pulled me aside and offered up his own bad news. "The old broad on your game with frosted hair is Carmina. A ballbuster. Blows a ton of money in here."

I nodded, understanding he meant be patient. I'd dealt to ballbuster degenerates over the years. One more would make no difference, not the day before karaoke, when I hoped to drink coffee with Audra. The dealer I relieved spread the cards. Her shirt pocket was stuffed with five-dollar chips. "Third base," she whispered, meaning the tipper was the man in the last seat.

The woman I figured to be Carmina placed two five-dollar chips in the betting circle and looked up. "I don't know you. Are you a cherry?"

"Yep, first time." I gathered up the cards and began shuffling.

"Shouldn't lie," she said.

"First time with you."

"Hey, Norm," she said, "this one's got a sense of humor!"

Norm strolled over to the table and chatted with Carmina as I finished the shuffle. She lit a cigarette, blew smoke in my face, and seemed to take some pleasure in doing it. I offered the cut to the man on third base. He declined, saying he was never lucky on his own cut.

"Don't you know it's unlucky to be superstitious?" I asked and passed the cut card to Carmina. She made a circle with it in the air, then plunged it into the deck.

"Good luck," I said.

"My ass," she said under her breath.

Now that I didn't need it, the insurance company offered four thousand dollars to settle the accident. But the pressure was off, so I'd told Friece to turn it down. For the time being I was Mr. Apathy, content to stand my shift, pay my bills, and get by. I tuned Carmina out and dealt as if my brain were in my fingers.

The table fell into a silent tug-of-war, the same approximate chips going back and forth, except for Carmina, who won five hands in a row, ten dollars every bet. It was obvious she played to lose, but got a little lucky. "You don't smile," she said. "How do expect to make a buck?"

By selling my soul, I thought. I winked and said, "Maybe when you start winning."

"Hells bells, I haven't won in twenty years."

I realized someone was gunning my game. I looked up and saw a tall man with long hair and sharp features, his jaw working up and down on a wad of gum as he eyeballed my game. I told him that I had an open seat. He pretended not to hear me, backpedaled a step, and slipped into the maze of slot machines. The player on third base signaled for a hit. I gave him a seven and waited as he made up his mind whether to stay or hit.

"I been playin' twenty-one years," Carmina said. "I won that first year. That's how they get you. You think you can undo twenty years of sliding?"

"Probably easier to walk on water," I said. I scanned the slot aisles, looking for the long-haired man. But he'd vanished.

Carmina put up a two-dollar bet for me and said, "Is Jude your real name? I never in my life met one before."

"Real name's Judas," I said, though it was a lie. The cut card came up. I broke the stack in two, took a quarter of each from the top.

"He sold out Christ," she said.

"My mother liked the name." I split the deck in half and shuffled. As I did I noticed that because of the thumb I'd dislocated, my dexterity was impeded and I could no longer riffle cards flawlessly off the felt surface and give the deck a thorough shuffle.

"Your father let her do that?"

I finished the shuffle and offered her the cut card. "I never asked."

"Why didn't you ask?"

"Never got around to it. Father's dead. So's Mother."

"It's sad to be alone. You got a girl?"

"Got a daughter."

"No. The other kind."

"Naw. Lost the last one to Mel Gibson."

Carmina laughed. I dealt out the hands. I thought about seeing Audra again. After all, what was there to endure, a few teenagers screaming off-key?

The cards turned against the players. I'd seen it thousands of times.

10 It was like breathing inside a Crock-Pot. Vegas was in day forty-three of one-hundred-degree temperatures and no rain. Heat waves danced on the asphalt, and seasonal clouds had gathered, towering billows that lay languorously on the tops of the Black Mountains and blanketed the valley south to Stateline.

Beth wasn't waiting, as was her habit. Five minutes passed before she showed up with her overnight bag.

"Got all your stuff?"

"I always do," she snarled, unlike the Beth I knew. Then too, she was a teenager.

"Well," I said, "let's go set music back a century."

She sat slumped against the door and stared out the car window. I thought of my own teenage years and hoped she wasn't suffering heartache. I asked if something was bothering her. She shrugged and said that summer was too long. I let it go. Given some distraction, her bad moods usually lifted in minutes, and pulling in the parking lot at Jitters did the trick.

Audra wasn't inside, nor was Katie. I gave Beth five dollars for a decaffeinated mocha. She walked straight to the clutch of mothers and daughters, and soon her voice blended into the general ruckus. I bought a regular coffee and a newspaper, then found a table in the corner so I could simultaneously watch the stage and the door.

The first song they sang was Aretha Franklin's "Respect." The rendition degenerated into a five-girl shout-a-rama. An elderly couple stepped inside, heard the singing, and retreated. Beth held the microphone. I stopped eyeing the door and acted captivated as the girls finished. They bowed, the women applauded, and the drill-sergeant mom glanced in my direction to see if I was clapping.

Then a woman dressed up as Madonna took the stage. She slung a stuffed lime-green snake over her shoulders and started gyrating to the Cindy Lauper song "Girls Just Want to Have Fun." Her voice was on-key and not what I'd call bad, but she was fifty pounds heavier than Madonna and waved her arms about and slapped her shoulders as if in a mosquito-killing competition. Finished, she held the toy snake to her crotch and squatted down on its puffy head. The moms sat staring off. When one clapped, the others cut looks in her direction.

A Buddy Holly emulator in horn rims followed the Madonna snake act. As he sang, he looked straight ahead with a deadpan expression and strummed a broom. Some among the girls sang along, "a love like yours will surely . . ." After the number, the deejay took the microphone and declared a short break. Beth crossed the room with a friend in tow and introduced her. The girl immediately left to join her other friends.

"She couldn't come," Beth said.

"She?"

Beth looked at the double glass doors. "I saw you watching for her."

"Who?"

"She's in New Mexico. At something called a sweat. Taos, I think Katie said. She's going to walk on hot coals."

The session continued, the girls first, followed by the Madonna impersonator, this time singing a Madonna song, and finally a Michael Jackson wannabe, who could moonwalk, but couldn't sing. When the Michael

Jackson impostor did a final pirouette, the deejay took the microphone and thanked everyone for participating. Beth crossed the floor and pecked my cheek. She asked if she could visit her friend's house, because the girls were going there and she'd go home later.

"Go home?"

"Where you live. I don't think of Mom's as home."

The friend Beth was going to ride with called across the room, saying that they were leaving now.

"Okay. Have a good time. Oh, and, Beth?"

"Huh?"

"I hope she doesn't burn her feet on those hot coals."

Beth hugged my neck and whispered, "She won't. I'll see you in an hour, maybe two."

The young, I thought, as she backed away. "I'll cook a great dinner."

"Make some pizza. Like Domino's."

"How about scallops and escargot?"

She pretended to gag, then raced to her friends. They giggled as they headed to the door.

LUCAS WAS SUPPOSED TO BE WITH HIS GIRLFRIEND, but his Prelude was parked in front of the house. I parked next to his Honda. Hell, I thought, my son drove a better car than I did, one paid for at that. I gathered the grocery bags and slid out of the car. I banged on the door with my elbow and hollered for someone to open it. No one responded. I set the groceries down and unlocked the door. Lucas and his friend Benjy sat on the living room couch listening to one of my Grand Funk Railroad albums.

"Hi, Dad. Mind if Benjy eats here?"

"Mind if one of you healthy young men picks up the groceries?"

Lucas jumped up to help. "You know, Dad, those old rockers weren't so bad."

"Righteous dudes," Benjy said.

They liked my turntable. Vinyls, they called the albums, with a sense of awe. I expected to see Beth as well, but she wasn't in the family room or the kitchen.

"Where's Beth?"

Lucas set the bags on the counter. "Hamburgers and potato salad. Extraordinary, Dad."

"I asked a question?"

"Upstairs. She got pissed when Benjy and I started playing 'Bumper Stickers You'll Never See.'"

Benjy laid his bag next to the ones Lucas had set down. "Like this— 'People Don't Kill, Guns Do,' 'The Best Way to Tan Is Be Born in Mexico.'"

"And that bothered her?" I started unpacking a bag.

"Not them. Benjy said the bumper sticker absolutely no one would ever print up is 'Say No to Pussy.'"

I turned around. "You said that, Benjy?"

"Yeah?"

"Jesus, you two! She's had a bad day."

"She's fourteen, Dad. Every day's a bad one."

"I thought you were going to be somewhere with Heather."

"She prefers choir practice to me."

"Smart girl. Right now, so do I."

Benjy drifted back to the living room. Lucas motioned with his thumb that he was going there as well. I nodded and began separating groceries and placing them appropriately. The boys played my *Layla* album. I was absorbed in my task when Beth entered silently and startled me.

"Dad?"

I snapped my head and looked over my shoulder. "Yes?"

"Can I help you cook?"

"Sure, glad to have you."

The phone rang. Beth answered it. She cupped the mouthpiece and said, "Are you here?"

"I feel like I am."

"It's Mom."

I recalled our last argument in 1991, just before Anne, after a dozen threats to do it, had filed for divorce. It was over the stereo, my listening to it too loudly. Apparently, she'd been holding back for months and shouted that all she wanted "was some peace. No," she'd corrected herself, "I want a goddamn divorce. And this time I mean it." She'd gotten all she wanted—the divorce, the house, the kids, and child support. All those years we'd tried off and on to pretend it was working, I suppose, the way many couples do, but a loveless marriage had finally taken a toll on both of us. Since the divorce we'd sniped at each other from time to time, usually over money, but had remained mostly civil around the children.

I took the receiver. "Hello, Anne. What's up?"

"Nothing. I just remembered something about Hefty and thought you might be interested."

"What's that?"

"He hit on me. It was clumsy, as you can imagine."

"Really?"

"Yeah, not once, but twice."

"What did you say to him?"

"I told him I was going out with you and that you'd kick his ass if I told you."

I couldn't hold back smiling as I looked at Beth. "I was never a fighter."

"He didn't know that."

"How clumsy was he?"

"Just shy the first time. Then he said something like he'd eat my panties if I wanted that."

"That qualifies as weird. Look, I'll get you the support for Beth soon. The new job's not much, but I'll make a check out in a week or two and get ahead later."

"Tell the kids I said . . . Never mind. I'll see them soon enough."

"I'll tell them anyhow. 'Bye."

I handed the receiver to Beth. It made sense that Hefty would hit on Anne. It struck me as odd that I rarely thought about my life with her. I didn't even remember if we'd ever been happy together. Other than my children, I couldn't recall any specific joy that came from the marriage, but for a time we got along. Then after the fire, the relationship dissolved, a small crisis at a time, probably in the way many marriages begin to fall apart. Despite her and my failings, we loved our children. Perhaps her having Beth, an unplanned pregnancy, wasn't a mistake, but a kind of desperate attempt to preserve something unsalvageable.

I was reminded of how attractive she was then, and even now. I had to admit that Anne had taken care of herself—the gym five times a week, regular spa treatments, and a couple of expensive visits to a surgeon, which of course she denied. Still, she was attractive and alluring to men, especially younger ones who liked to camp out at the house and mooch off her.

But she wasn't Audra.

11

Listelle, the graveyard cocktail waitress, leaned a hip against my table and set her empty tray on the layout. When work slowed and I was on a dead game, she'd taken to visiting with me.

"If I never picked up this cocktail tray again, it would do me just fine," she said.

"What are you studying tonight?"

"Calculus."

On break, she found a corner upstairs in the coffee shop and studied. The casino was merely a stopover to the rest of her life. She was completing a degree in biology and, though nearing forty, applying to medical schools. Her past was unusual. In her early twenties Listelle sold used cars. The summer she turned thirty, she'd fought forest fires in Idaho and Montana. While fighting a blaze, she'd carried a man with a broken leg on her shoulders out of the path of a fire and received an award for it.

"Slow, isn't it?"

"Yeah."

"I ask, what good is calculus going to do if I'm treating a four-year-old for strep throat?"

"You're asking the wrong guy. I'm just a dumb dealer."

"You're not the wrong guy. If I went for men, you'd do."

I couldn't hide my surprise. "Oh."

She smiled. "It's no secret I'm a lesbian. I don't announce it. I don't hide it."

"Why'd you tell me?"

She faced me. "You've been friendly. I was concerned you might hit on me. I didn't want it to get awkward."

"Okay. But if you went for men, I'd be dumbfounded if you went for me."

"Bet you do just fine with women."

I shook my head. "Once maybe. We get involved with people we see the most; that means casino people. It doesn't usually work, at least not in my experience. My ex and I met when we both worked at the Mint. Now she pushes cocktails at the Mirage and makes three hundred a day in tips. Me, I pay child support. But we have some great kids. I don't give her credit for it. Don't take any for it myself."

A white light flashed in the second bank of slots, a signal to summon a cocktail server.

Listelle looked at the light and yawned. "Probably Harriet wanting a double bourbon." She gathered up her tray. "She should will herself to science."

"I wasn't going to hit on you," I said.

"Why not? Something wrong with me?"

"No. But I'm interested in someone."

"Are you dating?"

"No. But now that I bought a car, I can ask her out."

"What makes her different?"

I said the first thing that came to mind. "She's been to prison."

"Yeah, that sounds like a good start, Jude. I gotta go, but first take a wise woman's advice. Run, don't walk. And in the opposite direction." She gathered up her tray and ambled off.

Bouncing it off Listelle, I realized how bizarre it seemed that I'd thought even of mentioning Audie's being in prison.

On schedule, the first of a caravan of buses from Orange County pulled into the south entrance. Passengers spilled into the casino and charged helter-skelter through the descending circles of slot machines. Within minutes, the tables filled up with blue-haired ladies waving free-play coupons and Vietnamese slapping down twenties. A group of college-age Vietnamese gathered at my table.

Roger, the relief pit boss, sidled up and whispered, "Bet there isn't a bowl of rice to be found between here and Costa Mesa."

"One hour to go," I said.

I was about to announce change for a hundred dollars when I noticed two uniformed Metro officers standing in the aisle nearby, looking at me. They exchanged glances and moved down the aisle. As they passed by, I called out change for a hundred-dollar bill. By the time I changed it up for chips and dropped the money in the box, they'd vanished.

The players, all young, enjoyed themselves, consulting one another on decisions or asking me what I'd do. In three hands, one turned a forty-dollar buy-in into two hundred.

"So, what you think, Jude? A soft seventeen I got. You with a three. Double down?"

I grinned. "If I had your luck, I'd double down on nineteen. But, me, if I went outside and it was raining beauty queens, a cow would land on my head."

The young man said he'd take that as a no and hit his hand. He caught a five and hit again. This time he drew a seven.

"Nineteen. I stay." He waved me off.

I turned over a queen and drew a nine.

He grinned and said, "I don't listen, you make a hand. Here." He tossed me a green chip.

The others at the table all put up bets for me. It was turning into a good day. I placed the tip behind the rack. As I did I saw the two cops standing at the edge of the pit with a security guard and Roger. I dealt out a hand. Out the corner of my eye I saw Roger closing Jennifer's game. Before I could deal the next, Jennifer tapped my shoulder and said, "See Roger." I clapped out and walked toward the end of the pit where he waited with the two cops.

"Hey, Jude. You forgot your tips," the young man called to me. I turned back, picked up the tips, and walked numbly to the toke box, where I dropped the chips.

"Jude Helms?" one of the cops asked.

I nodded. The officer held up a legal document, said it was a warrant, and I was under arrest.

"Must be a mistake," I said.

"Not according to the warrant," the officer said.

Though confused, I nodded and turned to Roger. "It's a mistake. I'll get it taken care of."

"Let's go," one of the cops said and pointed to the exit.

They didn't handcuff me until we were outside. The cop who frisked me asked if the handcuffs were too tight.

"No. I really don't understand this. I can't imagine what I did. I was in an accident, but the woman driving the other car was cited."

The warrant, the second one explained as they approached the squad car, charged me with battery. The lead cop placed a palm atop my head and eased me into the backseat.

On the way to jail the cops talked football—preseason games, rookie prospects, players over the hill. They didn't question me, and I didn't say a word until they stopped at the jail.

"I've never been arrested," I said. "Am I entitled to a call like in the movies?"

The driver looked into the rearview mirror. "A corrections officer will explain all that."

In the booking cage the officers ordered me to empty my pockets. One inventoried my property, a wallet with identification and fifty-six dollars, a tube of Chapstick, fingernail clippers, and car keys. He told me to strip. Another jailer sprayed yellow powder on my head, then my pubic area, and told me to turn around and spread my cheeks. I closed my eyes. One of the cops handed over a copy of the complaint attached to the warrant. I read the specifics twice.

Baffled, I said, "There must be a mistake. I never heard of a Stephen Edowski."

"No mistake. City attorney's office approved the complaint."

I read the complaint and closed my eyes. Edowski lived on Aberdeen—no doubt with an Afghan hound.

The corrections officer escorted me to a holding cell and locked me in with a dozen other prisoners. I asked when I could get a phone call. "After processing. For now, we're backed up."

The door slammed. I looked at the other inmates. They eyed me, much in the manner of dogs, hair up, teeth bared. The one nearest me asked what I was in for.

"Battery with dog shit, I guess."

The man turned to a nearby prisoner and said, "Probably murder."

I MADE BAIL just before five o'clock and took a cab to the New Laredo to get my car, a forty-one-dollar tab for the fare and five-dollar tip to a cabbie who smelled like discarded crab shells, and I didn't have anything left over for dinner. That was fine. I'd lost any appetite I might have had.

12

I stared at the wall as I held the receiver to my ear and asked Danny to repeat what he'd just said.

"I have to let you go."

"For being arrested on a misdemeanor?"

"For being arrested at work. I have no choice."

A day after my release, I couldn't fathom why they didn't arrest me at home or call and ask me to surrender. Cops show murderers that much consideration. How could the police even take Edowski seriously? Where was the evidence? I couldn't imagine a cop leaving the scene with a bag of dog turds and submitting the case to a prosecutor.

"Danny, it's a beef over a dog that shit on my lawn. Isn't a guy innocent until he's screwed by the courts?"

"Guilty or not, we had to close a game down with our eleven-o'clock bus tours in. We'll pay for a full shift, and you have tokes coming. I didn't want you to show up for work and find a termination slip waiting. I'll give you a good recommendation."

So much for loyalty, I thought. "Thanks, Danny. Take care of your mother."

"What does that mean?"

"Nothing. Just take care of her." I hung up.

13 I waited outside Anne's, weighing opposing prospects, whether to pursue a job at Wendy's or McDonald's or return to laying block. The idea of doing either didn't lift my spirits. Laying block walls in the Vegas heat after years of avoiding the sun held little appeal, and although there might be some work for a skilled mason, illegal immigrants had flooded construction and pushed down wages in Las Vegas to 1980s levels. The big advantage a fast food job had over construction was air-conditioning. The big disadvantage was low wages.

The living room window curtain opened, then the door opened, and Beth emerged. Head down, she rolled her overnight bag down the driveway.

I reached across the seat and threw open the door. "Hey, you."

"You were arrested. I heard Mom say it."

"It's true. I was arrested because I did a stupid thing."

"Really? How stupid?"

"This neighbor a couple of blocks over let his mutt do his business on the front lawn. I put it in a bag, followed the guy home, and dumped it on his shoes."

She looked off. When she looked back, she was grinning. "Really?"

"Afraid so."

"You totally did that? I mean, really, Dad, you know how crazy that sounds?"

"Pretty crazy, I bet."

"Can I tell the kids at school? They're always like telling weird-father stories. I only tell weird-mother stories." She looked at me pensively. "But who'll believe it?"

"Apparently, the cops."

She nodded, then turned on the radio and tuned it to a contemporary rock station. It was too loud, so I turned it down. She reached over to raise the volume. I shook my head. She stuck out her tongue. I put the car in gear.

"If you were a doctor or something," she said, "then I could live with you. You'd have the money to fight for me."

I wasn't a doctor, just a dealer, unemployed and facing a court case. I'd used equity in the house as collateral for bail and couldn't even consider selling now until the case was adjudicated. On top of all that, without money to retain one, no attorney would represent me.

I reached over and stroked her cheek with the back of my hand. I could tell from the way her eyes sparkled she had something more on her mind. "What?"

"Why couldn't I have normal parents?"

"That's the same question every child probably asks. So, what's on the agenda?"

"Karaoke tomorrow."

For the first time in two days, I felt hope.

14   Audra, as I'd come to think of her by that name and not Audie, was there and sitting alone, looking as casual as a tourist on vacation in her blue tank top, white cotton skirt, and leather sandals. She offered a short, noncommittal wave. I raised my hand, careful to make the gesture appear impersonal. I didn't want to appear anxious.

"It's okay, Dad."

"What?"

"Don't pretend you don't know." Beth hurried over to friends before I could speak.

I paid $1.80 for a mug and filled it with Kenya AA from an urn on the counter. As I stirred in sweetener, I glanced in Audie's direction. She was watching. Instead of walking over, as I wanted, and asking if I could join her, I retreated to a corner table and stared at the mug.

The girls flocked around the new master of ceremonies, a young, energetic black man who, in trying to organize the chaos, kept saying, "One at a time. One at a time, ladies."

I was listening to them shouting at the beleaguered man when Audie, coffee mug in hand, approached. She said in a soft tone, "Hi. I'm Audie and you're Beth's father."

"That's me." Close up she was even more appealing. "Jude." I offered my hand.

"I'm Katie's mom," she said, shaking my hand once and letting go. "But you knew that."

I wanted her to sit and join me. I wanted her to go away. Mostly, because others were watching, I wanted to be invisible or elsewhere. I took a sip of coffee.

She pointed at the door. "Why don't we go out and save our eardrums some pain?"

Before I could speak, she turned and headed for the exit. I lagged behind and watched the way the hem of her skirt fluttered at her calves. It reminded me of a younger Anne, whose walk had been what had first attracted me to her. I'd long forgotten the courting rules that applied when I was young and had a kind of clumsy and unearned confidence that I could score, for then it was all about scoring. Now I wasn't sure what any of it was about. Sex? Love? Romance? I was pretty certain that courting had influence on relationships.

She paused at the door and looked back, obviously waiting for me to open it.

"Here, let me get it," I said. Stupid, I thought.

We sat under a strand of misters that made the heat nearly bearable.

"It's too hot for coffee," she said.

I took a sip and nodded.

The girls' muted off-key singing drifted out. "Sounds much better out here," Audie said.

I smiled, nodded again, and cupped the mug in both hands.

"You ever talk?" she asked.

"Sure I do." It was an opening for me, but I didn't take it. What would I talk about? Being fired a second time in four weeks?

She crossed her legs at the knees and swung the top one back and forth. Her toenails were trimmed precisely and painted a deep red. She stared at the smoke-colored glass doors to the bistro next to Jitters. The girls' bad singing and the hum of car engines from the boulevard made the silence more pronounced. The hustle was so easy years ago. Now I couldn't carry on a simple conversation. At least I knew what topics to avoid—Anne, the divorce, personal subjects that ring of bitterness and strained conversations. In two decades of listening to women talk across tables in the break rooms, I'd learned that much. Medical problems and operations were out as well.

She set her mug down. "I heard you're having problems. Lost a job, right?"

"Kids talk," I said, uncertain as to how much of my recent history Beth had revealed.

"We have occasional bad days."

"Mine have extended into a season." I smiled to make light of the comment. "So, should I call you Audra or Audie?"

"Either one. My dad tagged me with Audie because he wanted to name me Audre. My mom wanted to name me Audra and always hated Dad calling me Audie. They actually had arguments over it." She tapped her fingers on the tabletop, then said, "Do you find me attractive?"

The question caught me off guard. "Huh?"

She arched an eyebrow. "You heard the question."

"Yes. I mean, I heard it. And . . . well, sure. My eyes see just fine. You're very attractive."

"I'm not looking for compliments. I just wanted to break the ice. And I didn't want to talk about daughters. Unless that's what you want to talk about."

"Well, actually I was going to talk about my daughter's obvious big mouth."

"She and my daughter were on the phone for an hour last night." She grinned. "Katie tells me most everything. I encourage it. Tell me, did you really dump dog turds on a guy's shoes?"

I wondered how she knew that, considering I'd just mentioned it to Beth. I was determined to handle it casually. I kept eye contact and nodded, this time slowly as I measured her expression. "I guess I did."

"Now, that's different."

"Yeah. I probably shouldn't discuss it, though I don't have to because my daughter does."

She didn't take the bait. Instead, she lightened the mood by telling a story of her daughter gluing earrings on herself when she was seven because her ears weren't pierced. I told of Beth coming home with a frog that a neighbor's dog had tried to eat.

"She had held it up and asked me to fix it. It was heartbreaking to tell her I couldn't. I helped her dig a grave for it in the backyard."

The storytelling turned into a lighthearted competition. She told about Katie dressing up a neighbor's cat in a doll's dress and placing it in a toy carriage. "The woman came over screaming that she was going to call the cops or the animal society. Can you imagine?"

"Yeah, my son once . . ." I told her how Lucas had turned off the water feed to the toilet and Anne had called a plumber to fix it. "Eighty dollars for a professional to turn a valve."

It was safe talk, stories that brought a chuckle or grimace. I relaxed.

People came and went, unnoticed by us. Sounds inside and those coming from the roadway receded. Everything was just background framing her. It went on that way until she said she felt the temperature drop. I looked where clouds hung over Red Rock.

"Looks like rain," I said. "That'll be a relief."

She held up her wristwatch. "It's been almost an hour. Maybe we should go inside."

I peeked inside before opening the door. Beth and three other girls formed a half circle around the microphone. I held the door open and followed her inside. We sat at a table near the entrance. The other mothers looked at us with obvious disapproval. She ignored them.

When the girls finished their song and surrendered the microphone to the emcee, Audra leaned forward and rested her elbows on the table. "I'll be straightforward with you."

It'd had gone well up to then. My mouth went dry. I was certain she was going to warn me not to misinterpret her friendliness and say that we were parents who shared a common interest in our daughters and their friendship. Something along those lines.

"Yes?"

"Like I said, Katie tells me everything. She said you just got fired from a job."

I looked at the girls, all of them alight. Everything else seemed heavy. The clouds outside. The weight of her eyes on me. "Yeah. Two jobs actually. Sounds like I'm a flake, but . . ."

"If you want me to mind my own business, tell me to, but I think I can get you work."

"Besides dealing, all I know is laying patios or block walls."

"I know people in the business."

"Thanks, I, uh . . ." I started to say I was going to try other work. Instead, I held up my thumb. "Can't shuffle like I used to. Probably wouldn't pass an audition."

She took my hand abruptly in hers and examined it. Her touch stirred hairs on my arm and back of my neck. A nearby soccer mom coughed to let tell us we weren't going unnoticed.

Audie let go. "I have a friend I can call."

Why would someone, a stranger, arrange a job for me? A kickback from tokes? Doing a favor for her? "In the slow season, you can still get me a job? You don't even know me."

"You're the father of my daughter's best friend. That's a pretty good recommendation."

Though I'd come to despise even the idea of casinos, I felt oddly relieved at the prospect of returning to dealing, something I was both comfortable and uncomfortable with, an ambiguity I reconciled on the spot with all that hung over me now, the prospect of impending attorney's fees, child support, and a mortgage payment coming due. "You don't have to."

"It's no bother."

The emcee announced that we were in for a treat. He stepped down from the stage, and a silicone-enhanced Dolly Parton imitator wearing a checkered blouse and carrying a footwide lollipop stepped up to the microphone.

Audie shook her head and said, "This could be painful."

"Your friend, why would he want to help?"

"Did I say it was a man?" She raised an eyebrow. "Let's go back out. I can't handle all these women looking at us."

Outside we took the same seats.

She looked west. "Do you think it'll rain?"

I decided to take a risk. "If it does, I'll take you to dinner?"

She smiled. "You can't do that."

My throat tightened. I stared at the clouds gathering on the mountains.

A couple of seconds passed, then she reached over and touched the back of my hand. I was amazed at how her touched softened everything.

"How about this? I'll take you to dinner . . . if it rains," she said and withdrew her hand.

It rained that afternoon. She called.

15 Audie, for I had decided to start calling her that, pulled her BMW into the circular driveway of a three-story house in the Scotch 80s, a tract of exclusive homes southeast of Rancho Circle. Edwardian in design with stone and stucco walls, stained-glass windows, and a faux slate roof, it looked out of place in the desert. It wasn't the type of house someone like me was invited into.

She shut off the engine and gazed at the tall double doors. "He'll ask questions. Answer his, but don't ask any."

"Why not?"

She smiled. "That's exactly what I'm talking about."

I wondered why I shouldn't ask questions, but assumed I'd find out soon enough.

I half-expected a butler to answer the bell. Instead, a Hispanic woman in a navy-blue dress opened the door and greeted Audie as *la señora*. We stepped into an entry flooded with light from overhead. A spiral staircase led to upper floors. Next to the stairs was an elevator with oak doors. The housekeeper motioned for us to follow and started down the hallway, her skirt whistling like crepe paper.

"Who the hell's this friend?" I whispered.

Audie placed a finger to her lips. "Remember. No questions. Wait."

I sighed intentionally to show my frustration, but kept silent. The housekeeper knocked on the fourth door on the right and immediately retreated back down the hallway.

"Coming," a man said. The door opened, and a guy in his fifties stepped into the hallway. He kissed Audie's cheek and smiled at me. "Hello there," he said.

"Ben, this is Jude."

He gripped my hand in a well-practiced handshake, firm, little movement. Letting go, he looked me in the eye. He had a practiced smile as well and had obviously spent lavishly to control the riptides of age—daily workouts, surgery on the eyes and throat, white caps on his too straight teeth, salt-and-pepper hair razor cut. "Glad you came," he said and let go of my hand.

His face wasn't familiar, but his type was—perpetually tanned, the kind who favored gaudy jewelry and flashy women, men used to controlling those around them, dapper men who could hold a gaming license and knew who to call to get things done, in a boardroom or a back room. I worked with his kind, ones who'd fronted for the outfit before Spilotro and others killed the golden goose.

He motioned us into a room the size of my entire house, garage included. Its walls rose up thirty feet to a vaulted ceiling. In addition to chairs and couches, it was furnished with three blackjack tables, slot machines, and stools. It seemed some kind of eccentric indulgence.

Ben pointed to a bar at the far wall. "I have any kind of fruit juice you'd like, made fresh, pulp and all, and kept chilled. What can I get you, Jude?"

"I don't drink much fruit juice."

"I'll fix a mango frappé. Why don't you and Audie wait at the center black-jack game? Have a seat. We'll get to know each other in a minute, and I'd like to see you work."

She sat on a stool at the center table. I sat so that a seat separated us. I wanted to determine the lay of things. For all I knew, she might be Ben's mistress. After all, our brief dinner date had ended on a walk to her car, where we'd made plans to come here. She'd said she'd had a nice evening and left matters at that, no kiss, no hug, not even a handshake.

"So, Providence brought you here, Jude."

"No, Audie did. In a BMW."

Ben grinned and looked at Audie. "Funny guy you brought."

She propped her chin on her hand, her expression indicating disapproval. Ben continued pouring drinks. I wondered about Audie and him, who slept under whose sheets. He sprinkled ice into tumblers, stirred each, tasted his, stirred more, tasted again, and nodded.

He turned to Audie. "Two hands, three drinks. A little help, dear."

Audie whispered as she stood, "It's not what you think."

Part of me said, hit the door and don't look back. Another part said, hang around to see what she is about. She crossed the room. I imagined her in a backless dress, her hips dimpled. She picked up two glasses and muttered something I couldn't hear.

Ben said, "I'll be back in a minute," and abruptly walked to the door.

I took my glass from her. "Are you going to tell me what's up?"

She shook her head and placed her drink on the blackjack layout.

I took a sip. "Not bad. So, who is Ben?"

She took the glass from me, set it on the table next to hers, and shook her head. Without any warning, she gripped my neck in one hand, pulled my face to hers, and kissed me. Her tongue parting my lips, she pressed her groin against my knee, then placed her palms on my chest and pried herself away, leaving me with an incipient erection.

She looked unabashedly at my groin. "Well, Jude's alive." She picked up her drink and sipped. "Don't you like the taste it leaves on your tongue?" Her mouth spread into an enigmatic smile. "Ben's my uncle," she said, "figuratively."

This, the strangest week of my life, was taking yet another oddball turn.

The door opened and Ben stood in the threshold. He asked if he was interrupting. He didn't wait for an answer, just crossed the room and sat on the stool beside me. "Like the drink? Tastes better with lipstick, I'll bet," he said, brushing his lips with the back of his hand.

I wiped off the lipstick.

"Tell me something unusual about yourself," Ben said.

I thought a moment and said, "Nothing. I'm an ordinary guy."

"Think. There's something dark about you, Jude. You're scarred." He pointed to my solar plexis. "Did your father beat you? Were you molested by a priest?"

I'd experienced some odd job interviews in recent weeks, clerks asking if I'd gone camping with my parents or played hooky from school, but this was more like the one-grand seminars Anne described attending before she started channeling the ancient dead, or whatever it was she now did. "What kind of questions are those?"

"Were you molested? It's not that uncommon. Boys are molested by males more often than girls are by females. What's unusual is for a man to admit it."

"This sounds like my ex-wife's witch-doctor crap."

"What makes you so different that Audie has taken an interest in you?"

I didn't know how or care to answer the questions, and I wanted to leave now. I'd heard how men had broken down at Anne's seminars. I wasn't about to curl into a fetal position and cry for my mother. I answered by giving him the obvious. "I've been fired twice for no reason."

"That's a start. But there's more."

"Lemme see. I was arrested for dumping dog shit on a man's shoes."

Ben waved his hand like a conductor signaling to an orchestra. "Something bigger, Jude."

I was feeling less comfortable with each question. "Is this supposed to be therapy?"

"Just answer. If you could turn yourself inside out and show the world the real Jude, what thing about you makes you different from the rest of mankind?"

"I don't know. Nothing. I'm just a guy."

"Think."

I noticed the chandelier hanging above and pictured it falling and flames bursting from the ceiling. I recalled the events I tried to avoid remembering— Randy lurching about, curling in on himself like a blazing question mark, until he vanished; smoke rising above the skyline; the dark confinement under a faux-leather shell as I crabbed along over carpet, disoriented, nearly sapped of strength, and terrified. I pictured people plunging down from windows, time and time again, as if they had to repeat the act in order to get it right, the same people every time, faceless, nameless. I remembered clearly being overcome by exhaustion as I pulled to a stop in front of my house. I'd sat in the car, staring at my front door and wondering how I'd be received. Every step that followed was as clear as if the event had happened just yesterday. I saw myself as I had been more than twenty years ago in the aftermath, my fumbling with the keys at the front door, then my staggering in. Anne, in a blue summer dress and barefoot, was seated in front of the television, watching coverage of the fire. I limped to the couch and stood at the arm. She'd gazed up and said it must have been tough. Tough? I lifted my cuff and exposed the burn. She'd asked, "Why? Why didn't you go to the hospital? Jesus." I don't know what I had expected, but not that. No doubt, it had been the postpartum blues talking, but it had hurt all the same and had planted a foundation for the icy wall that later separated us. I said, "Because I needed to come home." I'd left her sitting with her head in her hands and went to the bedroom, where I swooped Lucas up from the bassinet and held him until the feel of his baby breaths had restored some sense of life in me.

How do you tell somebody that happened and have them believe it? How? I said, "I'm just another guy. Nothing unusual."

There was a lengthy pause. Both Audie and Ben stared at me, but I didn't see them. I was as alone as the moment I stepped out on the sidewalk and realized in the scheme of things human life, mine included, wasn't as valuable as a painting, and that my plans for a future were like old newspapers blown about in the wind.

"What was it like?" Ben asked.

"What was what like?"

"We know you survived the MGM fire."

How did they know? I never told my children. Neither did Anne that I knew of. I closed my eyes. What had it been like? Simultaneously fast and slow. Frightening. I couldn't describe it so that they could feel it. "You could say it was hot."

Another silence followed. I heard Audie swirling ice in her glass. I looked at her. She seemed absorbed in looking at her feet. Ben was in thought. I finished my drink and set the glass aside. I was ready to leave.

Ben broke the silence. "I understand you want a job?"

"Yes. I need a job."

Ben and Audie exchanged glances. Something indiscernible passed between them, like two schoolkids privy to a piece of gossip. Ben made a clicking noise with his tongue, patted my shoulder, and said, "There are five decks in the shoe. Shuffle."

I went to the other side of the table and stood behind the rack. I looked at the cards and realized that I despised them. Despite that, I would do it because dealing was familiar, a forum where people gathered in a semicircle and hope and despair played off each other, where a dealer is reduced to little more than a soulless machine installed behind a layout to ensure the mathematics of profit.

"Ever wonder what a good dealer is worth, Jude?"

"No."

Ben sipped his drink, savoring it a moment before talking. "The average clerk dealing a five-deck shoe shuffles approximately two thousand two hundred times a year. By adopting automatic shufflers, casinos save the three minutes devoted to shuffling a deck on each shoe dealt. That translates to picking up the equivalent of five shifts per dealer per year."

As he talked, I shuffled. Ben paid particular attention to the way I riffled the cards. I was self-consciously aware that my left thumb strayed upward involuntarily. If this were a casino audition and a boss noticed it, I probably wouldn't get hired.

"The same person who calculated the shuffles," Ben said, "also determined that on the average a Strip dealer contributes in the range of $260,000 per year in revenue to a casino. The faster and more accurate the dealers, the more they're worth. A dealer working high-limit games may be worth a half-million to a million in gross capital. In fact, one's worth $40 a day to a casino, and whatever he and his fellow workers can squeeze out of the players in tokes."

Finished with the shuffle, I offered the cut card to Ben. "What's the point?"

"A good question." Ben didn't take the cut card. "The point is you're a good investment for a casino, but the casino doesn't see it that way. How often do casinos raise wages to reflect the profit picture? I'll tell you. Never. They expand the casino or build another one, and another, and then another. They've expanded everywhere in this country they can, so now they're moving profits overseas, more building as they slowly choke the life out of Las Vegas. That's the future. It's in the cards. You don't need a crystal ball to see it coming."

"You sound like a union organizer."

Ben laughed and took the cut card. "So I do. But I'm not. Never. Unions for dealers are a bad bet. You'll see that I don't make bad bets."

I presented the deck with my right hand as conditioned to do.

"No, the left hand," Ben said.

Ben studied the deck, then ran the plastic cut card over the corner of the deck once, then sliced into the deck about a quarter from the top. "Go ahead. Load the shoe."

I looked at Audra, then fit the cards in, and as I had thousands of times over twenty years buried the top card.

"Pretend these are real." Ben laid chips on three squares. "Twenty-five on the first square and a thousand on the next two. Now deal."

"Faceup or -down?" I asked.

"Faceup."

I dealt out the hands—a sixteen to the first spot, a blackjack to the second, and a twenty to the third.

"I stay on all three," Ben said.

I paid the blackjack, then turned over my hole card, revealing a sixteen. I hit and busted.

"Shuffle again, but spread the cards on the layout first."

"What?"

Ben took a wallet out of his pocket, counted out a thousand dollars, and set it behind the betting squares. "Shuffle again. If I win the big bet, you get the thousand."

I looked at the bills. "What's going on?"

"Can you use money, Jude? If you can, shuffle. Take a chance. I'll bet the big bet gets a blackjack." He laid an additional two hundred dollars beside the thousand. "If I don't get the blackjack, you make eight hundred for the shuffle. You can't lose."

"If you don't make a blackjack?"

"That's right."

Audie grinned as if at an inside joke. I fanned the cards out on the layout, backs up.

"Faceup," Ben said.

I picked up the cards, turned the deck over, and spread it faceup.

"Every dealer has a signature. It's in the way cards are spread on a dead game. In the way a dealer pitches cards or turns them over or shuffles. Go ahead, shuffle."

I shuffled and presented the cut card to Ben. He ran the plastic card over the edge before slicing it into the deck. The heaviest wager was in the first betting box. I dealt. As predicted, the hand was a blackjack, an ace of diamonds and jack of clubs.

"You're richer by twelve hundred," Ben said.

The money was the easiest I'd ever earned and greatly appreciated. How it happened, I had no idea, but the game wasn't on the square. In gambling there were no mysteries, just gimmicks called gypsy moves. I knew them, the old ones cross-roaders used. My dad worked the flat stores in Montana, and when I was nine, he'd shown how deuces were dealt, how a hole card was switched. He had an entire catalog of stories about cheating. He showed me that sleight of hand worked because people's minds and eyes fail to catch what's obvious. The shuffle had been normal. Ben cut. I buried the top card. Ben had done something. Counting cards was a slow-percentage strategy and by itself never guaranteed specific results. Somehow Ben had "put the chump to sleep," as my dad used to say.

"The deck's marked, right?" I said.

"Look close."

I looked closely at the cards on the layout, saw nothing unusual, no bends, no scratches, no daub. If the deck were marked, Ben would have read it on the backs of cards.

"How?"

"Shuffle again."

I smiled. "How much is this shuffle worth?"

"Maybe a million dollars over time. First fan the cards out like you did before."

"Tell me. What are you doing?"

"Just shuffle."

I was up twelve hundred. Why not? As instructed, I shuffled.

Halfway through the shuffle, Ben said, "It's no mystery. You clump cards."

"What?"

"Your right thumb riffles the deck consistently, but your left doesn't. You're leaving blocks of cards together. I can run a cut card down the deck, locate the clump and cut for the first hand or second hand. It's called tracking. I cut for aces and face cards to show. Getting the cards first, I have the advantage. The rest is memory. The way you shuffle clumps in, if we went through the entire shoe, I'd find a soft spot or two and bet on them. No one the wiser."

"It's cheating."

"Prove it."

I considered that a moment. He was right. Preventable, but unprovable.

"It's still cheating."

Ben came around and stood beside me. He picked up the twelve hundred dollars and stuffed it in my shirt pocket. "I can get you a spot worth a couple of thousand a week. In addition to tokes and salary, you'll make a hundred grand a year just because of your thumb. No taxes on that. Or you can leave now and forget everything that occurred."

"I don't know."

"Think, Jude. What have casinos ever done for you? Are you rich? Can you take a month off and go to Europe or a week even to go to Hawaii? Is your car paid for? Follow me on this. You have two kids and for years have paid child support or college tuition. On your days off you putter around, cleaning the house, mowing the lawn, and pretend it's pleasure. You may or may not go to a movie. You stay home when you take vacations because you want to be with your kids, but your ex-wife gets to go wherever she wants to. You pay taxes. You show up to work on time. You're a good employee. Oh, you may not love your job, but you do it. And what's the reward, Jude? Debt? Being fired? Two times? You tell me."

"Three times, actually. Fired three times. And terminated because of the fire. How do you know about the vacations?"

"Okay, let's say four times."

I looked at Audie. She took my gaze squarely. I wanted to know what she was thinking, wanted to know if she was a bribe or if she'd felt a stirring toward me as I had for her. She'd certainly briefed Ben well on what she knew of me. I knew much of what he knew had gone from my daughter's lips to Audie's ears. But the rest was a mystery. How much had he guessed? How much had he discovered and how? Except for glancing at one another, the three of us sat motionless for a moment, our breathing the only sound in the room.

Then I said, "But I've been a good dealer. I've never cheated."

"Will that be on your tombstone?" Ben asked.

"I warned you he was a nice guy," Audie said.

Ben cut an eye in her direction as if to scold her. "Nice guys get desperate." He turned to me. "This is a chance to make money," he said softly. "I could wait until you're out working and take the same advantage of your shuffle. But I'm offering you a good job, a fair cut. Who's given you an even shake? Fired for no reason. Four times, you say. How much, if anything, did the MGM give you for the fire? For your pain?"

Audie reached over and took my hand. "Tell me really, what it was like."

The past is a foreign land, in this case, not one I wanted to visit. I looked at my hand in hers. The kindness of a security guard had kept life from falling apart that day. I looked at the door as if looking for an exit, then at Audie as she waited for an answer. I felt a cramping in the chest as if two heavy objects were pressing in from both sides.

I pulled my hand away from hers, looked at the ceiling, then the bar where Ben had fixed drinks. How was all this paid for? Not off dealer's tokes. I'd beaten the fire and lived to feel like a cheat, who'd been cheated. Cards. Insurance. Is it the same? I thought of Dad lying on orange and red and black carpet, chest convulsing in pain, no one coming to his aid, my uncle walking in a darkened bar for a serendipitous meeting with an armed kid who had nothing to lose.

Ben said, "Jude, you've been to hell, literally. Did the business care? Anyone in it?"

"There was a painting," I said. "I saved a painting, a valuable one."

"You were burned, weren't you?" Audie said.

I blinked. I couldn't continue the line of talk. "I've been burned worse since."

"Jude, couldn't you have just punched him?" Ben asked.

"Who?"

"The dog man."

"Him." I shrugged. "No, I guess I wanted to make a point."

"True, but don't you get the real point?"

"Yeah, the real point is I didn't want his dog crapping on my lawn."

"No, Jude. The real point is you've had so much shit dumped on you, you just wanted to give a little back. We all do. Think. Did you deserve to be fired?"

I didn't know what I deserved. Everybody gets a share of bad luck. What does anyone deserve? What I did know was my good sense told me to leave and never return.

"I'm not a thief." I took the money out of my shirt pocket and laid it on the table next to the deck of cards.

16 The room was full of human smells—stale tobacco smoke on clothes, wet diapers, milk, candy—and the line of the unemployed coiled through three switchbacks, extending to the rear of the building some fifty feet. I took my place in it, now an unemployed statistic entitled to a few weeks of benefits for having spent years bending over a table hearing myself referred to in the third *non*person. The low grumble of adult talk filled the background, and the sounds of unruly children filled the foreground. Some parents scolded or swatted their miscreant children. Others didn't bother doing either. A woman near the front of the line held a screaming infant in her arms and polished her nails, managing neither very well. Another ignored two sons who argued over whose turn it was with a handheld computer game. A few people read papers and magazines. I'd not thought ahead, or I would have brought a book to block out my surroundings.

I'd never been unemployed in the needy sense. Following the fire I'd forgone receiving unemployment checks, and after my abrupt exit from the Maxim, I'd been hired within two weeks at the Monaco. Now, I was one among a multitude looking for bread and feeling troubled about it. I should have felt better, though. I had some reason to, declining Ben's proposition as I had. But in the process, I'd fumbled any chance I had with Audie. If I ever actually had one.

"Can't even smoke," a sandy-headed man in front of me complained.

One good thing in all this, I thought. I nodded politely. "I don't smoke."

"I can dig that. Wish I could quit. Know how much smokes cost?"

"Too much."

"You can say that again."

The line moved two steps. I looked back. The file now spilled outside on the sidewalk. I watched an apathetic caseworker interview a man in Spanish. She stared at the form in front of her as he rattled on passionately about whatever brought him here. What misery, I thought.

I recalled my attorney's instructions, the dos and don'ts of preparing to go to court. I was all but healed; still, he insisted I follow a regimen of therapy three days a week and consume a collection of prescribed pills for all manner of imagined aches and ailments. Part of the insurance opera. There was the other opera, the Audie opera, full of real ailment. After we'd left Ben's we'd sat holding hands in her car in the driveway to her house. After a few minutes, she'd let go of my hand, kissed me, and run her hand inside my shirt. She'd told me to come back if I changed my mind; otherwise, matters would be too complicated. Change my mind? I couldn't change my mind or put her out of it, even though now I knew how far she was out of my league and far more complication than I was prepared to handle.

"Damn line hasn't moved in ten minutes," the man who wanted to smoke said.

I nodded absentmindedly. I wondered how Audie managed a mortgage and car payment on a BMW. Not from standing in unemployment lines. From Ben?

"I was laid off a construction crew when we finished a project," the man in the next position said. "I go through this all the time. What about you?"

I looked him, leather skinned, about my age, thin. "I was fired for no reason."

"No reason. You ain't union?"

I could smell alcohol on his breath. "I'm a dealer."

"You guys need a union. I been in lines like this off and on all my working days, but the union always finds me a job before benefits run out. I'm a framer."

"Why would you be laid off?" The line moved a couple of steps.

"The illegals workin' for ten bucks an hour." The man turned again. "Say, tell me somethin'. Do you guys cheat? I mean, I ain't never beat any of you."

I turned away from his whiskey breath. "It's numbers, an equation, just like the distance between the earth and stars."

"Sure it is, pal."

Just then the infant that had been crying earlier bellowed. The wail silenced the room. Every eye cast a look at the young mother, who continued applying nail polish.

"If they was a bit faster, that woman could attend to her baby," the man said.

I looked at the back of the line. It was no longer a congregation of people, but a thing itself, compressed under its own weight. I noticed the sky framing the building across the street. I thought of a drive with my mother and father to Caliente. The sky had been deep blue, as if the whole of creation began with that day.

The baby screamed again. I thought of Beth, how I'd stayed up with her when she'd been colicky. I studied the desperate and bored faces and understood, in full, the meaning of "stay in line." It meant be safe, conform, think first about security, play by the rules—all choices I'd made. It also suggested I'd been a willing participant in all that led me to be here. Don't step out of line. It resonated in my head. Then I stepped out of line.

The man in front asked if I wanted my place saved. I waved him off and turned toward the exit. People glad that the line was moving forward one more step looked ahead as I passed by. At the door I glanced at the sky blue-ing over the roofs of the office building across the street. Unsure of where I was heading or what to do next, I stepped out into the hot day.

SUN BORING DOWN ON MY BACK, I stood on the stoop of one among a few dozen tract homes slapped together in Summerlin in the early '90s. Twice I'd started to press the bell, but instead agonized over even coming here. I'd done so mostly because I wanted to know if I was just a chump she was recruiting into a scam. If so, why me? I hesitated a few seconds longer before deciding I lacked even the resolve to press a doorbell.

I headed for the car. At the curb I paused and looked back. She was on the other side of the door. I wondered if she knew I was out here. I paced the sidewalk and saw the blinds crack in a window across the street and thought how I must appear to curious neighbors. This time I stepped up to the door and without deliberation pressed the doorbell, counted to five, and pressed again.

Then the door flew open.

"It took you long enough," she said and reached for my hand. She pulled me inside and slammed the door shut. Her hair was wrapped in a towel that looked like a turban, and she wore a red cotton robe that stopped at midthigh.

I hadn't known what to expect, but I especially hadn't expected her to greet me that way.

"Mrs. Long called," she said, "and told me a strange man was hanging around. She wanted to call the police."

"I didn't mean to get the neighbors upset."

"Never mind her. Come on." She took my wrist and led me past the front room to the family room.

All manner of conflict inside my head, I searched her face for approval. "I shouldn't have just come over like this."

"It's hot. You probably needed a cold drink."

She sat me on a leather couch in a family room adjacent to the kitchen and left me. Her sandaled feet clopped over the terra-cotta tiles.

I couldn't help but noticed her legs, calves shapely and strong. "You ever dance?"

She looked over her shoulder. "When I was a girl."

"I meant like ballet."

She opened the refrigerator and grabbed a half-gallon bottle. "My mother pushed me to be a ballerina so hard that one day I stopped. It takes more discipline than I ever had."

A few landscape paintings, the kind seen on calendars, hung on the walls. She had one of those entertainment centers, flat-screen television, stereo, and DVD in one. Suddenly I wanted small talk, safe talk. "So, how do you afford all this? You never told me what kind of work . . ."

She arched an eyebrow and shook her head. "In time." She poured two glasses of iced tea and brought them to the couch. "So what brings you?"

Twenty years earlier when I was brash and confident, I might have said I was there to fuck her. In those days privacy and maybe a joint were all the aphrodisiacs people required. I had no answer for what I was doing, any more than a man standing on the edge of a cliff searching for the courage to leap or the good sense to walk away. My initial purpose, or so I rationalized it, was to tell her I wasn't a thief, that she had me all wrong. I had to think of some explanation, but my thoughts were in a jumble.

"Impulse."

"Impulse, huh? Here's mint tea over melon-flavored ice. It'll cut the effect of the heat." She handed me a glass and sank into the cushion. "I'm not surprised you're here."

"No?"

"No. The question is, what do you want?"

She smelled of things feminine, of spice shampoo and lavender.

"Go ahead, drink. I promise it's not poisoned." She raised the glass and studied me, her expression flat. "I know in part why you came. You want answers to . . . fill in some blanks?"

I took a drink and held the glass on my lap with both hands. "I guess I do."

"Go ahead. Start with what's most on your mind."

"Were you in prison?"

"Yes."

"What for?"

"That gets complicated. My senior year in college, I took a summer job at Harvey's on Tahoe's South Shore, waiting tables. Five college kids from

California renting a log cabin. I was drawn to the back trails through ponderosa forests, the gorgeous lake. It was an adventure of sorts. Money was far better than what I'd made at Denny's in Santa Rosa, and the nightlife, it was . . . well, insane. A summer job became a year-round job. By winter I was hooked on skiing.

"Drugs were a big part of that world. Any party you went to, marijuana was served up like hors d'oeuvres. I bought into it all. Days on the slopes. Nights earning money for rent and ski passes. I quit waiting tables and picked up dealing blackjack. I skied and got high."

She looked me in the eye, gauging my reaction. Who was I to judge? I'd smoked weed in my break-in years and once snorted a powder someone claimed was cocaine. All it had done was clog my nose and convince me never to try it again.

"Were you convicted of drugs?"

She took a breath and said, "Just hear me out. My second year as a dealer I saw this guy with long brown hair ski the gun barrel faster than anyone I'd ever seen. He took the moguls at the bottom on the fly. I met him later at the Way Station, a club on Pioneer Trail. He had wild brown eyes and endless amounts of money. I was twenty-three, open to anything. I lacked the will to resist him or the worldliness to see through him.

"He turned me on to cocaine, gave me whatever I wanted. It wasn't long before I dialed myself up with it daily. We skied and partied, a life with no sweat until he taught me to cheat. That was how he made his money. I was in love. You could say I fell under his spell and went along with whatever he said. For nearly six months we—him, his friends, and me—ripped off Harvey's. It came to an end when I got busted taking a cooler."

"A cooler?" I hadn't heard the term for some time.

"You know, a cold deck. Prison for eleven months. Douglas County wanted to make an example. I was pregnant when they sentenced me. Katie."

"And him? The guy you were involved with?"

"In prison. Another case, two years later. He's my husband."

"You're married?"

She nodded. "Katie's father."

"I see." She didn't flinch in telling her past. Nor was there a hint of remorse for her crime. I'd considered that she and Ben might be a feature, but a husband in prison blindsided me. It was best to leave. I took a swallow and set the glass on the coffee table.

"You see what?"

"That you're married."

She locked her eyes on me and said in an abrupt shift in conversation, "You like the tea?"

"Yes, thanks." I wondered what it was behind the dark-eyed stare. "I guess I'll go."

"Stop saying that. I haven't been with him for over nine years. I've asked for a divorce, but there are complications. Property and . . . Look, I just wanted to be up front."

"That's fair."

"'Fair.' That's all you're going to say?"

"I don't know what else to say. Lately, things have been pretty confusing."

She went silent and avoided my gaze. I felt like a jerk. I'd invited her to air her history, and she hadn't backed off a bit. She picked up her drink and took a sip. A bit of shine returned to her eyes. "Don't go just yet. Tell me about you."

"About me? Seems you already know more than . . . Beth's got big-mouth disease."

She laid her hand on the back of mine. "Tell me, how'd you get in the business? I mean, I got into it by accident, and what kid's ambition is to grow up to be a dealer?"

I leaned back in the couch. "Not much to tell. My dad was in the business. So was Uncle Frank who laid patios and block walls on the side. When my parents divorced, Dad got custody of me, and my mother took my younger brother and sister. She remarried. Dad never did, and when he died of a heart attack, my uncle took me in, no papers, no court. Starting at fourteen, I worked weekends, mixing hod, wheeling cement for patios.

"Uncle Frank taught me masonry, even how to estimate jobs. By then he'd quit the casinos and intended to make me a partner. He and I already had decided on F and J Custom Block and Patio as the name of our company. He printed up business cards. He used to say one day the valley would be buried under story after story of concrete and we'd lay the ground floor. He laughed, like it was a joke. But he was pretty much right.

"His laugh could make you laugh. He was happy. The only bad days he ever had followed my dad's death. You know, 'close like brothers' is not always the case, but they were. They made each other roar with laughter, telling the same old stories time after time." I paused as she took a sip of tea, then asked, "Is this sounding like a shaggy-dog story?"

"No. You listened to me. Go ahead."

"It's life. No happy ending. When I was nineteen, Uncle Frank walked into a bar to pick up a check from a client. Three men were robbing the place. Witnesses said he smiled and said, 'Bad timing,' and that was the last thing he ever said. One of the punks blew my uncle's face off with a shotgun."

"Jesus." Audie gripped my wrist. "Were they caught?"

"The kid with the shotgun was twenty. He got life, but was released two years ago."

"I'm sorry."

"My uncle stashed two thousand in insurance money from Dad's death for me. I used it to try to keep the business going for my aunt, but no one would do business with a twenty-year-old, so I lived with Uncle Frank's wife and worked for another contractor until I was almost twenty-two. One day it was 115 out. The foreman started ranting about the pace I was working. I decided if I was going to work for assholes, it'd be in air-conditioning.

"Now, I'm nearing the age my father was when he died. No job. Not much in the bank. And the assholes are as bad now as they were when I was laying block. That's a long way of telling you how I got in the business of dealing."

We sat for a time, swirling ice and sipping from our glasses, neither of us talking. Then she stretched across me and placed her drink on a coaster. She made no effort to cloak her nakedness beneath the robe, and she didn't back away when I reached for her, just touched her forefinger to my lips and said, "Not so fast."

She untied a sandal strap and let the sandal drop to the floor, then the next one, after which she picked up her glass and snuggled into the far corner of the couch, her knees together, her feet beneath her. I wanted her, but an annoying voice in my head whispered for me to leave. I didn't listen. Instead, I sat waiting for her to make the next move.

"Why else did you come?"

The line of people in a dejected state popped to mind. "I had to get out of the unemployment office. All those people crowded together like . . ."

"No, I mean, what is it you want?"

"I shouldn't have. I mean, Beth is your daughter's friend."

She scooted next to me, took the glass from my hand, hooked her hand around my neck, and pulled my face to hers. "Ben said you'd come around."

She kissed me, slowly at first, then began exploring my mouth with the tip of her tongue. Her lips were cool, and her mouth tasted of tea. She pulled away and sat at arm's length, just looking at me, a smile on her face.

"Go ahead," she said.

"Go ahead?"

"Yes."

I reached over and untied her robe. She shrugged it off her shoulders, then unknotted the towel and let her hair fall. I fingered a damp strand and kissed it.

"Here's fine," she whispered as she settled into the cushion. "Right here."

It was late afternoon when I left. And I had agreed to meet Ben again.

17 Ben answered the door. He smiled and stepped aside for Audie and me. I felt bolder this trip and wondered if Audie could sense a change in me. Did she see herself as the catalyst? Inside was pleasantly cool and less intimidating this time. The hallway smelled of incense, and sunlight glistened on the tile. As I looked again at the paintings on walls and the rugs on floors, I thought of high rollers I'd dealt to, how they lived, steeped in money, luxury, and privilege.

Ben walked us to the kitchen and asked if we were hungry. Audie said it was hot outside and a peach or tangerine was fine. Ben methodically pinched several peaches before selecting one. He rinsed it slowly under the faucet and placed it on a plate that he handed to Audie along with a knife and a napkin. He was the kind who put thought into whatever he did, from rinsing fruit to the way he held the plate.

"Jude, do you drink coffee?"

"How else could I make it through twenty years in the casino?"

"French roast or Kenya double A?"

"You pick." I sat with my hands on my lap, feeling foolish.

Ben said, "A movie was released a few years back, Jude, *The Croupier*. Did you see it?"

"No."

"British film. Not bad. The dealer hated his job. Did you hate yours?"

"Sure, sometimes. Does anyone like dealing?"

"A rhetorical question, I assume. But I'll answer. Some do. Maybe it's just money they like, or the mindless repetition, or meeting people. Did you like any of it, Jude?"

"Punching the time clock on the way out?"

Audie looked up from peeling her peach and winked.

"When the coffee's done, we'll talk a bit and go to work," Ben said.

What work? I thought, and said, "Fine. I guess."

The coffee gurgled to a finish. Ben set out two mugs. As if a parent laying down rules, he said, "Your cut will be 20 percent, no more. You have to prove yourself deserving first."

"Deserving?" His tone troubled me, but I'd come this far and there was Audie to consider. She looked especially seductive as she chewed a slice of peach.

Once the coffee was poured, Ben settled on a chair on the opposite side of the table. He stirred sugar in his coffee. "Your father was in the business, right?"

"A dealer and later a floorman." I looked at Audie, who looked away. "I'm guessing you already know this."

"My family was kind of in the business as well," Ben said. "My father and three others died in an airplane crash between Reno and Carson City in 1963. I was nineteen. They tried to fly into Reno from Vegas in a storm. Hit the side of a mountain. They were the best in the business. Manny could lay down paint or work up a deck with the bend, Glen could string or key any slot machine in the world, and Angie was their rounder, could distract any dealer or a pit boss by tilting her head. Not unlike Audie. You agree, Jude, that she could distract you?"

I stirred my coffee and looked at her. She took a bite of peach and looked out the window to where a hummingbird hovered over a feeder. "Yes. She's distracting."

"Stop talking about me like I'm not here," she said.

"Anyhow," Ben said, "Dad was on his way to cold-deck Harrah's at the lake. That was when getting caught meant broken hands or worse. There was risk in doing what they did, but getting in a private plane and tackling a storm to turn a dollar was an unnecessary risk. You wouldn't take unnecessary risks, Jude, would you?"

I was almost ashamed to say it, but I said, "I've never taken any risks."

"There's good and bad in that. Dad worked Mob joints first, Hot Springs, New Orleans, all over Nevada, started at age eighteen as a bust-out dealer, then went the other way." He paused and took a drink of coffee. "You're wondering where this is going." He glanced at Audie. She looked at him, then at me, and nodded once.

"I learned from them and passed what I knew on to a few, including Audie's husband, who was too greedy and got nailed. Do you know why Audie's husband is in prison?"

"I think so."

Audie's full attention was on Ben.

"First he got Audie busted, then to pay off her attorney, he took up with another dealer, a blonde. This is while Audie was pregnant and serving time. Am I missing anything, Audie?"

I looked at her. She avoided looking back as she answered. "That kind of covers it."

"Working with that dealer," Ben said, "he set up the joint. Ran a few cold decks in at King's Castle. I heard three at least. A boss was in on it."

I was still looking at Audie. As if reading my thoughts, Ben stopped, took a drink of coffee, and said, "Having second thoughts?"

"About her?"

Audie stood. "If you two insist on talking about me like I'm not here, I'm going outside."

Ben picked up where he'd left off. "The eye in the sky wasn't in on the switch. The killer is surveillance. Time was it was easy to get around cameras. Not now. What my father taught me is mostly worthless, not because people now running the joints have the sense to figure anything out, but because they can watch videos endlessly until they pick up on the scam."

I was confused. My not being unable to riffle the bottom few cards of a deck had no relation to the scams he was describing. It was a quirk caused by an accident. It certainly wasn't a move video equipment would catch, even if surveillance thought the play was unusual.

None of us spoke. Ben took a drink of coffee. Audie walked to the French doors leading to the patio and stood in the sunlight, her bare legs outlined through the fabric of her crepe skirt, its white pleats gathered at her small waist. I recalled watching her walk the first time we stepped outside at Jitters, the motion of her hips like liquid.

"She's a beautiful woman," Ben said in a near whisper.

I blinked and looked at him.

"Audie, Jude agrees you're beautiful."

"Really, I don't want you discussing my looks." She stepped outside and closed the door.

Ben laughed. "Sassy, always has been." He rested his weight on his elbows and leaned toward me. "We play safe. Nothing taped or provable.

People who land on your game will know you. You won't know them. Every week you get an envelope. You trust my calculations. Clear?"

My stomach churned. I couldn't believe what I was considering. It wasn't me sitting there, not the me I'd been for nearly forty-eight years. "Yeah, clear."

"Does the idea make you nervous. Scared perhaps?"

"Yes."

"Good. Then you won't take chances? See, this *is* serious. We don't want snitches."

I didn't speak. Nor did he for a time. Apparently, my silence sealed a covenant.

Finally, he spoke up. "You have a minor legal problem to clean up before I can get you hired. Assault with dog shit, right?"

I nodded.

"Here's the name of an attorney." He handed over a business card. "If anyone can convince the DA or whoever that the case is bogus, he can."

The card was Charles Braverman's. I knew his reputation. Good, but expensive. "I can't afford him."

"I'll guarantee your bill and take it out of your cut later. You in or out, Jude, which?"

The dog case all but evaporated from my mind. The other reasons to say yes spooled through my brain. Enough money to give me independence. Money for my kids. And *her*, Audie? I looked outside, where she leaned against a white column, her profile lovely. She was elusive and way beyond me. What else she was, I couldn't be sure. I was certain, however, that I wasn't the kind of man who wove a spell over her kind of a woman. Self-deception has amazing power, but I wasn't ready to succumb to it. I'd lived too long in the world of probability and chance and knew, over time, house odds predict final outcomes. But I was ready to buck the odds.

"In," I said.

"Okay then. See Braverman."

As if on cue, Audie opened the door and stepped inside. She came straight to me and wrapped her arms around my neck, the first affection she'd displayed since picking me up.

"How's it going?" she asked as if she didn't already know.

"Fine," Ben said. "We'll start here tomorrow. I'll get him a good spot where dealers do the shuffling."

She said, "I'll drive him to Braverman's office if you can arrange for him to see Jude before the afternoon."

He looked at me. "Be here tomorrow afternoon."

"Okay, tomorrow."

Ben picked up a phone from the countertop and dialed Braverman's office to make an appointment. Audie lifted my arm over her shoulder and snuggled close. I felt her breath on my neck, her breasts against my chest. The feel of her against me instantly stirred a desire for her and numbed me to any thought of doubt.

BRAVERMAN HAD A SQUARE FACE, a wide brow, and solid jaw line, thick with the trendy two-day unshaven look. I sat as he talked in legal code over the phone. He motioned for me to be patient, then looked at the ceiling as he grunted in response to the other party.

The walls in the reception area were filled with sheepskins and plaques, but Braverman's private office spoke of a man who allowed no clutter. It was wallpapered and bare save for three large photographs, one of him with a young wife and daughter, one of him holding a thirty-pound lake trout taken at Lake Tahoe, and one as a youth shaking hands with Martin Luther King. The only concessions to decor were the several indoor plants strategically placed around the room.

The lawyer finally said good-bye to the caller and cradled the receiver. He cleared his throat and looked intently at me. "Let me get this straight. You really followed a guy home with a bag of dog shit and dumped it on his shoes?"

"It was his dog's shit, not mine. It's not like I went looking for dog shit to drop on him."

"Do you often do things like that?"

"It was a first."

"The city attorney had the audacity to file a case. No wonder justice moves at a snail's pace. I can't imagine a prosecutor bringing this before a judge, at least not with a straight face. There must be something else. What other kinds of crimes have you been charged with?"

"I was caught shoplifting when I was thirteen. The store called my dad."

"Were you arrested? Not that juvenile offenses count."

"No."

Braverman scrunched his eyebrows in such a way that it appeared he had only one that ran from temple to temple. "Let's say we go court. What will you tell the judge?"

I thought before answering. "Something like the guy walked his dog on my lawn for weeks, let the dog relieve itself, and left the mess for me. I finally did something about it. I mean, how much crap do we have to endure?"

Braverman chuckled. "That'll get a laugh. You can't come up with a better story?"

If I was willing to steal, shouldn't I be willing to lie? But I wasn't. It was the thought of Beth and Lucas. I'd never lied to them except by omission. Up until today I'd never done a thing that might make them lose trust in me. "It's the truth. I couldn't . . ."

"Okay. That's good. I just have to know my client. We can probably work this through without a trial. Would you take a fine?"

"His dog pooped on my yard for weeks. I lost my job because I was arrested at work."

Braverman seemed to weigh all this before he said, "There will be no jury, so you've got to persuade the judge that you're not a nut. The court won't care about how you were injured. It's unfortunate that way. What the court will want to weigh is the damage you did and perhaps your motive. We can take it to trial, which will be more expensive for you. Or make a deal. Go ahead. Make it tough or make it easy."

I considered that Audie was waiting for me in the outer office where I left her reading a magazine. She wouldn't want me wasting everyone's time. "How much of a fine?"

"Trespassing. Maybe $250. Nothing's a guarantee until I talk to the city attorney."

"I'm not sure."

"Do you want this dismissed? Or perhaps get hit with a hefty fine or thirty days in jail?"

"I don't want that."

"Okay, here's what I'll do."

I listened to his strategy. Starting with the city attorney and ending with the judge, it seemed plausible. "But I never called Animal Control," I said when he hinted at it.

"No one knows that. This is a misdemeanor. No one investigates. Let's try."

I conceded that point. He tripped the intercom and asked his secretary to dial a man named Willark. He turned on the speaker phone and shuffled papers while he waited.

"Yeah," a man's gravelly baritone said. What he said next was partially drowned out by background noise. He sounded as if he'd been drinking. Then I figured out the all-too-familiar sounds, in the background—loud voices, the clatter of coins, the clink of glass. What a way to negotiate a case, my future, over a cell phone in the bar of a casino.

"You at your office, Johnny?" Braverman grinned to bring me into the joke.

"I'm at the Queens, stuck three bills on this damned double-bonus machine."

"Can you pull yourself away and go outside so we can talk?"

"This better be worth more than three bills."

Braverman raised his eyebrows. "Worth saving you a court date on a bum case."

"I'm going." Gradually, the noise faded and a moment later all but disappeared. Willark's voice came over clearly, asking what exactly it was Braverman wanted.

Braverman said, "I've got the dog-shit vigilante's case."

"The who?"

"The guy who's accused of dumping dog crap on a neighbor's shoes."

"Oh, yeah. The warrants guys told me about that one. You pulled me away from my machine to talk that case?"

"Give me a trespass on it and a fine, say a hundred."

"I don't have the file."

"We're going to file against the alleged victim if we can't deal and take him to civil court too. The guy's dog soiled my client's yard for months before my client acted. Animal Control didn't do anything about it, and my client lost sleep, lost his job because he was arrested, and is in need of therapy because of malicious prosecution. He's got a strong case against the whole system and a civil case against your victim and maybe Animal Control. Johnny, you know I don't bluff. We'll take the guy to the cleaners and pick up loose change from your bosses."

"I'll look at the file and give you a call. No guarantee on the fine. May have to be higher."

Braverman's face lit up. He tapped his chin. "Thank you, Johnny."

"I'm going back to my machine."

"You're hooked. You know that?"

"It's a diversion. Keeps me sane. Dog shit. What's next?" The line went dead.

Braverman said, "That's it. Two days. Three at the most."

I pointed at the picture of the trout. "Nice fish. What'd you use for bait?"

"Like any self-respecting attorney, I used my ex-wife," Braverman said with a belly laugh.

WHEN I GOT HOME, I found a message on my recorder from Friece. This is the day for attorneys, I thought. The secretary put me on hold to transfer the call.

"Jude?"

"Yes."

"The insurance company offered nine thousand for medical and pain and suffering."

"What about the car?"

"The adjuster totaled it. I don't have the figures broken down, but I think you get about sixty-seven hundred after they pay off the lender."

A net of sixty-seven hundred dollars. Two days before it would have been an attractive offer, a reasonable if not fair amount, and turning it down was taking a risk. The old me would have said take it. After all, it was just short of the seven-thousand-dollar down payment I'd lost on the car. But I was a changed man.

"Tell them I said thirty thousand," I said with unexpected confidence.

18 Audie sat at the counter trying to convince me of the advantages in owning a luxury car. In the presence of Ben, she was distant, seemingly untouchable, but in the evening reverted to her witty, lighthearted manner as we talked about the vicissitudes of rearing daughters.

"They're safer," she insisted.

"So are tanks. Tonight," I said, picking up a tomato, "a special macaroni."

"Why not go out to eat? It's easier and faster. I'll pay." She preferred eating out. I, on the other hand, enjoyed cleaving stems off broccoli. Nights I had Beth, she and I would drive to Audie's, and the four us would go out to dinner. One evening I packed a meal for all of us, and we drove to Spring Mountain Ranch and sat on the lawn watching *Oklahoma* performed under the stars. Audie seemed content that night, as she reached out and held my hand. I'd interpreted it as a sign she felt a connection. Normally, she didn't show affection. Sex with her, though wild and physical, seemed almost impersonal, almost as if it were a workout for her.

I sliced into a bell pepper and held it under her nose. "Smell it."

"Wonderful," she said. "Why don't you make a deodorant out of it?"

I set the pepper aside and cut into a tomato.

"I suppose tomatoes talk to you," she said.

"They sing the blues when you dice them."

"Why not the opera?"

"They only sing the blues. You have to know your vegetables."

"Tomatoes are fruit."

"Those too."

"I'm serious. You need to buy a better car."

"Why do I need a better car?"

"Because traffic doesn't seem as bad when you're locked inside a BMW."

"I liked my convertible," I said.

"That's the answer, a BMW convertible. That's what you'll buy."

"You've got me spending dream money on a dream car. I don't even have a job. Speaking of which, when is that going to happen?"

Her playful expression shifted. "Let's talk about something else."

I sliced more tomato into the salad. "I could have spent those mornings looking for work. How long can I wait?"

"He's giving you money."

"It's not work. Not real work."

She withdrew as she always did whenever I questioned the purpose of the drills. To get along, I mostly avoided the topic. I wanted to quit, thought about it regularly. Yet five mornings a week, Ben and I stood facing each other across a layout, me trying one gypsy move, then another, switching hole cards, rolling the deck, dealing seconds—moves used years ago when some joints were flat and deuce dealers fleeced customers. Some moves I found tough to execute. For one thing, my afflicted thumb made it difficult to bubble a top card and peek at it when dealing seconds. I couldn't mask the move. I proved better at the heel peek, but it was a harder move to disguise.

Ben, offering no explanation, continually coached and scolded. An undercurrent ran through the sessions. He criticized and on occasion praised. Praise or criticism, it seemed wasted on me. Ten days had passed since Braverman took my case and no movement made to resolve it. Ben maintained he couldn't place me in a casino until the case was adjudicated. I suspected that the delay was intentional. In the meantime, Ben paid me a hundred a session, enough that I kept up with the bills. But I wanted steady employment and enough money coming in to help the kids.

I sat the salad on the countertop. "If you don't want to talk about the job I'm supposed to get, okay. Let's talk about why Ben insists that I practice gypsy moves."

She shrugged. Her eyes seemed darker than usual. "Ask him."

"I did. He compared me to a baseball pitcher taking batting practice even though he wasn't going to be called on to hit home runs. It wasn't much of an answer, so I'm asking you."

She walked around the counter and faced me. "Do you want to stop?"

I reached in a drawer for the masher and turned my attention to the potatoes. "You mean practicing?"

"All of this? Do you want to stop it?"

"You mean quit, us included, is that what you're saying?"

She ran her tongue over her teeth, then nodded. "You told Ben you were in. There's no partial in or maybes. No half-dead or half-pregnant."

When I didn't speak up, she gathered her purse from the table and started for the door. I spent years as a man who'd solved problems largely by avoiding them. She was married to a convict, herself a felon. She'd orchestrated my meeting Ben, another thief. She was all problem and no solution. If she left, she just left. I felt a sense of resolve and relief. Still, as she neared the door, my guts knotted.

Her hand touched the knob. She looked over her shoulder and said, "You're in or out!" paraphrasing Ben's question.

I didn't respond.

The door opened and slammed shut. My forehead damp, I stood momentarily under the fan in the kitchen, then hurried to the front door and flung it open. The dome light was on in her BMW. She was groping around in her purse. To an outsider, the scene might appear nothing but a lovers' quarrel. In a way it was, but as I watched her fumble in her purse for keys, I sensed her interest in me lay solely on my commitment to Ben's scheme. Still, I wanted her back. I pictured her nude in bed, reading a children's book she'd found on a shelf. She'd begun to read it aloud. It had been Beth's favorite when she was four or five. I'd kept it for sentimental reasons. As Audie read, I'd run my hand over contours and crevices of her body, felt the near-invisible hairs on her forearm, reached down to stroke the tuft of reddish hair on her pubic mound.

The engine fired up, the dome light went off, and the Beemer tore off, leaving a patch of rubber on the hardtop. If she had looked, she would have seen me on the sidewalk, hollering for her to come back.

19 Early in the evening two days after she stormed out, Audie stood at the threshold, head tilted seductively. I was in my apron, paring knife in hand, when I answered the doorbell. Her hasty departure had added another mess to the disarray that was my life. Now her showing up piled on even more. My birthday was in two days, and before her blowup, I'd planned on celebrating all forty-eight years of it with her. Afterward, I planned on a party for one, which consisted of breaking out my record collection and sitting in the living room, listening to rock and roll.

"Hi," she said.

"Sure, hi."

"Can I come in?"

"Why not? I'm cooking."

She stepped inside. "You're always cooking."

"What's an unemployed dealer supposed to do with so much time?" I shut the door and walked to the kitchen.

She strolled in and dropped her purse on the table.

I went to the sink where I'd been washing potatoes. "What brings you?"

"If you want, I can leave."

I picked up the peeler and went to work on a potato. She tapped her fingernails on the tabletop and watched. I kept at the potato. She grabbed her purse, turned away.

I dropped the potato in a pan of water. "Okay, stay," I said, "but level with me."

I walked around the counter, placed a hand on her shoulder, and nudged her over to the table. She slumped down in a chair and brushed my hand away. "I didn't come here for that."

"For what?"

"To fuck you."

I couldn't tell if her behavior was staged or sincere. "Then tell me why you did come."

Head bowed, she muttered, "I came to tell you he owns me."

"He?"

"Ben. Owns the house I live in, the car I drive, the food I eat."

"He's your, what, sugar daddy?"

"No. If it were only that easy. It's a long story that starts back when I was released from prison. Money first to pay my rent, to buy my silence, then to pay for my husband's lawyer."

She slumped down on a stool at the counter. "I told him you were out. He said I bungled everything, and if you went to the cops, he'd put me and Katie on the street. I don't have a job."

"That's two of us who won't have a job." The remark was a jab I felt entitled to.

"I told him you wouldn't tell the cops. He said you better not. He laid the titles to the car and house on his table and said they were mine if . . . if."

I nodded. "If I played along."

Since the night she'd walked out, I'd given thought to matters—vacations I'd never taken, my father's dying at age fifty-one with only two thousand dollars in the bank, a pittance after all his years of working. Since the fire, I'd thought that happiness, even the desire for it, was an illusion, but illusion or not, I wanted a taste of it and wondered if it was what she wanted.

"It was never me, was it?"

"At first, right guy, right place. But now . . . All that's changed. I mean, I do care."

I couldn't be certain if she was sincere, but if not, it didn't matter. She'd brought warmth again to my sheets and spread the complex smells of a woman around my house, and these had been absent from my life too long. From the time she'd reappeared at the door, I was prepared to pretend she did care for me even if she didn't.

"Tell me then, why does he want to teach me how to cheat?"

"Jesus, I don't know."

"You mean, you can't say."

"I keep paying for my mistake. And now you're paying for it."

"What do you want?"

"I want your help. He'll do what he says."

We'd never discussed her marriage. "Your husband—do you still love him?"

She didn't answer. I went to the cutting board and stood staring at the zucchini, took a deep breath, picked up the paring knife, and drove the blade down. It broke off as it slammed into the wood. Nothing is bad luck or good; it's bad life or good life. That's what I'd learned from the fire. Resign yourself to it, I thought.

"I'll be going now," she said.

"Go ahead. You're good at that."

I picked up a potato and began scraping at the peel. She said good-bye and walked to the door. It closed. After a few seconds it opened and shut again. Her footsteps padded across the carpet, then clicked against the tile in the hallway. Her purse landed with a thud on the kitchen counter. She bent forward, lifted her skirt, and slipped out of her panties. She tossed those on the counter. We stared at each other for a moment. I looked down at the lavender thong.

She came around the counter, placed a hand behind my neck, pressed her groin against my thigh, and pulled my face to hers. I slid my hands down her waist, resting my palms on the contour of her hips. Then I lifted her skirt slowly until it was bunched at her hips, reached down, and ran my hand over her pubic mound and between her legs. She was warm and already wet, and she moaned at my touch.

Later that night, after we'd eaten, we lay on the bed talking around the subject of us instead of talking about us. I was on my back. She rolled atop me and straddled my chest, ran her fingers over my throat, and then circled my nipple with a finger. I cupped her breasts. She pushed my hand away and bent forward as if to kiss my nipple. Instead of kissing it, she bit so hard that I thrust upward in pain and tossed her off the bed. She rolled onto the floor and sat, her porcelain skin glowing in the window-framed moonlight.

"What the hell was that about?"

She didn't answer, just crawled back onto the bed, took my shaft in hand, and began stroking. When I was erect, she worked her way down, kissing me until her mouth brushed my penis. She looked up at me and said, "The question now is, can you trust me?"

20 At the time I gave no thought to what Audie might have meant, nor did I consider the varied meaning of the words, when she'd said she hadn't come to the house to fuck me. Instead, I let myself believe that serendipity had brought her and all that was

ahead to me. I convinced myself that soon the hard times would be behind me, and despite my sore nipple or any reservations I still held, I returned to Ben's, contrite and ready to do whatever was asked of me. For his part, he welcomed me in and said that the past was just that and we had to focus now on the work.

My skills improved rapidly under Ben's demanding eye, but whatever his real purpose in teaching me he kept it to himself. He was relentless in his demands for perfection. "Excellence isn't good enough," he'd say and push me harder. The three- and sometimes four-hour sessions left me exhausted. A month passed, and we began a fresh regimen of moves, working up a deck from outside the layout, reading the bend, and hand switches. I became increasingly leery. What I was learning was far beyond the scope of what any dealer should know about cheating and more than enough to land me on the casinos' blacklist and in the Gaming Commission's Black Book alongside the likes of Lefty Rosenthal and Tony Spilotro.

Whenever Ben brought out a fresh deck and shuffled it, the sound stirred apprehension in me, a worry that someday I'd be asked to put these skills to the test. How and when exactly I had no idea, but it seemed inevitable. I took that dread home with me as Audie and I drove away each afternoon. Each day Ben handed over an envelope containing two hundred in cash, money that paid the bills, but did nothing to ease the constant rumbling in my stomach. The only respite from my worries was nights in the bedroom with Audie. Even then I was on guard, never sure what she might decide to bite on.

As July neared its end, Ben and I were practicing a card switch. He flashed his hand, a five and a king. I showed mine, an ace and a three. Audie, acting as the dealer, showed an eight. Ben pinned the king under a six-chip stack, leaving the five unpinned at a slight angle. The objective was for me, using one hand, to snatch up the five and drop my ace atop the king, then complete the move with a scraping motion over the felt as if asking for a hit.

Audie hit my hand with a six. I signaled for another card and busted. Ben flipped over the blackjack.

"That was perfect," Audie said. "I didn't catch the move."

In the last half hour we'd successfully executed card switches more than twenty times in sequence. I realized that she, like Ben, had been assessing my progress all along.

Ben nodded. "That's it for today."

Ben never ended sessions early. Always one more try, up to the final tick of the second hand. I sensed from the tenor of things that matters were edging closer to some kind of climax. I felt sick with uncertainty for what might be coming next.

That night after making love to Audie, I tossed and turned until an hour before dawn. I hadn't stolen since I was a thirteen when Dad, after catching me with a stolen model-car kit, walked me back to the store and made me return the model and apologize to the manager. The mere thought of going into a casino to cheat terrified me, but it seemed I was bound to do just that. I kept imagining Anne saying that I was subverting myself. I pictured uniformed guards pulling me by the arms away from a game, me struggling to free myself from their ever-tightening grasp. I'd seen this done in similar fashion before to troublemakers and cheaters. I finally calmed my fear by recalling what busy periods in casinos were like, players demanding markers, bosses distracted, dealers enduring a last few minutes before a much-wanted break. It was easiest to pull off a caper then.

THE NEXT MORNING Audie and I ate a quick breakfast at an IHOP before driving to Ben's. She was unusually quiet. I sensed something different ahead and that she knew what it was. Ben met us at the door as usual and asked me if I'd slept well. I lied and said I had.

"Well, you look like shit. Like you're hung over."

"Thanks."

"He's fine. We had a big breakfast," Audie said.

Ben walked us to the game room where a man sat at the blackjack table. He stood as we entered, looked at Audie, and smiled as if they were familiar. I felt a twinge of jealousy.

"Jude," Ben said, "this is Angel."

Angel stepped up and offered me his hand. He was tall and thin, in his thirties, with long sandy-brown hair parted down the middle. Had his hair been short, he might have been mistaken for a Kennedy. Something about him seemed familiar, but I couldn't figure what. Maybe he was just a type. I dismissed it as that and shook his hand. Angel turned to Audie and asked how she and Katie had been doing.

"Angel's down from Reno," Ben said.

Audie leaned into my arm, assuring me. "You'll practice with him today, and tomorrow you'll go out with him."

"I assume you don't mean a date," I said.

No one laughed. Angel looked confused, as if unsure if he was supposed to say something. Ben grinned as a doctor might when preparing a patient for bad news. Audie took the car keys from her purse and rattled them. I turned for the door, knowing another sleepless night faced me.

21 We waited at Ben's in the den for the fourth member of the crew to arrive, Angel with his eyes on a sports betting form, Audie in a recliner with an open newspaper in hand, me on a stool, steadying my sweating hands. Past noon, the temperature hung at 110 degrees. For two days the ever-darkening clouds had promised rainfall, but so far had delivered only a blanket of humidity that spread over the valley and sapped our energy. I looked out at the sky, clouded up again all the way south to Stateline. Between the heat and humidity and my jitters, I felt as if I'd just run a one-legged marathon.

Ignoring all of us, Audie turned a page and spread the paper again.

"Does the paper say rain?" I asked.

She glanced up at me, nodded, and flipped to the next page.

"Nice talking to me," I said.

She went on reading, or pretending to.

I'd lain awake much of the night, most of it in gut-turning anticipation. I feared I would lack guts enough to go through with whatever was to come or freeze in the middle of a play and bungle the caper. One slight error could result in jail for all of us. The thought scared me, and the humiliation it would cause my children truly disturbed me. They could laugh off a quirky act like dumping dog turds on someone's shoes, but my getting arrested for stealing from a casino would likely be unforgivable. As if dwelling on possible consequences wasn't enough to deal with, Audie's demeanor toward me was inexplicable. She'd brushed off my invitation to stay the night, didn't even come inside, just brushed my cheek lightly with her lips, and curtly told me to get a good sleep. This morning, on the drive to Ben's she'd barely spoken. When I asked how she'd slept, she'd shrugged and adjusted the rearview mirror. And when asked what was wrong, she'd said, "Nothing. Nothing's wrong. Let it go."

As I looked at her now, I wondered if I'd been duped. I thought it through for a few seconds and decided if I'd been duped, I'd duped myself into this. All I had to do was stand in an unemployment line, bide my time, and find a job, any job.

Ben sat beside Angel on a couch. "What do you think, Jude? This clown here, this Angel, risks getting busted so he can bet on football. Not just football—preseason games. Is that nuts?"

Angel waved his hands as if erasing Ben's comment. "How's it nuts? It's my money, and hey, a game don't mean nothin' if I don't have a wad on it. Where's the damned rush?"

"I never bet sports," I said. I looked at Angel, careful not to stare or make it obvious that I sensed something familiar about him that I still couldn't pin down.

"Never bet 'em?" Angel said, obviously astounded. "Weird."

"Jude's a family man," Audie said without looking up from the magazine. "Spends his money on his kids." She was irritated, maybe at Angel. Or the idea of his blowing money on betting sports. Perhaps me. I gathered from the way she dismissed Angel's remark that whatever reason she had for leaving abruptly last night, Angel wasn't it.

"Well, that's good," he said and looked at me. "What she ain't saying is that she and my ex are . . . were . . . friends. And Audie doesn't think I'm much at the fathering business. Hey, they get what they need. They're my kids. You know, I got feelings."

I shoved my shaking hands in my pockets to keep the others from seeing them. Audie set the paper aside, came over, and rested her hands on my shoulders. She dug her fingers in. I stiffened.

"Relax," she whispered. "You'll do fine."

Angel looked our way. "No secrets, kiddies."

"How's he doing?" Ben asked Audie.

"Ask him." Audie let her hands drop to her side. She walked to the recliner, where she sat and crossed her ankles.

"Okay." Ben got up and faced all of us. "Here it is. Because it's your first go, Jude, you bet third base and Angel will switch to you. If it looks like a no go, Angel will say it's tom. In that case, Jude, play a couple of hands and leave the game. If everything's jake, play it out the way I instructed."

"Got it," I said, knowing tom meant that the caper had soured.

Ben said that he'd decided on the Whiskey River, a downtown joint that catered to bus-ticket tourists and locals. The dealers dealt handheld single- and double-deck games and were mostly break-ins whose lapses kept bosses occupied correcting mistakes.

"One camera covers the entire pit. There are three exits in case the play's busted. Leave in a hurry, but walk." Ben looked at me. "If you think the camera's on you, cash out. If real trouble comes down, separate. Jude, you grab the chips and head for the back exit. Do not go to the car."

"Why not?"

"Just listen. If you think you've been made or someone's following you, take a taxi to the Sahara. That goes for all four of you."

"But there's only three of us," I said.

He pointed an index finger to silence me. "Otherwise, Jude, if you're sure you aren't being followed, go to Berdie's Bail Bonds on Third Street and ask for Russ."

I broke out in a fresh sweat.

"Audie will find the spot," Ben said.

The doorbell chimed. Everyone looked in the direction of the sound. The silence that pervaded the room was palpable. I tensed. My last hope sank. The best chance of getting out of this had been if whoever our fourth member to be was didn't show.

"Probably her," Angel said.

"A half hour late," Audie said. "It's her, no doubt."

"I'll get it," Angel said.

Ben cut Angel off. "I'll make sure." He hurried out, shutting the door behind him.

Angel watched the door. Audie stared at her paper.

"It's bound to rain," I said, perhaps just to hear my voice or test to see if it quavered.

A moment later the door opened, and Ben announced, "It's her. She had to use the toilet."

The wait drew toward ten minutes. With Ben in the room, the silence was less noticeable. Then finally the door opened, and the latecomer entered. Angel crossed the room, arms open, and took Patty Lane into an embrace. Hardly the fourth I expected to see. She wore pink shorts, the kind we as kids called crotch biters, and a pink halter top that emphasized her tanned, silicone-enhanced mounds. Her unbraided hair cascaded harmlessly down her back.

Angel led her by the hand to the center of the room and told her to turn around. "Look. What man in his right mind wouldn't pay attention to this?" He patted her butt.

The house in Spanish Oaks, trips to Europe, a Mercedes. All nothing now, I thought. The dealers at the Monaco would love to hear about this!

Ben stepped between them and walked Patty over to me. "Patty, this is Jude."

She smiled as if we were old friends, extended her hand, and said, "Hi, Jude." Then she asked as I took her hand, "Do I know you from somewhere?"

She wasn't being ironic because irony was beyond her. She'd spoken to me only once before, to apologize, at a boss's insistence, for her nearly blinding my eye with her ponytail.

I smiled back and said, "I don't think so."

AUDIE WAS INSIDE, scouting the pit. The rest of us waited outside, thunder clapping at a distance, sun shining overhead. Angel gnawed on a stick of gum. A camera hung from his neck, his attempt to look like one of the tourists who milled about Fremont Street snapping pictures. A few feet away, Patty Lane looked up and down the street as if waiting for someone.

The Fremont Street Experience had eyes everywhere, security cameras watching and recording. The synthetic screen top that closed off the sky and the lenses eyeballing the street made the mall seem small enough to induce claustrophobia. The street that had once been a canvas of motley human interaction was no longer a place of joy, where as teenagers my friends and I rode up and back from the Blue Angel to the Union Plaza, climbing from one moving automobile to another or passing a can of beer or a joint back and forth. No other place in the world had been like it. Now it wasn't a street. It was a mall, and that innocent past was gone and the person I'd become didn't belong here. But I was.

"Friday and Saturday nights," I said, "we used to start at Five Points East and drive up Fremont and back until curfew."

"Sounds boring," Angel said.

"I was a kid. What did I know? It was fun."

Angel's attention was on the Whiskey River. "Been in there a while."

I glanced at Patty Lane and Angel, and I realized where I recognized him from. His slack-jawed way of working his gum sparked a memory of a gum chewer who'd clocked my game at the New Laredo and walked away. He'd been sent to scout me out even before Audie drove me to the first meeting. It made sense now.

He furrowed his eyebrows. "Tell me, really, did you dump dog shit on a man's shoes?"

"Yeah, I guess I did."

"That's cool." He chomped away at his gum for a time, then said, "Met all kinds of thieves, a couple of murderers too. No dog-shit dumper before."

"Guess now you have."

"Yeah. Damn. Wonder what's takin' so long? Audie's a together babe, but a ballbuster." Angel frowned. "Sorry, I mean . . ."

"It's okay."

"How're you doin'?"

"Me?" I looked at him. "I'm okay."

"You dropped out for a minute. You scared?"

"I guess."

"It's the waiting. Here." Angel offered up a stick of gum. "Take one. It helps."

I popped the gum in and began to chew. I started to toss the wrapper, but thought, what if a cop saw me littering? I stuffed it in my pocket. I looked at the tall building that used to be the Mint, thought of my history with it, not just dealing there and meeting the mother of my children. At age five, I'd ridden the glass elevator to the top with Dad. I recalled the initial thrill as gravity pulled at my stomach, the fear I felt as I'd edged close to the glass and looked down, a fear similar to what I now felt.

"Here she comes," Angel said.

Audie, a large purse dangling at her side, stepped away from the casino. She hugged the purse to her hip and crossed the mall into the shadow of the plaza, where we stood. She said, "BJ eleven, fourth table on the right. Second pit," and walked on without looking back.

"Okay. It's time." Angel stepped from the curb.

I felt clammy all over, neck to waist, palms damp, fingers tingling, trepidation in every cell of my body. My mouth dry, I tailed Angel. Though it did little good to calm me, I chewed gum and fought the urge to turn and walk in the opposite direction. If I were to back out, it must be now. Independent of my thoughts, my feet somehow kept me moving toward the entrance.

A step ahead of me, Angel grabbed the brass handle to the glass door, looked back, and said, "Don't fuck it up."

I wiped my hands on my trousers, took a deep breath, and entered. The air-conditioning hit my face like a slap.

Angel went directly to the table and angled himself to block anyone from taking the last seat. He laid two twenties on the layout. The dealer glanced over and finished dealing the hand to the player in the middle seat. I circled the pit from the opposite side and approached the table.

"Excuse me," I said to Angel. "Are you going to play two spots?"

"No, help yourself."

I scooted the stool back and sat on third base. So far, so good, I thought, an odd notion because nothing at all had yet happened. Still, I felt better about it all.

The dealer's name tag read Dean. He was old for a break-in, perhaps forty, his fingers calloused and cumbersome, stubby digits that had done hard labor for most of their days. His belly bulged over his belt. Watching him cut the chips on the layout, I thought, soft as a quail's breast. Audie had sized up the right dealer, the kind destined to dead-end in some midlevel casino and earn a tough living.

"Dean, my man, I hope you're lucky for me," Angel said.

Dean changed the forty into five-dollar chips and handed them to Angel. "Good luck."

"I like your style, Dean," Angel said and laid down another twenty. "Give me ones with that, so I can help you out."

Dean changed up the bills, and Angel put out a five-dollar bet for himself and a dollar bet in front of the circle for Dean. "I win, you win."

I laid down four twenty-dollar bills. The idea was not to flash big bills. Ben said a gypsy move worked because it was preceded by a con, the simpler the better. I brushed my palms over the felt and said, "All reds, please."

Dean spread the bills in front of him and called out, "Change eighty!"

A floorman, no more than twenty-five, cut an eye at the game and told Dean to change it up. The young boss was stuck watching five games, four of them busy. Dean's face strained from concentration as he shuffled and stripped the deck. He nearly fumbled one strip.

Angel turned his head, faked a cough, and whispered, "This is jake."

Confident now we could pull it off, I laid two chips in the betting circle. I would follow the plan, start small, build up bets—the goal a thousand dollars, then walk. If someone wises up, grab the checks and hustle out, but don't run. As Dean offered the deck for a cut, Patty Lane eased down on first base. She leaned forward and placed a twenty-dollar bill in the betting circle.

Dean's eyes snapped in her direction. "You want the money to play, ma'am?"

"What does that mean?" she asked.

"Do you want to bet the whole twenty?"

"Do I have to?"

She's got him on the hook, I thought. I had to wonder myself if it was an act or if she was sincere. In either case, she was ideal bait to reel him in.

"No, ma'am."

She looked at the two-dollar-minimum sign and said, "Oh, I see. Just . . . two dollars."

"I'll change it up for you."

She smiled up at him. "Thanks."

Intent as he was on estimating Patty Lane's cup size, Dean failed to case the layout before pitching the cards. His delivery wasn't graceful, but he managed to get the cards to all of us. I held my first card faceup, a six, so Angel could see it. He flashed his discretely—a five. We'd likely go for an eleven to make the hand or double down if Dean showed a three through a seven. Angel's second card was a nine, mine an eight. Dean's up card was a seven. I pinned the six underneath my chips and laid the eight on top. Patty Lane leaned forward so that her breasts pressed together. She exposed her cards, two queens. "Should I split these?" she asked.

That was all the distraction Angel needed. His hand whisked over the felt. He snatched up my eight and simultaneously dropped the five, the exchange so smooth even I couldn't see it. I turned over my cards and matched my bet. Dean, entranced by Patty Lane's tan cleavage, was still explaining the risk of splitting tens. The man playing the middle, also mesmerized, pinned his cards under the money without looking at them. The floorman, eyes wide, glanced at Patty Lane, looked at another game, then back at her. Dean, the floorman, the man in the middle seat, all rendered hormone dumb.

Angel took a card and stayed. The dealer pinned a card behind my bet, wished me good luck, and turned over his hole card. He had a seventeen and seemed pleased that he did. His eyes straying toward Patty Lane, he exposed my double-down card, a nine. He nearly knocked the chips over as he paid off my bet. He pushed with Angel, then turned over the cards of the man in the center spot and looked around as if seeking a witness.

When he gathered his wits, Dean said, "Did you know you stayed on a nine, sir?"

The man grinned meekly. "It's a new strategy."

Dean locked up the man's bet and moved to Patty Lane.

"Guess we know what you got." He smiled and paid her.

As Dean turned over Patty Lane's hand, an unexpected sensation took a grip on me. Blood rushed to my head, then drained away an instant later. My pulse slowed. The bells and buzzers coming from the slots, the subdued roar of human voices, and all the blended other noise that so defines a casino seemed to diminish. I looked about and saw objects with the kind of acuity I'd had as a teenager.

"You should be betting more," the man in the center seat said to Patty Lane.

"And you should have taken a hit." Patty Lane looked up at Dean. "Should I bet more?"

"Ma'am, I can't say."

She looked at Angel, then me. "What do you two think?"

"I'm betting more," Angel said. "Dean here is our lucky dealer." He put another five on his hand and another dollar bet out for Dean. "We're pressin', my man."

The con proceeded just as Ben had mapped it out. I bumped my bet to thirty. I won five more hands, then reduced the bet and lost it intentionally. In setting up my hand, Angel often improved his own. Even Patty Lane was making money.

A few hands later the floorman came over, introduced himself to each player. He asked if we'd like drinks. Ben had advised me not to worry if a boss stood close to the table. The best way to detect a gypsy move was in the peripheral vision, from a distance. Nor did a boss expect anyone to cheat right under his nose.

I took a hit on a thirteen against the dealer's nine and busted. The con couldn't have been better timed. Dumb floorman, I thought, and said, "I'll have a diet Coke."

"I'll get the girl." The boss walked to the podium.

I bet fifty dollars and placed a five-dollar chip in front of the betting circle for Dean.

Little by little, it became easier. Angel had deft hands, and if there was an inkling we were being watched, we didn't switch. I came to sense those times. When I caught a natural, I was strangely disappointed; I didn't want to lose the rhythm of the move.

When Dean's relief arrived to send him on break, I stood and asked the dealer to color me up, said my lucky dealer was leaving and that I'd had enough. The new dealer was a woman no more than twenty-three. She seemed angry about my leaving. I exchanged reds and picked up three green and eight black checks. Eleven hundred seventy-five, a nice score.

"Think I'll cash out too," Angel said.

From buy in to cash out, the scam had taken thirty-two minutes. I folded eleven hundred in bills in my wallet and walked out into a world that seemed newly hatched. I'd committed a crime, but oddly I didn't feel like a criminal. At a trash basket on Fremont I rid myself of the stale gum and glanced up through the light show at what had once been the Mint. The elevator was rising and I was on it, a five-year-old again looking down, scared and elated.

A wall of clouds surrounded the Sheep Range. A dusklike sky darkened the street, and the air was cool. The storm was closing on the city. Anxious to tell Audie of our success, I picked up the pace and hurried to the car. Even if I had reservations about us, I wanted her to be proud of me for pulling it off. She was parked on the second floor of the Horseshoe, listening to an FM rock station.

I slid in, spread the wallet, and thumbed the bills. "All without a hitch. It was great."

I intended to tell her that I'd been dead for twenty years, that I was thankful for today, but before I could, she reached over, changed the station, and said, "Should I be impressed?"

Just then Angel lumbered up to the back door, opened it, and sank into the seat. He reached over and patted my shoulder. "You did good, Jude."

"Where's Patty?" Audie asked.

"A Slow Sally. Probably still cashing out. No clue and she still won most of her bets. Maybe I'll have her pick some teams for me. Hell, it'd probably be as good as my system."

"Here she comes," Audie said.

Patty Lane climbed in the back beside Angel and kissed him. She heard the music and said, "Ick. Find us some soft rock."

I breathed in the heavy air, exhaled, and set the radio dial. Audie backed out, turned, and drove down the ramp. She took Fourth Street to the freeway. Lightning sparked in the sky. Audie drove, eyes fixed on the road. Angel and Patty Lane held hands like high school kids. My pulse sounded at my temples. Not since the fire, I thought, not since then.

BEN USHERED US IN, said that he was on the phone, refreshments waited in the den, and we knew how to make ourselves comfortable. Audie lagged behind, saying she had to use the toilet. Liverwurst sandwiches sat on a mahogany service tray. Liverwurst was exactly what I wanted. I poured a glass of mint tea. Angel and Patty Lane filled their plates with fruit.

I sat on the leather couch and bit into the sandwich. My imagination took off—a couch like this, marble floors, original art on the walls. I considered the life money afforded people, envisioned a new one for myself, in which I could spoil my kids and I wouldn't be just a two-second afterthought to dealers in a break room. Audie came in, laid her purse behind the blackjack table, and sank into a recliner. She drew her legs up, wrapped her arms around her knees, and stared out the window. Then a few seconds later, as if bitten, she sprang up, selected a cigar from Ben's humidor, and said, "I'll be on the patio." On the way, she picked up Ben's Tiffany lighter.

"Might rain," I said.

She gave me a look that sliced into me. "I'm smart enough to come in out of the rain." She threw the door open and slammed it behind her.

"She's got a nose full of somethin'," Angel said after she was gone.

"It'll stain her teeth," Patty Lane said.

"What?" Angel asked.

"The cigar. Tobacco's terrible on teeth."

Angel gave Patty Lane a patient, loving look.

You're either in or out, I thought. Now that I was in with Ben, was I out with Audie?

Ben entered and said he was pleased we'd helped ourselves. He asked where Audie was.

Angel said, "Outside."

Ben poured a glass of fruit tea, cut a slice of cheddar, and stood nibbling it and sipping from the glass. Audie sat poolside, puffing slowly on the cigar. He said, "Eighty-dollar Havana. That should come out of her cut." He stared off as if something weighty occupied his mind. After a few seconds, he turned to me. "I just got off the phone with an old acquaintance, Jude. I got a little present for you. You start dealing this week."

I should've been pleased, and would have been if his present hadn't been wrapped in such ominous paper. I looked outside at her. So, Audie, what now, I wondered, now that your friend owns part of me too? I was too wired to give much thought to what had gone down or my role in it. One important thing that escaped was that the proceeds we'd netted from the scam, when split five ways, wouldn't put a dent into the lifestyles that Ben and Patty Lane enjoyed. If I'd thought on it, I would have realized that what had happened in the Whiskey River was never intended to be about money.

22 Thursday and the kids would be over. The final fifty minutes of eight hours were clicking down toward shift's end, and I had two days off coming. I felt a headache coming on. The battering sounds of the casino and cigarette smoke added to a dull throb at my temples. I offered up the deck to first base to cut. He ran the cut card over the edge and sliced the deck. Out of the gate he laid down a two-hundred-dollar bet, then doubled down on a ten, according to basic strategy a percentage bet against my nine showing. I gave him a down card and wished him good luck. The young woman on the next seat signaled for a hit. I gave her an eight. She smiled and tucked her cards under the bet. Her eyes were dark and her hair long and straight. She'd said that she felt lucky and had stopped on her way to finish her final semester at law school in Tucson. No one else needed a hit.

The players stared at their chips in the betting circles as if contemplating the vastness of the universe. I turned over my hole card, busted a thirteen with a queen. "Twenty-three," I said. "Beats twenty-one." The stale joke rarely got a laugh. Here it wasn't even heard. I turned over the down card on first base. He'd caught an ace. I wondered, was it luck or was he Ben's agent?

"Overkill," I said, another rusty line used to loosen players up. It too was wasted. Nothing short of a mask and a .38 was going to get a tip out of them. I hollered, "Blacks out!" and paid the four hundred. The boss looked over. In the Le Grande, a four-hundred-dollar laydown went all but unnoticed, especially with a junket of players from Taiwan firing up five grand a hand in the main pit. The floorman stifled a yawn and looked away.

The standing and constant motion had taken their toll, sore feet and aching back. On this, the end of my fifth week on the job, I would receive envelope number five from Ben, something worth looking forward to. I shuffled and stripped the cards, my mind on matters I'd imagined before—buying land or otherwise investing. The thoughts fostered worries, concerns such as how to spend or invest cash without alerting the IRS, and suspicions such as who I could trust. The previous four envelopes had contained more than two thousand each. Still, I wondered if Ben had been shorting me. It seemed participating in a crime fostered paranoia.

I finished the deck, shuffled, and offered the cut to the young woman. She too ran the cut card across the edge of the deck. "For luck," she said. The player on first base increased his bet to five hundred, and the woman raised hers to six greens, a hefty wager for a college student.

She asked, "Can I make a bet for you?"

I smiled. "Sure."

She placed a five-dollar chip on the front edge of her betting circle. I dealt the next hand. A slot machine buzzer went off. I slipped my down card under an eight of clubs. The man's hand was good. The young woman took a hit and pinned hers. I broke, shuffled, dealt the next hand, and the next. Hands one billion and one billion and one. The player on first bet ten dollars on both occasions and left. I broke the deck in half and began shuffling again. The headache owned me now. I handed the cut card to the young woman again and watched her run the red plastic card up the edge and plunged it into the deck. I slipped the bottom half to the top and buried the first card in the discard rack. Relax, I thought, don't look at her . . . in case.

"Is it too late to raise my bet?" she asked.

"No."

"Can I change my bet after I see the cards?" she asked and smiled.

"That's called cheating, ma'am."

She placed four more greens on her stack. I dealt. She pinned her cards. I turned over a nineteen and exposed her hand. A twenty, another winner. She played three small hands and left.

I felt a tap on the shoulder and glanced at my watch. Norma, my relief, had arrived two minutes early. The first dealer to speak to me the day I came to work, she had a name tag that said she was from Wisconsin. I'd asked about her southern accent. She said she was born in Arkansas, but when Clinton became president, she'd had her name tag changed.

She whispered, "Mack wants to see you."

Mack was the boss who'd auditioned me and recommended me for immediate hiring. I'd not talked to him since, not even in passing. "I've got the early out."

"Just passing on the message. And I like your car."

I'd wanted to buy another Mustang. Instead, I'd purchased a two-year-old Nissan that was still under the original warranty. It was hard to fathom anyone liking it, white and ordinary as it was. But it was affordable and reliable, for the time being all I needed. I spread the cards and clapped out. As I did, Norma brushed my arm with her palm. When I turned away, she winked and called me handsome.

She settled in behind the table and said, "How y'all doin'? Was Jude nice or mean?"

I walked away a bit baffled. Since taking the job, all had seemed to go well. What would a boss want? My head throbbed. I wondered if the eye in the sky had noticed something. My stiff-thumb shuffle, perhaps. I dropped my tips in the toke box and went looking. Mack was watching a roulette game in pit 2 from the end of the apron. He riffled two stacks of chips into one. The ball slowed and dropped in the twenty-four. The dealer marked the winner and began sweeping the layout. Mack walked a chip across the backs of his knuckles, then looked at me. "Just wanted to know how it was going, Jude."

"Fine."

Mack flipped the lone chip on the layout. "You being treated okay?"

I sensed something in Mack's tone, in his trying too hard to be friendly. But why? Despite Ben's warnings that I just deal, I was curious about who was or wasn't in on the scam. How high up did Ben's influence go? "Sure. Just fine."

"Any problems, bring 'em to me."

"Thanks, but everyone's been good to me. I like it here."

"I hoped to hear that. Well, no need to waste time standing in the pit." The roulette dealer spun the ball. Mack cut a stack of roulette chips in two and shuffled both halves into one stack again. "Go on home."

As I punched out at the time office, I thought, a strange end to an ordinary day. I wondered what Audie was doing and when would I see her again. Ever since the day we ripped off the Whiskey River she'd changed. We'd gone to dinner a few times and had sex twice, the groping and thrashing-about kind that was over too fast. She'd otherwise avoided me.

23 Lucas's car shined in the glow from the corner streetlight. It made me want a nicer car, but the Nissan would do for now. Wasn't it best to drive something inconspicuous and avoid drawing attention to myself? Isn't that what smart thieves did? Still, something in me wanted that better car. I was reminded of the time I wanted only a small nibble or two from the American pie. A modest business. A sign over a door. The small wants of a normal life. I wondered if it was human to stop wanting, if people who had everything stopped wanting more.

I found an unaddressed envelope in my mailbox, my week's cut from the scam, and stuffed it in my pocket. In addition to what the scam brought in, I averaged, in tips and wages, well over a deuce a day. Five grand a month. For the first time in my life, I was flush and all because of a thumb. The irony didn't escape me. I felt so rich now that when the woman's insurance company upped the settlement offer that week to eleven thousand, I turned it down.

I bent over at the edge of the driveway and picked up the paper. As I did, I heard leaves rustle. I thought I spotted movement out of the corner of my eye, in the bushes at the near side of Mel's yard. I stared into the shadows of the swaying oleanders, but saw nothing unusual. A cat, maybe. Neighborhood was full of them. I tucked the paper under my arm and keyed the lock. Footfalls came from somewhere up the block. I snapped my head in that direction and again saw nothing. I dismissed it as a neighborhood kid hoping for a peek at Gay, who once answered the door in the buff to accept a package from the mailman. The story had circulated through most everyone on the block.

Beth and Lucas sat zombielike in the dark, watching television. Light flickered on their faces. They usually mimicked the characters' language after watching an episode. I waved as I passed by. "Bad on your eyes to watch in the dark. What're you watching?"

Without looking up, Lucas said, "Summer reruns. *Friends.*"

"I've seen this one. It's okay," Beth said. "I mean, for a brain drainer."

"Lucas, on your way in you could have picked up the paper," I said.

"I knew you'd get it, Dad."

"Right," I said and went up to my bedroom, where I opened a dresser drawer and took out an envelope stuffed with cash. I added thirteen hundred from this week's take. Nine thousand two hundred forty dollars total. It occurred as I shut the drawer that I should find a safer place to keep the money.

As the kids watched, I heated up some sauce from the night before. "Hand over the olive oil. Did either of you hear someone outside a while ago?"

Lucas handed me the bottle. "No. But there was someone—"

"Yeah, Dad," Beth cut in. "Why's a guy watching us from across the street?"

Watching? What guy? I poured the pasta into boiling water and dropped the spoon into the pan, splashing water on the floor. I couldn't stop the alarm going off inside my head. "Shit." I opened the silverware drawer and pulled out another. "Lucas, wipe that up. What guy, honey?"

"The one in the gray Honda."

"Dad, I told her there are a thousand gray Hondas in town," Lucas said.

"No one's watching anyone," I said, assuring her.

Lucas said, "Probably watching Mel's, just waiting for a peek at him going at it with—"

I bumped him with my hip. "Let it go."

At the table as we ate, Lucas began talking about his former college algebra teacher. I was glad the conversation shifted away from the man in the Honda. But nothing else other than the man was on my mind. I wondered if he was the one whose footsteps I'd heard.

I ate half of my meal and said, "I'm going to lie down for a minute." I folded my napkin and stood. "You two clean up. We'll go out for strawberry pie. We haven't done it for a while."

I went upstairs, turned off the bedroom light, and cracked the blinds to peek out. No gray Honda, no prowler, nothing out of the ordinary. The streetlight illuminated the asphalt. A film of water from the sprinklers on the lawn across the street glistened on the sidewalk. Nothing to spark concern, except I was concerned. What if he was after my money? Or some type of cop? I hoped Lucas was right. Hondas were everywhere, many of them gray. Beth could be mistaken.

I was too beat from dealing to think about any cloak-and-dagger. I lay down on the bed and calculated the future. Sixty thousand extra or more a year, cold cash, and what it meant—a vacation in the Caribbean, a cabin, paying for Lucas's honeymoon when he got married. I couldn't yet bring myself to think of Beth ever marrying. It was the father in me. What man could be good enough for her?

A car turned the corner. I return to the blinds and spread them with my fingertips in time to see the taillights drift around the next corner. I swallowed and pulled my fingers back from the blinds, then sat on the edge of the bed and listened to the sprinklers go on in my own yard.

24

I started to nod off after an hour and a half of listening to traffic cases and disturbing-the-peace complaints.

Braverman tapped my knee and motioned toward the front of the courtroom. "We're up."

I followed him to the rail. He held the gate, and I stepped in and stood before the bench as dozens of traffic violators had. Braverman waited calmly. He'd indicated the case would be reduced, but nothing was absolute. I would have had reservations no matter what he said. The longer the judge fumbled with papers, the more my stomach talked to me. He finally set the last papers aside and picked up the file to his right. He looked from Braverman to me, then to the city attorney.

"*City of Las Vegas versus Jude Holmes,* charge battery. Are the sides ready to proceed?"

"The defendant's name is Helms, Your Honor. And we are ready," Braverman said.

"I stand corrected."

"The city's ready, Your Honor."

"Good. How does your client plead, Mr. Braverman?"

"Not guilty."

"I see. Is the victim present?"

A man stood up. He wore a black suit with a black tie. He'd been seated in the bench in front of us, and I hadn't recognized him.

"Well, let's start."

The bailiff swore in Stephen Edowski and told him to be seated on the witness stand. The city attorney asked his name and address, then commenced presenting the city's case. Edowski answered a series of questions that set up a story of an incident only remotely resembling what had happened that night. He claimed to be in his house when a stranger rang his bell, threatened him, and dumped dog feces on his shoes. He pointed me out as the culprit. The attorney showed him a plastic bag that contained a pair of shoes and asked Edowski to identify them. Edowski said they were his. The attorney pointed out the stains on the shoes to the judge.

"Were you walking your dog earlier?"

"No, sir."

"So you did nothing to provoke this battery?"

"No, sir."

"Had you ever seen the accused before?"

"No, sir."

"The city rests its case, Your Honor."

The judge looked at Braverman. "Does the accused wish to examine the witness?"

Braverman smiled at Edowski. "Yes, Your Honor. It won't take long. Mr. Edowski, were the droppings that landed on your shoes fresh?"

"Yes."

"Messy fresh?"

"Yes."

"Thank you. I have no more questions of the witness. I'd like to call Officer Trent to the stand."

"Is Officer Trent present?" the judge asked.

A man in a beige uniform stood and moved to the front of the courtroom. The bailiff held the gate open for him and swore him in. On the witness stand, the Animal Control officer said that he'd handled two complaints at Edowski's house on Aberdeen, both involving neighborhood complaints about his using other people's yards to relieve his dog.

"Did you cite him?"

"The second time, yes."

"Why was that?"

"Because his dog was off its leash."

"Thank you. I have no further questions for the witness. I call Mr. Helms to the stand."

The bailiff swore me in with a Bible, and I eased into the witness chair and took a breath. Braverman told me to tell my version of the evening's events. I told my side in every detail, first mentioning how I had witnessed Edowski over a period of several weeks lead his dog onto my yard to do its business. I finished by admitting to the court that I'd dropped the feces on Edowski's shoes, but only after I followed him home.

"You see, it was his property and figured he'd want it returned. I tried to hand it to him, but he wouldn't take the bag. The bag was mine. I couldn't just give it to him."

"So you dumped the contents."

"Yes, sir."

The hint of a smile appeared on the judge's lips.

"What kind of dog was this?"

"An Afghan."

The judge lowered his glasses and shouted to the courtroom, "Mr. Edowski!" Edowski stood up in front of his seat.

"What kind of dog do you have?"

"Sir?"

"Let me remind you, you're still under oath."

"An Afghan."

"Officer Trent, is that the dog that was off the leash?"

"Yes, Your Honor."

The judge said, "I'd like to speak to counsel at the bench."

Braverman grinned and stood from his chair. The city attorney was having difficulty hiding his own amusement as he stepped up to the judge. They conferred for two minutes, each nodding to the judge, then they returned to their respective tables. Braverman winked at me.

The judge called the bailiff over and whispered something, then cleared his throat. "Mr. Edowski, I assume from your address that you live in a residence with a yard. If you have a pet, that's the pet's toilet. The neighborhood is not. You wouldn't be here today if you didn't randomly abuse your neighbors. Stop that behavior. And don't ever fib in a court of law. It is a crime to lie under oath."

"But I . . . I was—"

"Mr. Edowski, I'm tempted to have you try on these shoes to prove they're yours. Now, before you dig your hole too deep, sit. And you, Mr. Helms, are you some kind of vigilante?"

"I'm a blackjack dealer, Your Honor."

"Right. Well, I'm reducing the case to littering and fining you twenty-five dollars. You can pay the clerk." He grinned. "And have a nice day. Next case."

I paid the fine to a clerk who grinned as she wrote a receipt. Most everyone in the courtroom smiled at me as we walked the aisle to the exit. Several gave me a thumbs-up. Out of sight of the judge, Braverman dug in his wallet and handed me a twenty-dollar bill and said he owed me five, that the entertainment was worth it.

I left the courtroom thinking that I would call Audie later in the day and see if she wanted to celebrate. I wasn't ready to give up on her. I figured she would get a bang out of the story.

THAT EVENING as I pulled in the driveway, I saw the gray Honda, engine off, its driver in the seat. I threw open my door and dashed across the street before the driver could pull away. His window was rolled down. "Can I help you?" I asked. "You're scaring my daughter."

He rolled up his window and started the engine.

"Stop!" I called, but the car was already moving. I banged on his window. He calmly pressed the accelerator and left me red-faced and panting in the middle of the street. I caught some numbers on the license, a California plate. When I turned around, I saw my daughter standing on the lawn, her lips trembling as she gasped for air. I hurried to her.

She caught her breath and said, "Dad, you shouldn't have done that. Dad . . ."

I pulled her close and said everything was going to be all right, something I didn't truly believe.

25 The gun was dark metallic blue, and its checkered stocks shined. Using a soft cloth to protect the finish, the clerk opened the cylinder and offered the gun for me to examine. I held it with a sense of awe and apprehension, sort of the way I'd felt when the nurse handed Lucas to me for the first time. Before then, I'd never held a baby. Before now, I'd never held a real gun.

"It's a beauty, S&W Model Twenty-seven," the clerk said. "Kinda powerful for home defense. Just make sure you don't shoot through a wall. Bullet might not stop till it killed a neighbor two doors down. Don't many people buy revolvers no more, but for my money they're the most accurate. Well, truth is that actually depends on whether you know how to shoot."

I gripped the stock. Its heft surprised me. I held it at arm's length. "I had no idea guns were so expensive."

"Ain't it the truth. Thing is, they're like houses. A house appreciates in value in a good neighborhood. Same with a gun. I can sell somethin' cheaper. I got a .25 caliber that costs under a hundred. It's good for shooting cockroaches, and 'at's about it."

I handed the revolver back to the clerk. "I'll take this one."

The clerk reached in a drawer and pulled out a paper form, which he set on the glass countertop. "I need to see a driver's license." His big belly pressed against the glass as he took out the box, wiped the revolver, and placed it in the box.

I laid my license on the glass. The clerk confirmed the picture and handed it back. He placed a pen on the form. "Fill out this form. I'll have to call Metro."

"Why's that?"

"You ain't never bought a gun before, have you?"

"No."

"Never shot one neither, I'll bet."

I started to lie, then changed my mind. "No."

"The call registers the gun." The clerk opened his own wallet and gave me a card. "Best shootin' range in town. They carry wad cutters and offer instructions on how to shoot." I must have looked confused, because the clerk said, "Man, wad cutters is reloads for target shooting. Make clean holes in paper, but ugly holes in anything else, but not like hollow points. No, sir!"

"Hollow points?"

"Fill out that paperwork and I'll get you a box. One'll do 'less you use them for hunting. You're not planning on hunting, are you?"

I looked at the closed box. "No."

I SAT PARKED IN FRONT OF HER HOUSE, gathering the courage to knock on her door. I had to talk to her if for no reason other than finding an explanation for the man in the Honda. Her garage opened, and she backed out in her BMW. She looked at me as she pulled out of the driveway. I rolled down my window and waved. She drove past, shaking her head.

"I just want to talk!" I shouted.

26 I was dealing to a lone woman when Felicia, the assistant pit boss, sidled up to my game. She said business was slow and asked if I wanted to leave at half-shift. In her midthirties, she was married to a golf pro, always dressed in something blue, and smelled like a basket of fruit. "You keep looking around like you want to escape."

Though there was nothing more I wanted to do at the moment, I had to be on a game in case one of Ben's agents showed. "I'll stick it out. It may get busy later. The kids need things."

"Don't they always? Look, keep your eyes on the layout," Felicia whispered. "The eye in the sky may be watching."

"Sure."

I'd weighed telling Ben I was through. Even if I dropped out from our arrangement, he'd keep sending players to my game and I would be out a share of it. And I owed my job to him. He could get me fired just as easily as he got me hired. Then, too, he'd brought a stalker into my life. Who was he? A spy? A cop? A Gaming Control agent? A fed? Had I been thinking, I would have gotten the full license plate before confronting him. And what then? Tell Ben?

A woman sat down. I shuffled, dealt cards, and kept my head down. She looked at her hand and shook her head. "Can't you do better?" She pinned her cards under the bet and said, "I went to college in Louisville. The Cardinals, not the baseball kind, but we did have a baseball team. It's always interested me that St. Louis and Louisville both have Cardinals."

"I never thought about it."

"Most people don't. Then there's Stanford. I don't get it."

It was obvious she was one of those souls who wanted to interact with someone, but the subject was so off-the-cuff, I temporarily lost track of what I was doing.

"Are you going to turn over your card?" she said.

I exposed my down card and busted out, hitting a sixteen. I turned over her cards and paid her.

"I think it all started with the Catholics," she said. "The College of Cardinals. I mean, who would use birds as a mascot?"

"Right," I said and thereafter smiled and nodded, all the while thinking how lonely it must be for those who come seeking small talk in a casino.

She caught a short streak, six or seven hands, talking all the while, harmless chitchat about her job, her mother, her children, the dinner she'd eaten last night. I smiled and pretended interest. On my mind was the man in the Honda. What if he was a nutcase after my daughter?

When her streak ended and she lost three hands, she said, "Does anyone ever win at this game?"

The casinos, I thought.

"My ex-husband won one time, something like three hundred dollars."

"Good for him. Let's hope you can do it."

She won the next hand and put up a bet for me. "Let's see if it can happen twice."

What seemed just another ordinary day shifted to bizarre when I glanced up and noticed my former coworker Gus, his lips in a closed, somewhat mocking smile. He was looking directly at me. He lit a cigarette and nodded at me. I returned the nod and dealt the next hand. A moment later he stubbed out his cigarette, crossed the aisle, and stood at arm's length from the table. I recalled the last conversation I had with him shortly before I was fired at the Monaco and remembered knowing nothing personal of him beyond the story of his escape from Cuba. The woman pinned her cards. I busted my hand, paid her, and thanked her for the tip, then glanced up at Gus as I placed the two red checks behind the discard rack.

Gus asked the woman, "Ees okay if I play here?"

She said, "Of course."

"Good." Feigning no sign of recognizing me, Gus peeled five bills from a roll of hundreds, placed them on the layout, and eased himself onto the first-base stool.

"Change five hundred!" I spread the bills on the layout.

"All green," he said. "I'll wait for the shuffle. I don' wanna ruin this lady's luck."

"Go ahead," she said. "My luck's mostly bad."

"I'll jus' wait."

What happened next came as no surprise, as the pattern of Gus's play was all too obvious. Following my next shuffle, he scraped the cut card down the edge of the deck and laid a $150 bet in the circle and won it, that bet and two more, $750 off one shuffle. He gathered up his winnings, stood back from his stool, and walked to the casino cage, leaving no tip, offering no thank-you, and saying no adieus. I smiled. It struck me I was little more than one card in a stacked deck, as were Gus and Patty Lane and Angel, and Ben was in a back room somewhere dealing out the cards and raking in the money.

27 Though the table was busy, I looked up by chance and saw him, leaning against a slot machine, the gray-Honda man. At least I thought so. I'd glimpsed him only briefly, inside a moving car, and I couldn't be positive. A bit under six feet tall, medium build, late thirties, he was the kind who otherwise blended into any crowd. But it seemed he wanted me to see him. I paid a bet, lowered my head, and kept dealing. When I looked up again, he was gone.

On break, I dropped my tokes into the box and headed for the cafeteria. Nearing the end of the pit, I saw him by the doors to the help's hall. I considered confronting him, but couldn't afford to make a scene at work, so I walked on and pushed through the swinging doors. Halfway down the hall, I heard footsteps closing in from behind. I looked ahead and kept walking. A few steps later, a voice called me by name. I turned around, but didn't see who I expected.

He was round faced, squat, on the heavy side, nearing fifty, his hair gray. He approached and extended a hand to me, in it a business card. I faced him and backpedaled slowly toward the door.

"Here. For you." He advanced two steps, reached out, and shoved the card in my shirt pocket. "Call," he said, then turned and headed back toward the casino. Two dealers entered the hallway. He slipped between them and disappeared through the doors.

I poured a cup of coffee and studied the card, ordinary, white with black print, on it the name G. Blitzstein and a phone number. Scribbled on the back side were the words "Don't tell Ben." Tell him what? Nearby, a group of animated dealers gathered around two adjoining tables and began the ritual rumor chasing and complaining. It seemed sort of carefree. I wondered if I'd ever again slip back into bitching about tokes and players and bosses. It occurred that since Audie had come along, matters had changed so drastically that other than my children, my thoughts had narrowed pretty much to two things—who was the Honda man watching me and why, and her. For three weeks now there had been no dinners, no lovemaking, no answering my phone calls. And no explanation for any of this. Now, I had a fat stranger added into the mix.

The last hours of the shift dragged. I thought of nothing but the card in my wallet. I didn't phone Ben about the encounter, mostly because I didn't trust him any more than I trusted the man who handed me the card. Besides, Ben had cautioned me to call only in an emergency, in which case I was not to say why or what, but simply name a time. The meeting place was predesignated—the Roadrunner at Buffalo and Summerlin Parkway.

On my last break, I called from a pay phone. The number rang several times. "Gabe here," the man finally answered. Background noise filtered in over the cell phone.

"G. Blitzstein?"

"Yeah, Jude. I've been waiting for your call. You ready to talk?"

"About what? Give me a hint."

"Meet me at Albino's on Paradise at eight fifteen. I'll tell you then. Did you call Ben?"

I didn't want to admit anything compromising. This could be another of Ben's elaborate tests, as the card switching had been. "I don't know a Ben."

"Then why'd you call?"

"Curious about who's stalking me."

The man chuckled. "See you there, Jude."

I called home. Beth was supposed to be there. She wasn't. My thoughts went immediately to the Honda man. She'd nagged me about being the only girl in school without a cell phone. I wished I gotten her one. I left a message saying I'd be late.

GABE HAD PICKED A CORNER BOOTH at the far end of the restaurant. He stood and waved, both unnecessary. I'd spotted him immediately. I slid into a seat opposite him and looked around for anyone who might be watching.

"Drink?" Gabe asked.

I shook my head. I wanted only to confront the matter and leave. "What do you want?"

Gabe smiled. "Relax. Let's have a late dinner and talk."

"Okay, then, if you won't tell me that, who are you?"

"Berdie's Bail Bonds."

I recognized it as where Ben had instructed me to go if things went sour at the Whiskey River. "So, tell me something else."

"How about, I know Ben. Let's have a drink and eat."

"I ate at work."

"A drink then."

I looked around a second time, wondering what exactly I was looking for. How would I spot anything unusual? I was no good at this cloak-and-dagger shit. I hadn't even thought to bring the gun. If I had, what then? I decided it best to assume Gabe was a cop and I was a suspect. "Okay. I give. Who's Ben?"

"Ben's the reason we're both here. This isn't playground games." Blitzstein took an exasperated breath and looked at the ceiling. His upper teeth were splayed. Advanced periodontal disease, I figured.

The waiter arrived just then and took our drink orders. Gabe asked for a Gray Goose and tonic. I ordered a margarita, hardly the kind of drink a man sitting with a cop or a crook should drink, but then this wasn't television. Gabe looked up from studying the menu.

"They have interesting dishes here, Italian-Cajun hybrid. So you're in business with Ben."

"I don't know who Ben is."

"Back to grade school, huh? Well, let's pretend you do, and you're making—what? A thousand, eleven hundred a week? You should be making double that. Double."

"I'm a blackjack dealer eking out a living."

"Then why'd you come?"

I hesitated before saying, "No one's ever stalked my family."

"Stalking your family? I didn't know you had one. Drink. I'll eat. We'll talk afterward."

Afterward followed a three-course herb-chicken dinner, berry ice-cream dessert, and a double Hennessy VSO. Meanwhile, I nursed a second margarita and listened to a piano player plunk out '60s rhythm-and-blues tunes on a baby grand. Blue smoke spiraled up to the ceiling. On occasion, Gabe looked up from his meal to grunt approval. Of the food or the music, I was uncertain. All I was sure of was that the night was another strange one.

After Gabe ordered his second double Hennessy, he looked up, left eye half-closed, and said, "Ben owns you. The hammer just hasn't dropped."

I recalled Audie saying that Ben owned her. Now me? I knew the answer. I looked at my hands, then at the piano player, and finally at Gabe. I'd avoided incriminating myself and felt safe in leaving. I stood.

"Stay. I'll make it worth your while. You know a guy named Angel? A broad named Audie? Unusual name, huh?"

I didn't answer.

"Okay, here's the pitch. He's shorting you. With me, you'd make two grand a week and you'll know who's in, because that's who I want to cut the deck every time. That's a hundred thousand a year, plus you still do business with Ben. Three years you can lock up half a million. No one the wiser. With what you make with me, him, and the job, you can retire in four or five years. All safe."

"All safe doing what?"

He leaned close and whispered. "You know, locating cards. Ever hear of it?"

The piano player began a jazzy version of "We All Live in a Yellow Submarine."

"I'm not in the cheating business, Gabe," I said. "It's not safe. I'd be careful if I were you." As I slid out of the booth, I felt bold. "And keep your buddy away from my daughter."

Gabe sat back and smiled up at me. "Whoa. Check the hostility. I don't know your daughter or nothing about a buddy. What I said, it's a legitimate offer. You got the number."

I chuckled. "Legitimate offer?"

Gabe, confused at first, laughed, then said, "He's setting you up for a big score."

I sat back down. "Again, I don't know what you're talking about."

"I'm talking about you taking a cold deck."

"Never. That's cheating . . ." I started to further protest, to say I would never cheat, but stopped short.

"I know what it is. Like I said, he owns you. Here's my deal. You tell me when it's going down, and I'll run in my own people and make it worth your while. How does a million sound to you?"

Scary, I thought, too scary.

WHEN I ARRIVED HOME, Beth was still not there. The meal I'd left for her to warm up was in the refrigerator. I searched the rooms for evidence she'd been home. It was obvious she hadn't. I telephoned Anne's, expecting Lucas to answer. Instead, Anne did. I didn't want to talk to her, but did out of concern for Beth. "Have you seen Beth?"

"You don't know where she is?"

"Not at the moment."

A key rattled in the door. I cupped a hand over the receiver. "Beth?"

"Yeah, Dad." She stood in the entry to the family room. She seemed upset.

Anne was still talking. I held the receiver away and shouted that Beth had just come in. I apologized to Anne for bothering her, said, "I'll talk to you about it later," and hung up.

"Where've you been?"

She crossed the room, put her arms around my neck, and began to cry.

"What?"

When her tears subsided, she wiped her eyes with the back of her hand and said, "Katie got picked up for shoplifting. I went with Audie to juvie. I left a message for you." She pointed to the blinking answering-machine light.

I sat her down at the table. "Why'd Audie ask you?"

"Because Katie's my friend."

She sniffled again as if it were a prelude to more crying. I ripped a paper towel off the rack and handed it to her.

"Dad! You don't give a girl who's crying a paper towel." She smiled.

The phone rang. I was thankful, as it gave me reason to avoid a conversation I didn't wanted to have—with Beth or myself. Especially myself.

"That'll be your mother. You get it. I'm not in the mood."

I smelled of casino and bar, cigarettes and booze, and was too tired at the moment to think. Beth was home. Nothing else seemed important, not even the fact that Audie had dropped her off and not bothered to come in and explain what had happened. I went upstairs to clean up and change. I unbuttoned my shirt and pulled out the tail. I wanted the taste of triple sec off my tongue. I was brushing my teeth when Beth knocked at the door.

"Come in."

She stood in the open doorway, staring at me bent over the sink. I looked at her through the mirror. She was upset. "I saw him again, Dad. You said it would be okay. It's not." She wheeled about and left.

"I'll take care of it," I said, but I didn't even know what *it* was, who he was, and in many ways who I was. I sat on the edge of the bed. Only once before had I felt this alone, and that was crawling out of the fire. At least then I hadn't let anyone down.

28 The *Monday Night Football* crowd hogged the tables by the bar. I watched for Ben and waited for the waitress to bring my order. I'd called and told him we needed to talk. I wanted out. I wasn't going to offer an explanation—just out. I hoped to keep the straight dealing job. A year or two, I could save enough to start a masonry business, put casinos behind me forever. There was no use blaming anyone. I wasn't cut out to be a crook or deal with strangers watching my house or handing me business cards. How could I trust that Gabe was who he claimed to be? He might easily have been a cop, and the meeting could have been a setup.

The waitress set my order down. The apple crisp was too sweet, the coffee too bitter. The bar erupted in cheers. I turned to see the final few yards of a kickoff return for a touchdown. The runner jumped up, spiked the ball over the goalposts, and began a celebration dance. When I turned again, Ben was seated across from me.

"Hello, Jude."

I pointed toward the big screen. "Hundred-yard return."

"I leave football to Angel. I assume you have a good reason for calling."

I nodded. I called initially to see whether Gabe was some kind of cop or as he claimed, an opportunist trying to cut himself in, but I'd since decided not to bring him up. Ben tapped his fingers on the table and stared at me. I took a sip and set the cup down. The waitress approached and asked Ben if he wanted to order food or a drink.

"Gray Goose and tonic."

How many people drank Gray Goose? I hadn't even heard of it until I sat with Gabe and heard him order it. Though I had no intention of mentioning Gabe, I saw the drink as a possible link between the two of them and wondered if the meeting had been a test of sorts to see if I'd implicate myself or Ben and the others in a scam. If not, then Gabe was on square about cutting in on Ben's operation. I felt compelled to establish that I wasn't going to involve myself with another scam. All I wanted to do was quit and, at the same time, keep my job.

"So?"

"I met a man named Gabe. You know him? Stubby guy."

Ben scratched his nose, then offered an ironic grin. "Yeah. He's a chaser."

"A chaser?"

"Bounty hunter. Chases bond skippers for Russ at Berdie's. How'd you meet him?"

"He showed up at work and gave me a card with a note on the back that said not to tell you. I met him at a restaurant. You know, just to see what was on his mind."

Ben waved me silent as the waitress placed the drink down.

"Anything else?" she asked.

"No, fine. Go ahead and give me the check."

When she left, I started to tell Ben that I wasn't cut out to be a cheater, but he spoke first.

"So you met him, and I'm guessing he wanted to cut in on the action."

I shrugged. He tapped the table as he waited for my answer.

"I thought he was a cop trying to set me up."

"So, you went to meet a man you thought was a cop?" He entwined his fingers and looked away. "Blitz was a card man. He could lay down paint, work the bend, or slip in a deck. He once ran in a cooler at Harvey's with the casino manager and a pit boss watching the game."

"Blitz."

"Billy Blitzstein. Gabe's dad."

"Look, Ben, I didn't give up anything, but . . . that's not important. What is important is that I don't want creeps watching my house, don't want . . ."

"Watching your house?"

"Yeah, someone's been watching the house and watching me at work as well. Probably best if I quit, you know . . ."

The crowd screamed again. A man sitting at the bar stood up and did the twist. Ben took a drink and held the glass in both hands, his gaze fixed on me. "No quitting. You're in. That's it."

I was a head taller than Ben, forty pounds heavier. If it came to it, I could pummel him. I placed my elbows on the table, leaned toward him to emphasize my greater size, and doubled my hands into fists. "I think I can make that decision."

Ben inched even closer and grinned smugly. "If you don't want a cut, fine. Everything goes the same. No, actually you're committed to something else."

I'd lost. I leaned back. "Let's be reasonable. I . . ."

Another outburst of cheers from the football crowd muffled out the music from the speaker overhead. People at the bar hugged one another and jumped up and down. I waited, and when the noise subsided, I said, "I just wanted to tell you. Figured I owed it to you to let you know about Blitzstein."

"And you did."

Ben slid out of the booth and walked out the door. I considered cornering him in the parking lot and settling the matter. Then I looked at the unfinished drink and the twenty-dollar bill on the table, and I realized it had been settled. I just didn't know the terms.

THE SUMMER had cooked itself out. The evening was as beautiful as any I'd experienced, a little under seventy degrees with a soft western breeze, the pale autumn moon hanging above the horizon. I recalled times when my friends and I rode out to Red Rock on nights like this, smoked a joint if we had one, and laughed ourselves into exhaustion over the slightest thing. Afterward, we'd lie on the warm sandstone and gaze at the moon. Did Beth or Lucas do similar things? Who were my kids when they weren't with me? I hoped they enjoyed the joys of youth, but I also worried about them succumbing to the temptations always present in the landscape of Las Vegas culture. Now I had become my own example. I put the key in the car door.

I climbed the stairs as if I had a sack of stones on my back. Lately, I hated returning home to an empty house. As I passed Beth's room, I saw the curtains spread. I went to close them and glimpsed Mel and Gay in the spa, Mel's arm draped over her shoulders. They were talking, blissfully unaware of the rest of the world.

The phone rang. I hurried to the bedroom and picked up the receiver. "Hello."

"You told him, didn't you?"

"What?"

"You heard me. Your daughter's at your ex-wife's."

I went cold. I nodded as if answering a question and looked at the bedside table where the revolver lay at rest in the top drawer. I knew what I had to say and had to sound as if I meant it, because I'd never said anything like it before. "Go near her, and you'll wish you were dead."

"Yeah, okay, bad guy. Get this. It's not a game."

The line went dead. My hands trembled as I laid the receiver in its cradle. I checked the caller ID display. The number was private. Didn't matter. I didn't need a number. I'd recognized the voice. What did Gabe do but deal with criminals? How hard would it be to find someone to do the kind of dirty work that he seemed capable of?

29 No change came of my meeting with Ben. A month passed with no threatening calls. I still had the job, Ben's agents continued to land on my game and win, and at the end of each week I found an envelope with cash in my mailbox. One thing that did change was my taking on new habits. I joined a gym and worked out before reporting for my shift at the Le Grande. I routinely called Anne's from work on my last break to check on my daughter. If Beth wasn't there, I was perturbed until I could get to my house and call again. No matter what else occupied me, when at home I kept an eye on the phone, anticipating the next threatening call or some tragic news about Beth. School days, whenever possible, I drove Beth to Clark High, a magnet school for high achievers.

Had I really jeopardized my daughter's safety? No matter how I approached the question, the answer was invariably yes. Guilt is a powerful master, and I was guilty of introducing danger to my family. Some nights after work I parked down the street from Anne's and watched until the lights went out, often lingering long after the house went dark. Except when inside the casino, I kept the revolver at hand. Though dreading the idea that I might have to use it, I wondered if I was capable of using it, or if the day would come when I didn't feel a need for the weapon, a day when our lives would again be safe. Until then and although I knew I was acting on an illusion that I could protect Beth, I'd remain constantly armed and keep watch. Who better understood that, at best, safety is an illusion? But I needed the illusion to meliorate some of the guilt.

The second week in November I finished two miles on the treadmill, picked up a coffee to go, and drove to Anne's. Beth had called the night before to say she had a ride to school. I parked behind a camper so as not to be seen. After Audie passed through the intersection, I counted to three and pulled out. I lagged behind a quarter mile.

Had I exaggerated all this? Was I overreacting? How much could I protect her? When school ended, I would be halfway through my shift, and Beth would be vulnerable. It came down to the fact that days would run their course. I couldn't guard her around the clock. What more could I do, but what I was doing?

Audie's brake lights came on as she slowed in front of the school. I pulled to the curb and watched Beth and Katie get out. I questioned my sanity and my judgment, me a middle-aged man with a gun concealed under my seat parked a block away from a school. What would a cop think if one saw me? Once the girls were on the school grounds, I made a U-turn.

On the drive home I relaxed a bit. It was a cool, pleasant day. Poplar, fruitless mulberry, and Chinese elms were coloring up on the side streets. I didn't have to clock in at the Le Grande for three more hours and decided to take my troubles on a tour of the older parts of the city, the town I missed whenever I thought about the new Vegas where everything was regulated by homeowners' associations. Still, the population growth and construction boom provided me hope. At the amount I was saving, I'd have enough in a year to start a masonry business and meet my bills for a few weeks, this provided I could figure a way to legitimize the money. I drove aimlessly and eventually found myself in the Scotch 80s, a block west from Ben's house. At the corner, I pulled to a stop and parked, thinking I wouldn't be noticed. I had no idea what I would accomplish by it. The problem was Blitzstein, not Ben. I fired the engine. Just then Audie's BMW turned the corner and pulled into the driveway. She walked straight to the front door, where she let herself in. No doorbell. No Ben.

Common sense told me to leave, that I'd seen more than I should. Still, I sat in the car a few more seconds as matters took full shape in my mind. It was time to be smart.

When I got home a message awaited me on the recorder. I flipped the switch.

"I don't appreciate being followed. Stop it."

She'd gone completely cold on me, but I couldn't let it lie, not so long as my daughter stayed involved with hers. I called and left a message on her recorder. "Beth was safe until you came into my life. I'm off tomorrow. Meet me at Jitters if you want to discuss it. Two o'clock."

I didn't expect her to meet me, and I wasn't disappointed in my belief.

30

I walked into the break room at the Le Grande and looked around for an empty table. This was my last shift before two days off, and I wanted to be alone with my thoughts. Somehow I had to take my life back and do so without endangering Beth. Six weeks had passed since the phone call, and though Gabe Blitzstein's threat was beginning to seem all bluff, it still unsettled me, owing to my lack of circumspection at the start of all this. Dad had mentioned his being propositioned from time to time when he was a dealer and later as a boss. He'd said that casino scams weren't uncommon, that wherever so much money passed through so many hands, scams were inevitable. I'd asked why he never went for one. "Thieves," he'd said. That was all.

Now I was one, caught in my own trap. I was sure, if he were alive and aware of what I was involved with, Dad would have been disappointed. I found little consolation that tonight I'd pick up an envelope stuffed with my weekly take. At the cost of my daughter's safety? The profit-to-risk ratio was widely disproportionate. A daughter for a dollar? For a million? Ten million? Dad wouldn't be disappointed in me. He'd be ashamed, just as I was.

At the Le Grande, we worked staggered shifts. Usually, a few empty tables were available in the break room, but today most dealers from the early shift were on break at once and spread around the room. The few tables where dealers from my shift sat were full. I wove a path through the narrow aisles until I spotted two empty chairs where Norma sat. She saw me at the same time and signaled me over. Jesus and Eric, both blackjack dealers, sat with her. Over the weeks, I'd made friends with Norma and often sat with her if we were on breaks together. She was witty and sometimes flamboyant. She had a self-deprecating sense of humor and was quick with a turn of a phrase when telling a clever anecdote. What she never was was boring. She could spin a piece of gossip without seeming mean-spirited and color a superficial conversation with images that kept others engaged. In short, she was entertaining and I needed to be entertained. On the other hand, I also figured that inside that shell of easy humor was someone substantial, someone I might under other circumstances want to know better.

"Have a seat, handsome," she said. "We've got news."

I looked around, pretending it wasn't me she meant.

"It's okay, Jude. You have my permission to sit until someone handsome shows up. Hell, look at the company I'm keeping."

I nodded to Jesus, a nice guy who'd fled El Salvador during the civil war, then to Eric, a pretty-boy type about thirty, too impressed with being a Strip dealer for my liking. I turned a chair around, swung a leg over, and crossed my arms on the back. "What news?"

Norma knew how to string an audience along. "You have to guess."

"Were tokes a new record low?"

"No."

"The casino is going into bankruptcy?"

"Don't be ridiculous."

"Okay, I'm no good at guessing," I said and sipped my coffee, admiring her red hair and hazel eyes as I did. "It must be big if it trumps bad news about tokes."

"You worked at the Monaco, didn't you?"

"Guilty."

"Its casino manager quit."

I said, "The dealers there will celebrate."

For an instant I was pleased, at first thinking that perhaps Hefty might end up in an unemployment line, but then I thought, so what? Management in casinos changed as often as chefs switched aprons. It was the nature of the business. There had to be something more to this; otherwise, why mention it?

"Well, we won't," Eric said. "He quit to come here. Starts next week as casino manager."

I gagged on my coffee, set the cup down, and wiped my chin with a napkin. Gradually, I cleared my throat as the others stared at me. "You guys are putting me on, right?"

Norma raised an open palm as if swearing an oath. "On my mother's head."

As I slowly digested it, I found the news amusing. I grinned as I picked up my cup. Hefty would be my ticket out of the scam. No scam, no Blitzstein. If I didn't have to worry whether Beth was safe, I could quit packing a revolver and start getting a full night's sleep.

"What's so funny?" Norma asked.

"Private joke," I said.

"Well, here's where the joke dies, my friend," Eric said. "We'll be pumping cards in an endless stream. Right, Norma?"

"No downtime. We're getting shuffling machines," Norma said. "I already heard."

"She ever been wrong?" Jesus asked.

"No," I said. "Never wrong, especially when she's the bearer of bad news."

This unexpected turn was a blessing. No shuffle, no scam. It might take an additional year at best, but I'd keep the job until I could fund a start-up business. The worst that would come was if Hefty fired me again, I'd be free of Ben and probably the mystery man in the Honda.

"What are you thinking, Jude?" Norma asked.

"Nothing. Why?"

"You were smiling."

"I was thinking I like red hair," I said flippantly.

"Really? Ever notice that I have red hair?"

"Yep. But you know the test."

She jabbed me in the arm. "I can pass it."

"What we were wondering is, did he fire you?" Eric asked.

I pictured Hefty on the other side of his desk. "Yes, and with no expression on his face."

I SET THE REVOLVER ON THE COUNTER and took the envelopes out of the mailbox along with the flyers and coupons. I stuffed the envelopes and the power bill under my arm and dumped the junk mail in the garbage. I set the bills on the coffee table without opening the envelopes, including the manila one with my cut of the take in it. The house was a mess. Lucas had been over two days before. He'd left wrappers from corn chips and soft drink cans on the coffee table. Half a lemon lay in a bowl. I got a garbage bag and began scooping up his mess.

The doorbell rang. I grabbed the gun and walked to the front door. Gun in one hand, garbage bag in the other, I flipped on the porch light and looked through the peephole. A man in a sports jacket stood in front of the peephole and said, "Jude Helms?"

"Yeah."

He held a leather holder up to the peephole, then let it flop open to expose a six-point gold star and identification card with his picture on it. "Detective Beardsley, Metro Homicide."

Homicide? I panicked. "Not Beth. Please."

The man lowered the badge. "Beth?"

"Yes, my daughter."

"Mr. Helms, I'm not here about a Beth. How about you open the door? We'll talk."

I felt the weight of the gun in my hand. It seemed a great deal heavier. I took a breath and said, "Just a second. I was changing clothes."

Hands trembling, I stashed the gun under the cushion on the big chair, pulled out my shirttail, then returned to the door and fumbled with the lock as I opened the door. "Don't get many people knocking on my door at night, especially cops," I said and stepped aside. I tucked in my shirttail as the detective stepped inside.

He looked about and nodded, prompted by what, I had no idea. He handed me a business card. It read, "Detective James Beardsley, Homicide and Crimes Against the Person."

"Have a seat." I pointed to the couch.

"Thank you."

We sat facing one another. I realized I was still holding the garbage bag. I set it aside.

"I thought you were changing clothes." Detective Beardsley pointed at the garbage bag.

"I was and taking the garbage out. You're sure you're not here about Beth?"

"Should I be?"

"I don't know. That's why I'm asking."

"Do you have reason to think something's happened to her?"

"She's my daughter. A teenager. I always worry about her. Would you like something to drink? I've got soft drinks, tea, coffee."

"No, thanks." The detective looked at the envelopes on the coffee table. "You get mail that has no address."

"Tips. They put my tips in an envelope." I rubbed my chin.

The detective stared at the envelope as if measuring its bulk. My knowledge of law was limited to what I'd seen on television or in movies. I couldn't imagine what a homicide detective might want and didn't know if he even had the right to interrogate me in my own house.

"As far as I know, she's okay. This is why I'm here." The detective took something out of his shirt and looked at it before he handed it to me.

The photo was a mug shot of Gabe taken in his thirties. I held the picture at arm's length and looked as if trying to place the face.

"You know him?"

I shook my head.

"Had your name on a card with the shift you work, your address, and phone number."

I shrugged. "I see hundreds of faces every day."

"You do work at the Le Grande? I mean, your work card indicates you do."

"Yeah."

"I subpoenaed his cell phone records. Someone from the Le Grande called him some six weeks ago. From the hall outside the employees' break room at 6:44. That ring a bell?"

I rested my back on the cushions and tried to appear mystified. "I don't know what this is about. Or how information about me ended up on a card."

"Just a routine investigation."

"If my daughter's okay, I'm not going to worry about a man I've never heard of." I leaned forward as if to stand, but seeing that Detective Beardsley wasn't ready to leave, I sat back and rested my hands on my knees to keep them from shaking.

"He called your house as well. As I said, I've got phone records. Someone answered."

I shrugged. "Could be a wrong number."

"Could be. Funny coincidence, though." The detective's expression suggested he'd scored several unanswered points. "I'm curious. Why, when a homicide investigator showed up at your door, was your first concern about your daughter?"

"I explained that."

The cop nodded several times. "Well, Gabriel Blitzstein is not exactly an upstanding sort. If he's gone for good, no one with any human virtue is going to mourn him, but my job is to try to find him. He's been missing about five weeks. You'll probably read about it in tomorrow's paper. Who knows? With his background, he might have skipped town and is in South America."

"I wouldn't know."

"Mr. Helms, I don't think that's the case. He was the kind of guy who pissed off a lot of people. Did he piss you off?"

"I said I didn't know him. I'm sorry he's missing. Maybe someone knows where he is, but I don't. Aren't you supposed to advise me of my rights or something?"

"If you're a suspect." The detective raised his eyebrows. "Are you?"

I shook my head. "A suspect in what?"

"You tell me."

"I've done nothing. Excuse me, but it's getting late and I haven't eaten."

The detective nodded. Standing, he told me to call the number on the card if I had any thoughts. Any thoughts? What else did I have but thoughts? I walked him to the door. At the threshold, he locked his eyes on me. "You've got a .357 magnum registered to you."

"Yeah."

"Why'd you buy it?"

"Why not?"

"It seems strange that you live to your midforties and never have a gun, at least not legally, then one day you buy one out of the blue. And right after Blitzstein calls your house and just before he disappears."

"Not out of the blue. I read the papers. This isn't a safe world."

"No, I guess it's not. Hell, some people even dump dog shit on others. Don't let that gun disappear just yet. We may want to take a look at it down the way. Well, good night. Aren't you going to open your mail?"

"What?"

"The mail. By the way, my cousin deals at the Le Grande. They don't put tips in an envelope. You get them on your paycheck. See you."

I stood at the open door and watched him drive off, thinking I would gladly trade this for a ten-year nightmare. One encounter with Blitzstein and suddenly I was a suspect. In what? I figured it was a good time to be paranoid. Ben might know something. I'd been cautioned never to show up without first calling. For now, I thought it unwise to call from home. I opened the envelope and stuffed the bills in my pocket without bothering to count them.

I circled the neighborhood until assured I wasn't being followed, then drove off. What was it Anne had told me? Control is an illusion. You gain it by giving up the illusion. Mumbo jumbo. I took Jones Boulevard to the freeway, exited at Valley View, turned left on Alta, and headed to Rancho. Traffic thinned as I approached Rancho Circle. By the time I reached Shadow Lane I'd traveled a dozen miles to go five, but mine was the only car on the road. I couldn't find a pay phone anywhere. It hadn't occurred to me that pay phones were all but extinct. I made a U-turn and drove to Bonanza, then east.

I searched the old Greater Vegas area for a pay phone. The neighborhood had deteriorated considerably since I'd lived here as a boy. I hadn't seen the East Stewart house in years. I thought about my parents, neither of whom I knew, though I'd lived with Dad until his death. Was it happenstance that I'd replicated the pattern of their life, a failed marriage, me a dealer, my ex-wife a cocktail waitress, ours a broken home? Except for a homicide detective knocking at my door and my involving myself in a cheating scam, I felt like the typical Las Vegas cliché.

I slowed as I came to the house. The windows were dark. A group of Hispanic teenagers leaned on the fenders and doors of a '63 Thunderbird. They eyed me.

"Hey, man, what'chu want?" one shouted.

One jumped off the curb and made gestures that I assumed were gang signs. That brought me to my senses. What would a cop see? A man cruising the hood, a pocketful of money and a gun under my seat. I drove off. At Five Points East I caught a red light. A cop cruiser stopped beside me. When the light changed, I looked straight ahead and accelerated slowly. I figured to find a phone in the Showboat. When I reached the Showboat, I discovered the name had changed and it was now the Castaways. I parked on the Atlantic Street side and waited until satisfied I wasn't tailed. Still, to be safe I drove as if I was being tailed by the cops. I circled the parking lot and found a spot under a light.

I opened the door and entered the back hallway where I immediately confronted a wall of stale odors, mostly from cigarette smoke accumulated over fifty years. A single set of feet trailed behind me, but I played it cool and didn't look back. I walked past the bowling lanes, bypassed the bingo room, and looked for a pay phone along the way. To kill time and see if someone was actually following me, I strolled the slot aisles, looking around casually and at the same time looking for a change girl. I saw none. The slots, even nickel machines, took only bills or credit cards. I hadn't pulled a handle since my break-in days at the Mint. These machines didn't even have handles. I stopped in front of one with a monitor that flashed Loony Tune characters hiding behind trees and peering out. I slipped a twenty in the money slot. The machine gobbled up the bill and registered twenty credits on a display. The credits vanished in seven plays. I stuffed another in, pressed the button several times, and won ten credits, but couldn't figure out exactly why. I pressed the button again and again. When three bars lined up on the pay line, it registered more credits. I looked for a button to cash out. The machine didn't pay in coins, only with a credit ticket that had to be redeemed.

I just wanted change for a phone. Two machines down a woman in her fifties, plain, hair braided on both sides of her head, was mumbling as she pressed the play button.

"Lady, this is a hot machine. It's got more than twenty credits. You want it? I'll give it up to you for two quarters."

She eyed me suspiciously.

"I'm taking a loss. Honest. I hit . . ."

"Don't play with me, mister. You just want my machine. Do I look stupid?"

I shrugged and played three credits. When the reels stopped, lights flashed overhead and the machine blacked out, then started blinking as a buzzer rang pandemonium overhead. A cocktail waitress passed by and said that a boss was on the way.

"What'd I win?"

She pointed to a flashing sign. "Nineteen thousand four hundred dollars."

I looked at the woman I'd offered the machine to. She glared. I smiled back.

The slot floorman and another boss arrived and confirmed the payout. They said I was welcome to stay at the hotel in a suite for nothing, food and beverages paid for. I thanked them but declined. When all the dots were connected, I gave the floorman a dollar and asked for change in quarters. He looked at me somewhat dumbfounded, but grudgingly took the dollar and said he'd get me change.

31

Rumors proved true; Hefty took over the joint. If he fired me, I welcomed it. I wanted Ben and all his agents and Hefty and Blitzstein, Detective Beardsley, and the clown in the gray Honda to watch me clock out for the last time. I had enough money to open up F and J Masonry. Until the night before I'd thought of luck as having an umbrella in the car when a storm hit. Now, I believed in luck as driving blindfolded behind the wheel of a car and surviving rush-hour traffic. A few dollars, next thing I knew I was royalty. Nearly twenty thousand on a fluke.

When I lined up for my table assignment, I expected and even hoped the boss would send me to the office to see Hefty. Instead, he assigned me to the high-limit pit. That came as a shock. The last time I'd dealt to high-end play or even been near a high-roller section was the evening Linus Berman had burned the Monaco on his seven-figure win streak. Standing behind a game with a mannequin smile on my face while waiting for some pampered rich guy to take a seat and ask for a marker wasn't how I would choose to spend the shift, or any shift. Until someone fired up the game, the idle hours there would make the day seem doubly long.

"Aren't there any five-dollar tables you could give me?"

"That's where they want you," he said. "I just follow orders. And so do you."

They who, I wondered, as I headed to the pit, which pit consisted of two blackjack tables and a mini baccarat table, each requiring a minimum five-hundred-dollar bet. It sat isolated from the rest of the casino by a swath of red carpet and an imported brass rail with intricate renderings of exotic birds. A dealer had told me the rail had been fabricated by hand in Spain and had cost a half-million dollars. I didn't doubt it. A guard stood constant watch at the entrance, and a cocktail waitress seated on a stool in the corner waited at the ready.

The tables were empty. The pit boss strolled over and took the minimum sign down and replaced it with a reserved sign. "For a new high roller."

"Who?"

"Some big player Mr. Hefty brought in with him."

I sidled in behind the rack and out of curiosity counted down the bank. The chips ranged from $5,000 to $100 and totaled $268,000, an impressive bank to start with. Standing idle behind that dead game, I had plenty of time to ponder what I gotten myself into, what would cause a homicide detective to visit me, and how best to extricate myself from the mess. By the end of my first hour standing idle I was resolved to take matters in hand and quit. If Hefty wouldn't fire me, why not? The scam was over, and anything else Ben had in mind for me, I didn't have a mind to do.

On my break I called Ben's answering service and left a message saying we had to meet that night. I wanted to tell him to his face, so that he would have no doubt about my determination to walk away and why.

BEN WAS WAITING in a booth near the entrance when I walked in. Business in the Roadrunner was sparse. He held a glass of iced vodka in both hands and swirled its contents. I slid into the booth opposite him.

"Hello," I said.

He grunted out a hello and took a drink from his glass. For a while he showed no interest in talking, just held the glass to his lips and sipped from it now and then. I decided to outwait him.

Finally, he swallowed the last of his drink and eyed me over the rim of the glass. "You want to eat first? Are you hungry?"

"No."

"Must be important to call me here."

I shook my head. "Depends, I guess. Is a cop visiting me important?"

"A cop?"

"Detective Beardsley. A homicide detective. He asked about Gabe Blitzstein."

Ben showed no reaction. The waitress came over, a young woman barely twenty-one with a sweet face, but so thin and shapeless she looked as if she'd been shrink-wrapped into her T-shirt and jeans. I ordered a glass of Syrah. She laid down a napkin with her twiglike fingers.

"Another of these," Ben said, holding up his glass.

I watched her walk away. "Yeah, about Blitzstein."

Ben said, "So, did you kill him?" He smiled. This time it seemed genuine.

"Who said he was dead?"

"A homicide detective investigates homicides. It's easy to assume."

"He's missing. Five weeks. No, six weeks now. Maybe you killed him."

"Or maybe he's in the parking lot watching your car."

"That's not funny."

"Why'd you wait a week to tell me?"

"I kind of figured you knew already."

"That a cop came to visit you?"

"No." I got to the point. "That's not why I wanted to see you. Hefty's the new casino manager at the Le Grande."

"I know."

"What else do you know?"

Ben looked bored with the question. "I don't see any emergency here."

"The casino's going to automatic shufflers. That will kill our arrangement. Guess that's emergency enough."

The waitress brought the drinks and set them down. "Do you want to order food?"

Ben looked up at her. "Do they serve food here?"

"Yes, sir."

"Then you should order something to eat."

She stood there stunned for a moment. "If you need something else, my name is Tiffany," she said, turned, and nearly fled out of the room.

"That was fucked up," I said.

Ben waved me off. "Forget the shufflers. There are ways, more profitable ways."

"Doesn't matter. I'm out."

"Didn't we have this conversation a few weeks back?"

"It's different now."

"Come to the house Thursday. That's your day off, right? You should see something."

I shook my head. "I can't go around wondering if someone's following me. And this detective thinks I'm involved with Gabe. I met him once."

"Harsh world, huh?"

I snorted. "Look, Hefty's probably going to fire me anyhow. He dumped me out of the Monaco."

"He won't." Ben said it as if it were a known fact.

"Just who are you, Ben?"

He stared at me over his drink. "What kind of question is that?"

"You've got a big house, a housekeeper, a Mercedes, everything people want. Why rip off casinos?"

"Are you wired, Jude?"

"No, just curious."

He smiled. "I don't indulge people's curiosity. Enjoy your wine. This time, you pick up the tab. Everyone has to pay his way from now on."

32 The following Thursday, Ben called me in the morning and woke me. He said he wanted me to come to his place around noon. I told him I would be busy and couldn't make it.

"Oh, I think you can make it. I've got something you must see."

"No, I really can't. I've got plans."

"Plans? Jude, you have no plans. You've never had a plan."

"I have lately."

"Okay, no games here. You wanted to know who I am. Let's start answering that by saying I'm someone who has your future in his hands. Forget your plans. Come over."

HE OPENED THE DOOR, said, "Glad you came. You've been on our minds, Jude," and motioned me inside, his tone now a complete switch from the menacing one I'd heard over the phone. Playing the debonair host Audie had first introduced me to, he pointed to a portable buffet in the den and told me to make myself at home, that his house was always open to me. Angel sat on a couch, his back to us. He looked over his shoulder and offered a curt hello.

"Angel, be polite," Ben said. "Jude's a friend."

Ben handed me a napkin and held up a silver platter of liverwurst sandwiches and deviled eggs. I hesitated.

"We're all friends here, Jude. And food goes well with entertainment."

"Entertainment?" I selected a liverwurst.

"Everything's better with a little food in the stomach." Ben set the platter down on a table and grinned. "I've got something to show you in the other room. Angel, come with us."

Ben told me to bring along the sandwich. He placed a hand on my back and guided me to the door. Angel followed us to the game room. The door was open. Ben told me to have a seat by the television. He picked up the remote and flicked on the television. A grainy image of the Fremont Street mall came on the screen. It had obviously been filmed using a compact camera. The video scanned to the brickwork on the street, the picture quivering as if either the ground or the camera was unstable. Despite the quality, I clearly saw myself on the screen, first me from the back side, then my profile as I entered the glass door of the Whiskey River.

I stiffened. "What's this?"

Ben said, "Watch."

My stomach tightened as the camera lost me for a moment, and then it picked me up inside the casino and followed my path to the table. I dropped the sandwich and napkin on the chair as the camera zoomed in and captured my eighty-dollar buy-in. Who? How? I hadn't seen a video camera. Although I was clearly in the video, as was the dealer's three-quarter profile, the only visible parts of Angel were his arm and hand. The lens was angled so he and Patty Lane were off camera. Every move I made was captured.

The video ran thirty-one minutes, each frame centered on me. It ended on a blurred image of me receiving $1,140 from a cashier. I forgot about Beth, the detective, Gabe, all the reasons I was prepared to quit. F and J Masonry vanished from my future, boxed, wrapped, and sealed inside that video. For a thousand dollars, split five ways. It had never been about money, just about his owning me. Ben, the man who left nothing to chance, owned me as Blitzstein had claimed. He'd needed someone with a clean background, someone he could slip into a position and control. How long had it been planned? The entire setup?

"Why? Why did you . . . Why the video?" I asked as if I hadn't figured it out.

Ben triggered the rewind. "This copy's yours. I have another. Technology. Amazing, huh? When video became so sophisticated that casinos started relying on it, I learned all I could about it. It can be constructive and instructive, as you can see. I find it fascinating. Nothing hurts our business, *your* business now, more than the electronic eye. In the old days we could go around the eye in the sky or buy an employee in surveillance. They make less than most dealers they watch. Isn't that right, Angel?"

"That's right."

"Angel started out as a dealer. Did business and got caught. No conviction. The camera wasn't on him. Only straight work he could get after that was in surveillance, because casinos don't hire thieves and put them on games, at least no longer. They did in your dad's day. I never told you I knew your dad. It was a small town then. Hell, the whole state was a small town in a sense. We learned our trade in flat stores, beating the squares." Ben grinned as if remembering something pleasant from the past. "I knew him from the New Frontier and the Sahara. He was a boss at the Sahara when he died, right?"

I nodded.

"When your father died, you were how old?"

"Twelve. I asked, why the video?"

"The real question you should ask is how."

I looked at Angel, who shrugged. "Okay, how?"

"Video cameras, so compact now, it's no problem to conceal one. Unzip a purse enough to expose the lens, aim it at the subject, press a button on a remote, the camera does the work."

Audie. That explained everything, but what Ben now had in mind.

He ejected the disc and handed to me. "The original's elsewhere. You know, only two or three casinos have gone to technology this clear."

"Why should I know that, or care?"

"You're working for one. Come." Ben walked me to the door. "Don't get any bad ideas unless you want a copy to end up in the Gaming Control Board's hands. And don't come around unless I call." As he shut the door, he added, "Remember, people disappear."

33 The video had changed matters. I watched it four times. Each viewing further fueled my anger. At first I looked at everything else other than myself to blame—Audie, Ben, Dad's dying so young, and the MGM fire. I laid the disc on the coffee table and stared at it for nearly an hour, my feelings shifting between fear and rage. I knew now why I'd been sent to the high-roller pit. Whatever Ben had in

mind, it involved my dealing high-limit blackjack. And I had a suspicion about what had happened to Blitzstein. The Mojave is a big desert, and the town had a history of people disappearing. Anyone who'd lived here since the '60s knew the story of Russian Louie's ride of no return. Blitzstein was just one more who vanished. I could easily be the next if I lost my value to Ben. What recourse did I have now but to submit to his bidding? I saw only one. I could keep the gun close.

When I'd finally thought matters through, I faced up to the fact that ultimately I alone was to blame. Audie hadn't betrayed me. She'd simply been loyal to Ben or herself. Or perhaps it was just true, as she'd claimed, that he owned her. After all, he now owned me, didn't he? I removed the disc and heaved it at the fireplace, smashed the case underfoot, and discarded the mess in a plastic garbage bag. In looking at the trash, I saw something I should have seen at first—the remainders of my choices. I realized I'd lost sight of something long ago in the flames of the MGM. Myself.

I SAT UNDER an annoyingly loud television and fumbled in a stack of pamphlets and magazine for something worth reading beside car brochures. I needed something, anything, to stop my mind from whittling away at the huge log of confusion that had become my life since Audie came into it. A woman with three daughters all under six years old sat opposite me. The youngest crawled in and out of the mother's lap as the others stared at the television screen. The man beside me reeked of cigarette smoke. The smell was getting to me. I stood to go out for some fresh air.

Following the fire at the MGM I hadn't thought it possible to control much of anything in life. But now as I saw it, by going without picking a direction and taking action, I would simply surrender myself to whatever Ben had in mind. I needed alternatives. In part the problem with coming up with a workable plan was that I wasn't sure in full who I was dealing with. Ben knew a great deal about me, but I knew little about him. Though I didn't know who he was, I knew the kind of man he was and what he might be capable of doing.

As I passed a car rental booth, an idea occurred, one that might set me at least on a path. One certainty was Ben had a scheme in mind that would drag me further into the tangle. A second was that I was no sleuth, knew nothing about that side of life. But I was alone in this and working with too many unknowns to make a plan. I had to become my own detective. I turned back and went to the parts department, where I studied the displays. When the parts clerk asked if he could help, I pointed to a particular stereo and asked if he had one in stock.

"Pretty sure I do."

"Good. And a set of these?" I indicated a chrome wheel.

"For some models."

"I want both on my car if you can get it done, say, by day after tomorrow."

He asked what kind of car I drove and concealed his surprise when I told him. He said he'd do what he could, but installation depended on the schedule of the service department. He made a couple of calls and said the items were in stock, but installation would take time because the service department was backed up.

"Can you bring your car back?"

I said, "I'll leave it and rent a car."

The rental clerk, a woman in her sixties, wanted to upgrade me to a high-end model, but I insisted on something small and plain. I needed to be inconspicuous.

"I have a beige Saturn."

"Perfect."

She took my credit card and license and filled out the paperwork. Twenty minutes later I was on the road. I wasn't sure if what I had in mind would pan out, but I had to try. I parked the car next to the curb under the shade of an ash tree and slouched down behind the steering wheel. Being a novice at this, I figured the best way to go undetected was by parking in shade with the rear of the car facing Ben's. That way I could slouch down in the seat and angle the side- and rearview mirrors to watch the place. I didn't know what I was expecting, just hoped for any sign that would shed light on my situation.

Parked in front of Ben's were two pickups with toolboxes mounted in their beds. One was loaded with rolls of carpet. A man wearing a carpenter's belt walked to a truck, opened a toolbox, and returned to the house with an electric drill. Shortly, two more appeared and walked to the second truck. They shouldered a roll of carpet and toted it inside.

I couldn't imagine what improvements Ben had in mind. Perhaps that's what people with money did, remodel what didn't need remodeling. I adjusted the rearview mirror to better see the driveway and front door. The carpet layers came and went three more times, after which nothing happened for the next fifty minutes, except for my legs cramping. I adjusted my position, stretched my legs over the console onto the passenger's seat, and readjusted the mirrors.

For a while the stakeout's only result was making my butt go numb. I didn't know how long to stay. An hour? Two? How did cops determine how much time to spend on a stakeout? I figured I'd given it long enough, dismissed it as a lame idea, and turned the ignition key. As soon as I did, Audie's BMW pulled into the driveway.

The driver's door swung open, and Ben got out. Before ringing the doorbell, he looked around the neighborhood as a visitor might. When the door opened, Audie greeted him. Behind her in the dim interior a man rested his hands on her shoulders. Audie backpedaled and Ben entered. The door closed. I didn't know how to interpret what I'd seen. It reasoned that whoever the man behind her was, he wasn't a member of the construction crew. Angel? Unlikely, considering the animosity between him and Audie.

I turned on the radio. A piece for a string quartet by Telemann was playing. I wondered what my kids would think, me slouched behind a wheel, playing gumshoe, with only the vaguest notion of what I was seeing. What if they heard I'd become a thief? An hour passed this way. Butt and toes numb, I surrendered. My knee cracked as I wriggled into a driving position. I started the engine and was about to shift the car into gear when the door opened, and Ben hurried out. He got in Audie's car and drove out of the circular driveway in my direction. I lay across the seat and waited for him to pass. Then, giving him a two-block lead, I followed.

He entered the freeway at Charleston Boulevard and in thick traffic drove south at a steady sixty-five miles per hour. I held back what I thought was a safe distance. At the approach to Flamingo Road, the BMW slipped into the right-hand lane. A mile later Ben took the next exit and followed the Tropicana flyover going east. Traffic thinned out as he neared the Strip. One car was between us, and he was about a hundred feet ahead. I slowed and let two cars pass me as a buffer. Ben turned south. A quarter mile later he slowed the BMW and steered to the right. I didn't have to speculate where he was headed.

He entered the high-rise parking structure. I coasted into the turn as he accelerated up the ramp. From the way he attacked the turns, Ben knew where he was going. I counted three before entering. Noise carried nicely inside. I lagged behind one floor below, rolled down my window, and followed the squeal of his tires. At the turn on the fourth floor, I glimpsed the BMW's brake lights as he pulled into a reserved space in D-level parking, in a section reserved for casino limousines and the personal cars of top executives.

I drove up one more floor and listened. The engine died. The door slammed. I counted to ten, then turned around and drove through general parking to the executive spaces. The BMW sat in a reserved space just left of the elevator. I knew who the general manager, the shift bosses, hosts, and pit bosses were on all shifts, and the chief of security as well. That left one possible executive position Ben could occupy. Head of casino surveillance. Of course. How else could the man who left nothing to chance have every base covered? I glanced at the video camera that monitored the parking level. No cameras, I thought, echoing Ben's words.

AS I STOOD IN LINE at the county recorder, I considered a hypothesis Anne had described, one she loosely hooked to something called chaos theory. She maintained that a butterfly, in choosing a particular flower over another, set off a chain reaction that determined the course of the universe. I applied the idea to my circumstances. Where did it really begin? Taking a job at the Mint in the late '70s? Forgetting Lucas's present? Being in the high-roller pit on a given shift? The theory resembled the shuffle of the deck, where one decision by a player altered the entire sequence. Hit, don't hit. Is that what the universe is based on and what makes the human condition operate?

The man in front stepped forward. Lines every day. How many now? Twenty thousand, each position in line being like an alternate flower the butterfly landed on? I was devising my own theory now. Jude's Theory. Nothing is as it appears. Believe in diminishing returns. Trust no one. Crawl until you're out of the fire, and then stand up and find a safe exit. I ran out of ideas to add to my theory as a station cleared. The clerk signaled me forward and asked how she could help. I handed her the address.

"I'll get you a microfiche that includes that plat." She pointed to the machines, where a dozen people were looking through viewers. "You can use one of those to look it up. Instructions are on the tape. Pencils and scratch paper are on the table. No charge for viewing the document, but there's a fee if you want a copy."

It took several minutes to scan the film, but I found the recorded deed. The mortgage was held by First Western States Fidelity in the name of Audra Amersen and Joel Moser. I stared at the names and dates a few seconds and rewound the tape. I was neither surprised nor upset. But whose house was whose? I thought about stepping back in line and checking the other address for ownership, but decided it wasn't important to know.

I dropped the tape in a return box. In the lobby I found a phone and opened the yellow pages. For no particular reason I picked the third listing and wrote down the number on my palm.

"Daryl Biggs Investigations," a woman's voice answered.

"Is Mr. Biggs in?"

"This is his answering service."

"Can you connect me?"

"One moment. I'll see."

I wondered if out of a big garden, I'd picked the right flower. The woman asked if I could copy down a number. She repeated it twice. I recorded it on my palm next to the other and hung up. I dialed the number. The phone buzzed. I heard some racket in the background.

"Daryl Biggs." His voice was a husky, throaty one.

"This is Jude Helms."

"Do I know you, Jude Helms?"

"No."

"Then this better be good. I'm stuck seventy dollars on this poker machine."

I recalled the attorney I'd heard on the conference line. "I need a detective."

"Most people who say that really need an attorney or a psychiatrist."

"I need all three, but one at a time."

"I like you already, Jude Helms. I'm in my office. Come see me."

"Where's that?"

"Big Dog's on West Sahara. You know it?"

I told him I would be there in twenty minutes.

"Ask for me at the bar."

BIG DOG'S WAS SMOKY, but because of several televisions mounted over the bar, it wasn't so dim that my eyes needed to adjust. The restaurant was bustling. A line of people waited to be seated. The bar was less so. I stood by the cashier's cage and scanned the bar for anyone who seemed to be expecting someone to arrive. No one looked like the movie versions of a detective, and no one seemed particularly interested in me. I asked the bartender, a brunette in her late thirties, if she knew a Daryl Biggs.

She jutted her chin. "The guy who's talking to the machine. What'll you have?"

"Nothing, but give him one of whatever he drinks." I laid a ten on the bar.

Daryl Biggs was bent over a video poker screen, a near-empty bottle of Heineken in his left hand. He was in his late fifties, his combed-back hair thinning and gray, his face somewhat bloated and his skin blotched. When I introduced myself, Biggs looked up for an instant, took in my face, then played off his hand.

Once finished, he said, "See this stool?"

I looked at his stool.

"Got my name engraved underneath the seat. What do you need?"

"To find out about two people. Maybe more."

"A hundred an hour, three hours minimum. I save on overhead by using this as an office. You got three hundred?"

I nodded. The bartender set a fresh Heineken in front of Biggs and laid the change on the bar. I told her to keep it.

Biggs took a swallow of beer and said, "You're contributing to inflation, my friend. A tip should always be less than half of what you're paying for."

"Here's what I need . . ."

I intended to give him the license plate number from Audie's BMW and the names from the deed, but Biggs shook his head. "Let's go outside."

We walked outside and away from the door. Biggs covered his eyes with sunglasses.

"Sun's poison, you know. At least it's fall. Hell, almost winter. Say you're in an alley, no escape. You're confronted by a gangbanger, a vicious Doberman, and an attorney. You have a gun, but just two bullets. What do you do?"

"Beats me."

"You shoot the attorney twice." Biggs laughed at his joke.

I'd heard it before and didn't. "Do I pay extra for the jokes?"

Biggs looked at me soberly. "No. I just love the joke. So what's the problem?"

"Problem? I didn't call about a problem."

"People don't call me if they're not in a jam. Can't collect a debt 'cause a guy skipped. Wife diddlin' the boss. You name it, people have it."

"It's not exactly a problem. I just need to know who Joel Moser and Audra Amersen-Moser are. Oh, and this license plate." I handed him a slip of paper with the number on it.

Biggs smiled. "That's all?"

"Yeah. Aren't you going to write their names down."

He shook his head. "How much information do you need? Addresses? Phone numbers?"

"I need to know who they are. You know, are they . . . have they been in trouble with the law? I've got two addresses and phone numbers."

"What's the address?"

I gave him the Scotch 8os address.

Biggs chuckled.

"What's so funny?"

"Well, that's a fine neighborhood, but the wrong address for Moser. He's in Carson City doing twenty or more, last I heard."

"You're sure?"

"One hundred dollars' worth of sure. I was on Metro when he finally went away. Ten to twenty, I think. Set up a casino scam that he got caught for. Then when he was out on bail for that, he ran a cold deck in at another casino. Got nailed again. Who knows, but they say he beat casinos out of a couple million over the years. Baccarat scams as well. I worked intelligence when he went down. He's suspected of two murders. No one could pin them on him. No bodies, just missing people."

The last sounded too familiar. "What about Audra Amersen?"

"His girlfriend or wife, I think. She sometimes used his name, but I don't think they were actually married. If you want me to check that out, I can. As I recall, she did a year, is an ex-con for hitting a casino in Reno or Tahoe. Some card caper. Happened years ago."

Biggs speed-dialed a number on his cell phone and turned his back to me. He called the person who answered "Hon," then looked back at me and winked. He walked a few feet away, small talking over the phone before giving the license plate. There was a pause as Biggs waited. He told me it would take a few seconds at most, but a few seconds became several minutes. He motioned for me to be patient, tucked the phone under his chin, and scratched something down in a notebook. He hung up and signaled me over.

"Your guy is Benjamin Goldman, a.k.a. Ben Gold, a.k.a. Benny the Fixer. His rap sheet is sealed, which tells me what I already knew. He's an old-timer. Once a cross-roader. He's got a work application at the Le Grande. His last place of employment before that was—"

"The Monaco." I pulled my wallet out and handed him one-hundred-dollar bills.

"Guess I'm supposed to take this and forget it."

"That's all I needed."

Biggs shook his head. "As I said, I like you, Jude Helms. So I'm going to tell you that whatever you needed to know this for won't solve the problem.

Even if it didn't show all over you, just asking about Moser tells me you got troubles." When he opened his wallet to fold the money inside, he pulled out a business card and jotted something on the back. "On the back are my cell and home numbers. I don't know what you're into, but these are bad people. Sometime soon, you'll be needing help, and my fee doesn't go down. Might go up, in fact."

"Thanks. I'll keep it in mind."

"And keep this in mind. Moser used to hang with some bad characters at the Horseshoe. You know some of the scum that place used to attract when Teddy was alive. Thanks for the beer." Biggs folded his cellular phone, slipped it in his shirt pocket, and stepped toward the door.

"You didn't tell me where Ben Goldman lives."

Biggs stopped and looked back. "1720 South Tomsik. Off Charleston near Oakey. Beer's getting warm." He opened the door and disappeared into the smoky dimness.

The address he'd given me was Audie's. I began to digest the information. I could fill in a few more blanks now, but as I did a fresh series of blanks appeared. So it was true Audie lived in a house owned by Ben, the one truth she'd probably told me. But Ben lived in a house that she and her husband, or whatever he was, owned. Why? It occurred to me as I opened the door to the rental car that I hadn't figure Patty Lane into any of questions or that she might be part of the answer to at least one of them. Who was behind all of this?

34 I spent the afternoon preparing dinner—flank steaks stuffed with banana peppers, bleu cheese, and chopped garlic; Caesar salad; vine-ripened tomato slices topped with provolone and fresh mint, smothered in wine vinegar and virgin olive oil; fresh asparagus steamed, lightly buttered; bow-tie pasta in Alfredo sauce; and a dessert of raspberries chilled in a bed of Gran Marnier. It was an adult meal, hardly the kind my kids appreciated, but I wanted them to experience something other than the usual steaks or burgers and baked potatoes, or the vegetarian dishes Anne subjected them to. I cooked also because I needed to reflect on life as I'd once thought it could be.

I was in the critical stages, tossing the salad, steaming asparagus, and broiling steaks, my attention divided evenly among the three, when Beth stepped into the kitchen. Lucas hung back. Any error might ruin a meal or turn it mediocre, which to my mind was worse. I told them to go away, that I'd call them when dinner was ready.

"Jeez," Lucas said. "It's not like you're Wolfgang Puck."

"Who?" I asked.

"Dad, Lucas has a kazoo up his butt," Beth said, an expression she'd gotten from me.

Lucas held his palms up to the sky. "It's natural. Everyone does it, even women. Dad, did you know the average woman farts thirteen times a day?"

"Who's Wolfgang Puck?" I asked again, playing dumb.

"Some famous guy who owns restaurants," Lucas said. "I figure Mom does more than the average woman."

"I don't care about your mother's farts. And don't talk about her that way."

"Smells good," Beth said.

"Thanks. Now, both of you, go away."

I took a deep breath, then another. I stirred the Alfredo sauce, checked the asparagus and put it on the hot plate, opened the oven, took a fork and turned the steaks, then set the salad on the table. I cupped my palms to my nose and smelled garlic, Parmesan, fresh lettuce. What I didn't smell was egg. Why can't we smell or see what is most obvious, I wondered. If I set the salad outside for a day, what I'd smell would be rotten egg.

I returned to the kitchen, poured water from the asparagus into the sink, added two tablespoons of butter, a pinch of fresh basil and balsamic vinegar, and stirred the mix. I poured it in a serving bowl. I imagined myself a chef and thought no job, other than being a general in a theater of war, demands more control. I was in control. On a roll. On a high. I sniffed the bowl. How can we be sure? The answer is when it smells right or wrong. Ether way, we know it's finished. Yes, of course. I hadn't seen far enough beyond what Audie meant to me. Whatever she stirred in me was rotting now. I could smell the scam and myself as one small ingredient in it.

I checked the bow tie. Al dente. Satisfied, I drained the pot, smothered the pasta with Alfredo sauce, and stirred until the noodles gleamed ivory. "It's ready!" I called out and opened the oven.

I told the kids to help cart the meal to the table, that I'd bring the steaks. Beth picked up the bowl of asparagus, Lucas the bow tie in Alfredo sauce. When they sat down, Lucas asked why I'd gone to so much trouble, when hamburgers would do.

"Because good things are worth the trouble. We owe ourselves a little trouble."

Lucas looked at Beth, who shrugged and said, "Dad, you're so weird."

"No," Lucas said, "that's pretty philosophical, Dad."

I forked a steak on Beth's plate, one on Lucas's, and last on my own. I turned to take the broiler pan to the kitchen, then stopped and eyed them.

"What now?" Beth asked.

"Okay, here it is. I fix a meal like this because I like cooking, but also because . . . well, of how much your mother can't cook."

"You got that right," Lucas said.

"That's okay. Don't trouble yourselves. I'll get the salad." I called from the kitchen, "If I asked you two to do something without questioning me, would you do exactly as I said? Would you think it was important enough?"

"Dad, you're being weird again," Beth said.

There was a silence, then Lucas spoke. "I would."

Then Beth said, "Dad, you're scaring me."

35 "So my mother looks at me and says, 'You know her. You met her.' And I say, 'No, I didn't.' But my mother doesn't believe me because she's got it in her head," Norma said.

"Mothers," I said, meaning nothing in particular. I smiled like the fool who accidentally found a pearl in an oyster. It was the best I could do.

The shufflers discouraged play, a pattern at the Monaco repeating itself here. Day to day, games in the high-end pit stood dead for hours, and I stood idle as my worries drumrolled in my head. What and when? When and what? And what was my part in it to be? For the first time in years I took to sitting among dealers on breaks and listening to the bitch sessions and the petty gossip I once abhorred. I did so mostly because Norma amused me and the company helped quiet my mind.

She drew on her cigarette and looked at me. "She's completely blocked out the fact that I never met her friends, any of them, and that I didn't talk to her for thirteen years. Is your mother like that, Jude?"

"She's dead."

"I'm sorry."

"No need."

"What was she like?"

"Tell the truth, I don't know. Pretty, I guess, and she changed the color of her hair a lot. They divorced when I was young. She took my younger brother and sister. Dad kept me. I went to visit her when she ended up in a hospice in Los Angeles. Her skin was almost transparent, and she didn't know who I was."

"That's depressing. A childhood without a mother."

"No, not really. My dad was a good father, but he died when I was twelve. My uncle, his brother, took me in. He taught me how to lay block and patios."

"But you didn't know your brother and sister, right?" She blew smoke at the ceiling.

"No. I have their phone numbers, but don't know—" I realized I was talking more about myself than I had for years, and it made me self-conscious. I pointed at her cigarette, and to avoid the conversation getting more personal, said, "You should quit smoking."

"And breathing casino air? What's that do for us? Really, you don't remember anything about your mother?"

I said, "Nothing significant." It saddened me to say so.

"You know, Jude, for a moment it seemed like you were actually human." Norma took a draw off her cigarette and stubbed it out. "Time to go."

"No. Too soon."

She walked the hallway to the casino with me. As we neared the main pit, she said, "I wonder if Linus Berman is going to play. Last time he was here, he didn't make a laydown on our shift. I'm thinking it's you. Maybe he sees bad omens. Maybe you've got toenail fungus or something."

"Gotta be the fungus, that or the automatic shufflers."

"They use the same shufflers we do on swing shift," she said.

"And he didn't play then either, did he?" I got a whiff of her perfume and asked, "What's that you're wearing?"

She glanced down at her blouse and tie and gave me a sly smile. "A uniform."

"I mean, you smell good."

"Jude, are you flirting with me?"

I didn't know what to say. I considered her a moment and realized she could interpret it that way, or maybe I was. She seemed embarrassed that I didn't answer.

"I'm kidding," she said. "You know me, the kidder. Besides, I'm probably not your type."

"What's my type?"

"You're a male dealer. Probably anything warm and wiggling."

I WAS SURPRISED to find a player firing five-hundred-dollar checks at the house. Middle Eastern, in his forties and clean shaven, in a Lincoln-green Fila jogging suit, in front of him more than thirty thousand in white and black chips. I tapped out Eric, who told me not to pay the player with pink checks. I saw Eric's pocket was empty. Just what we needed. A high-roller stiff. Millie, the pit boss, approached the table from behind and whispered for me to deal slowly. "Give Mr. Mashid time to make a decision."

Mashid tossed a black check on the layout in front of me. "Give to me all green."

I cut out four twenty-fives, locked up the hundred-dollar check, and waited for his bet. A cocktail waitress arrived with a black coffee and set it on a napkin atop the layout. Mashid tested the coffee, ran his tongue over his lips, and laid a green chip on her tray. He stood, pushed his chair aside, and spread three five-hundred-dollar bets in the squares. He was taller than I was by an inch and thin. His forehead was broad and his nose regally large.

"Don't pay in thousand dollar," he said. "Black and white only. Pink is girl's color."

He watched my every move as I dealt out the hands. I showed a king, checked my hole card, and waited. Mashid looked from his stack of chips to the king, then to his own hand. He matched the bet on the first hand for a double down and turned his cards over. I gave him a card facedown and said, "Good luck."

He held up an open palm. "I don't like how you look at me like I'm not who I am, but Osama bin Laden. And smiling too, like I'm a joke."

"Excuse me?"

"You heard."

I'd been through similar ordeals with tougher customers. I'd dealt to the infamous Dragon Lady, who tossed cards on the floor and threw ashtrays at dealers. To keep myself employed in the business I'd taken some monumental abuse in the past. It was part of the job, like the noise, the secondhand smoke, and the bosses with tenth-grade educations and inflated ideas of their intelligence, but today I didn't care if I was fired. Although I hadn't been smiling, I was now.

"Actually, I was thinking you looked like a movie star."

He blinked. "Me?"

"Yeah." I decided to savor the moment.

Mashid stood even taller. "Who you think?"

"Can't say. What do you want to do with that next hand?"

Mashid picked up the second hand, signaled for a hit, and pinned the cards under his bet. He picked up the next hand. "So, why you can't?"

I kept smiling while waiting for his decision on the third hand. He pinned the cards under the last white check. "I ask, why you can't say?"

I ignored him and, smiling, turned over my down card, a five, then hit to eighteen. I reached for Mashid's cards. "See, I can't remember his name. But he always plays an asshole."

Mashid had a nineteen. I paid with a white check. He pushed on the next hand and won the double down. I paid it with a pink chip. I began scooping up the cards and leaned toward him.

"He's kind of an evil guy, that kind of character. You've seen him."

Mashid squinted. "I don't see too much movie."

I laid the cards in the discard rack. I gauged Mashid as the type to explode and figured he would go off soon. "Ah, he's a big asshole anyhow, or plays those roles. Looks just like you."

He stared at the pink chip as if it were a viper. "You pay in pink?"

I looked at the bets. "I did?"

Instead of losing his temper, Mashid raked in the white chips from the double-down hand and let the pink one ride. He broke out in a broad smile and placed the three greens on each of the three squares in front of his bets. "I bet for you, okay, movie man?"

"Okay."

"You think pink is lucky, make me win. You make asshole happy, and you happy too. You and me, two assholes, huh?" He grinned.

I laughed. I couldn't even get myself fired by inferring to a customer that he was an asshole.

"Good. You like joke."

"Yeah, joke's on me," I said.

"What does it mean, the joke's on me?"

I dealt the top card out of the shoe—an ace. "It means you win."

By the time I was relieved, I'd made twelve hundred in tips for the dealers, and Mashid had won sixty thousand in pinks and whites. My problems had taken a vacation over the hour as he and I talked about everything from Michael Jackson to pizza as haute cuisine.

Eric tapped my shoulder and whispered, "How'd you loosen him up?"

"You don't want to know." I looked at Mashid and said, "Thanks, Mr. M. Keep an eye out for yourself on the big screen."

"The asshole," Mashid said and laughed.

NORMA WAS TELLING ANOTHER MOTHER STORY, which she called "Mama, Part 2: The Trip to the Dentist." The busboy called out my name, said I had a phone call, and placed the receiver down on top of the wall phone by the coffee machine. I picked up the receiver. "Jude here."

"Come over tomorrow night."

"Ben?"

"At nine."

Because I'd anticipated it for weeks, I thought I was ready for the phone call, but my hands went cold, my lips dry. I glanced at Norma, who looked concerned. I shrugged and smiled to ease any concern she had. Ben asked if I'd caught the time I was supposed to arrive.

"Yeah."

"Be there," Ben said and hung up.

Norma came over. "Are you okay?"

"Yeah, fine. Why?"

"You had a look on your face. That's all."

"Don't I always have a look on my face?"

She shook her head. "Sorry I brought it up." She turned to leave.

I awoke to the fact that she was sincerely concerned. "Norma?"

She ran her fingers through her hair and looked back at me. "What now?"

"What if I was flirting with you?"

"People have feelings, Jude," she said and walked away.

36 I had no one to confide in, but I wanted to establish some record in case events went south on me. I dialed my younger brother's number in Los Angeles, and as I waited for the line to ring through, I imagined his reaction to hearing the story, his wondering why after all these years I dragged him into a mess like this. And he'd be right in thinking it. He was in essence a stranger, one I'd talked to less than a half-dozen times in thirty years. I decided my story might sound like the ranting of a crazy man or someone being melodramatic. I hung up on the second ring and cradled the receiver. I had to do something other than sit and think. I gathered up my wallet and car keys off the counter, and with no clear idea what was facing me at Ben's, I left.

Sitting in front of Ben's house with the car's engine idling, I anticipated the worst. The engine sputtered as I cut the ignition. I wondered how many bodies ended up in desert graves because of a summons like this. After ringing the bell, I jammed my hands in my pockets to control the shaking. Ben let me in and signaled with a finger for me to follow.

I heard Angel ask, "Giants plus five at Philadelphia, whatta you think?"

A man whose voice was unfamiliar said, "I think betting sports is a loser's game."

I paused in the doorway. Every lamp in the room was turned on. Angel slouched on the nearest couch, studying a parlay card. He looked up, gave a halfhearted smile, said, "Speaking of losers," and returned to his parlay card.

Audie sat at the bar holding a wineglass. "Do you always have to be an asshole?" She wore a diamond on her ring finger, a marquee I calculated at three carats. I hadn't seen it before.

Angel shrugged. On a chair facing the couch sat a newcomer, my age, hair dark, skin pale. He took a sip from a wineglass and gazed up, his brown eyes unblinking. On a table beside him was an uncorked bottle of Zinfandel. He picked it up and refreshed his glass.

I looked at Ben, who said, "Don't stand in the doorway all night."

There was no red carpet and I was no star, but I felt like a row of cameras was covering my every move as I stepped into the room. "Hello, Audie."

"Have a seat, Jude." Ben motioned to a chair between him and the stranger.

I nodded to the man as I sat. "I'm Jude," I said. He didn't answer.

Ben sat angled to talk to both the newcomer and me. "We've decided to make you rich."

"Me? How's that?"

"In a minute. Jude, this is Wade."

The man stood and offered his hand to shake, but still didn't speak. He was shorter than I was by at least two inches and muscular, the type who spent a great deal of time pumping iron. His cheeks were scarred from acne, and he had a cleft chin. His deep-set eyes projected disdain and not much else. Audie ignored us and sipped from her glass. Ben asked if I wanted a drink.

"No, thanks."

No one spoke for a time, and then Ben said, "Well, let's go."

I glanced at Audie. She made eye contact for an instant and looked away. Angel was the last to stand. We filed out, Ben leading, followed by me, Wade, and Angel. We entered the room where Ben had drilled me on the blackjack table. Stunned, I stopped just inside the doorway and took in the room. Half was as it had been the last time I'd seen it. The remainder was a mock duplicate of a portion of the high-roller pit at the Le Grande, including brass rail and carpet. The layouts were identical, down to the chips that matched in both denomination and total amount in a table bank in the high-roller pit. "Impressed?" Ben said.

The detailing was impeccable. Gathering my wits, I said, "It's not how I'd remodel."

"What would you do?" Angel asked. "Orange shag carpet and strobe lights?"

Audie came up behind Wade. "Tell him, Ben," she said.

It sounded like an order coming from her, and I realized that it was an order.

"Training day, Jude. You learn a whole new trick."

"Yeah?" I felt relieved. At least my children were safe and I was alive. I took a stack of black checks from the rack, cut it in two, and shuffled them back into one. They felt the right weight. The inserts weren't authentic. The layouts, however, were.

"Look above you, Jude," Ben said as he sidled up next to me.

I looked up at the vaulted ceiling. The lens of a video camera mounted there was aimed at the center table. "What new trick?" I asked, though I'd figured it out.

"You're going to take a cooler," Audie said. She leaned a hip into the rail, arms crossed under her breasts, and gazed at me as she might a slice of moldy cheese. Then she turned away.

"How much did the brass birds cost?"

"Plastic. Made from molds," Ben said. "Besides the chips, the only thing not genuine."

I ignored him and addressed Audie. "A cooler. I take it that's not a drink."

"Cooler, cold deck, call it what you will. It's worth fifty thousand to you. You'll be the catcher. Angel will be the thrower."

"And Wade?" Jude asked.

Wade spoke for the first time. "That's none of your concern."

37

I placed a two of spades crossways on Linus Berman's double down. He shook his head and moved to the next hand, a sixteen. He hit it and lost. Two slot rows away a buzzer went off, signaling a big jackpot.

Berman looked over his shoulder. "Someone's got some luck."

Berman was stuck sixty grand in two hours. Even while losing, he'd put up bets for me. Why, I wondered, as did every dealer, can't a George seem to win? Then I remembered Berman's big score at the Monaco. "Mr. B, no one deserves to win more than you."

"But I don't play slots."

Berman moved to the last hand and took another bust. I turned over my hole card, a six.

"You had a stiff," he said. "Let's cruise 'til the deck's over."

The shuffler lifted the next deck into place. I waited for his bet. This time he spread two hands, a thousand on each. I dealt him a nineteen on the first and a sixteen on the second. I had a five showing. He signaled me off on both hands. I turned a thirteen, hit it with a two, then the cut card showed, signaling the end of the deck. I busted my hand on the next hit, a nine.

"Well, we finished on a winner," Berman said. "Glad to see that deck go."

I cleared the cards out of the shoe and placed them in the discard rack, then transferred the used deck to the rear compartment of the shuffler. I lifted the plastic door to the machine, pulled the fresh deck out, and offered up the cut card, the step-by-step procedure Ben had to overcome with his cold deck. How remained a mystery.

"Good luck, Mr. B."

He closed his eyes and plunged the plastic card into the deck. The shuffler whizzed into action, recycling the used deck, its metal arms riffling up the center of two even halves. Soon I was on autopilot, my thoughts regressing to three nights ago. The math was fuzzy, but I couldn't stop calculating potential outcomes. With a ten-thousand-dollar per-hand limit, how much could be made off a five-deck shoe that was set up? One deck had to be cut off the back, which left four, at an average of twenty to twenty-one hands per deck. Provided a player bet one hand at a time against the house. Those figures changed if the player went to five or six hands. Few players had that kind of money, even on high-end games.

But figuring one player betting one hand, the number came to roughly forty-two decisions per deck. A ten-thousand-dollar betting limit allowed for a player who won every hand to walk away with between four and five hundred thousand dollars, depending on how the deck was set up. On the other hand, if a player won forty or more decisions from a single shuffle of a five-deck shoe, it would alert security that something was out of order. If, in the same four decks, a player won six decisions to the house's one, the risk of drawing suspicion decreased. The play would be over before anyone was the wiser. The take could be more than a million dollars if the deck was set up to give the player a nominal amount of double downs and blackjacks.

I didn't know when the scam would go down. I was sure of only one thing: whoever the player, he had to be a high roller. No, a whale, a blue whale, nothing less. That was the river card needed to make a hand. The others had their plan to make it happen, but I was forming my own.

I felt a tap. I thanked Berman, stepped aside for Eric to deal, and left with a hundred and fifty in tokes in my pocket. I had a good idea what Norma's comments would be about Berman's losing. As if it were my doing. On the way to the break room, I stopped at the vending machine to buy a pack of gum. I'd cut back on coffee; didn't want shaky hands when the time came. As I stood back from retrieving the packet, I saw the gray-Honda man. I'd all but forgotten about him. I stalled any confrontation by dropping four more quarters in the machine and pressing a button.

He held his ground two steps away. I unwrapped the gum, tossed the foil in a wastebasket, reeled the gum into my mouth slowly. I nodded once and pushed through the swinging doors. I took a seat against the wall and alternately watched the door for him and Norma. I needed some diversion, a laugh, but her rotation had changed and she was still on a table. Sweating and watching the door, I spent my break wondering if Ben or Audie had sent the Honda man as a warning of sorts.

38 As Ben critiqued, Angel and I switched five-card decks, the house deck for the cold deck. At first I'd progressed fast, but improvement since then came in painfully slow increments, intentional on my part. In our second week of practice I was fumbling one out of every three tries as our speed increased. Once I even dropped a deck and caught hell for it. So far I'd somehow managed to make it appear the bungling was unintentional.

"You ready, Jude?"

"Yeah." We'd taken no breaks, except when Ben scolded us over a sloppy exchange. At the moment I didn't have to fake clumsiness.

I extended the deck in my left hand and offered up the cut card. Handicapped by a loose jacket with a huge pocket stitched inside, Angel had the tough part. He popped the Velcro strap that secured the deck, removed the cards from the pocket, handed them off, and slipped the house deck out of my hand. Simultaneously, he took the card from my right and cut the deck, the motion so smooth it looked like any normal cut. But it was still too slow. Ben's eyes said so.

"Try again," he said.

We did it again, a clean transfer. But this time following the exchange, I gripped the cold deck too loosely and dragged it across the layout. Angel shook his head.

"Lift the fuckin' thing and put it in the shoe."

"You're getting worse, Jude," Ben said and told me to keep a firm but relaxed grip. "Again."

I offered the deck. When Angel reached for it, the cards flew out of my hands and scattered over the layout and the floor. I'd held the deck too tightly and extended it too far for Angel. He looked at Ben and shrugged. I looked at my hands as if they belonged to someone else.

"It's not your hands, Jude," Ben said. "How many times do I have to say don't help him? You have to relax. Don't anticipate, just offer the deck like you would with any player and let Angel do the work. The objective is winning. You win best by deception. Never confront an overwhelming enemy—"

"What?" I said.

"It's from a book. *The Art of War.*"

Angel sighed and looked away. He'd apparently heard it before. Ben launched into a three-minute oration on how the principles applied to us, then said, "Now embrace them."

Two hundred and sixty cards fitted easily in my right hand. I'd been holding decks this size for more than twenty years, but even when I tried to hold it as I did at work, it seemed awkward. I bungled it again. Angel shook his head and slumped down on the stool.

"Are you trying to fuck up, Jude?" Ben asked.

I turned to Ben. "Yes. Actually, I want to fuck up in the middle of a high-limit pit with the world watching. What do you think? It's Angel's and my ass that will be hanging, not yours."

"Fuck it," Angel said. "I need a break." He left the room.

Ben and I eyed one another.

"You've got the hands. Touch and timing," Ben said. "Fifty thousand. Block the exchange out of your mind. Think about fifty grand and let your hands do the work."

I came around the layout and kneeled down to pick up cards. Audie's perfume announced her. I glanced up where she stood looking down at me. She wore a pink silk blouse and black midthigh skirt. I felt a reluctant admiration. Ben didn't call the shots, never had. The scam was hers all along. She planned. He handled details. The turn card in Texas hold 'em sets the stage for the last card to fill a hand, the river. That remained to be seen. I met her gaze with a smirk, then handed some cards to Ben and said, "Fifty thousand and you give me all the videos."

"It's not up to him," Audie said, and I caught a gleam from her diamond ring.

"Then *you* give me all the videos."

She strolled by and took a seat on the stool. Resting her elbows on the edge of the table, she looked at me the way a displeased parent might. "The decision isn't mine either."

"Well, tell whoever's in charge that's what I want."

"Or?"

I couldn't back up my ultimatum. I rose to my feet and handed the last of the cards to Ben. "Okay, then tell whoever's running it I think fifty thousand and the video copies is fair."

Ben said, "Let's take a break."

"How's this work for you guys?" Angel said.

He stood in the doorway wearing a light-brown pompadour wig. He'd tucked his hair inside the wig and glued bushy eyebrows over his own. A picture formed for me, a lanky customer stumbling into the pit and drenching Manny with a martini and Berman winning. Light-brown hair combed up and back, bushy eyebrows, mustache, and a knee-length coat. A woman was on his arm, a blonde wearing glasses. I'd caught only a fleeting glance of her. I looked at Audie and wondered what she would look like as a blonde wearing tortoise-shell glasses.

"Looks silly," Audie said.

"Why don't you just cut your hair?" Ben asked.

Angel grinned. "And end up like that Samsonite?"

"You mean Samson," Audie said.

"I mean, mind your own business."

Undaunted, Audie moved to the couch and picked up a *Sports Illustrated*.

Angel said, "Why's your nose in that, Audie? You don't know anything about sports."

Audie lowered the magazine and looked at him. "Don't push it."

"Push? He needs me," Angel said. "I know what I'm worth."

He? Who? I wondered.

"That's it. Let's all call it a day," Ben said. "We've got plenty of time left.

Jude, come with me. We'll take a look at something." He seemed tired, but I knew better. His exaggerated breaths merely emphasized his frustration.

Ben slipped a video in the feed to the VCR, then took a seat on the couch. He glanced at me, pressed the play button on the remote, and said, "Pay close attention. I think you'll find this interesting."

"Good, a movie. Is it a new release?" I said in a mocking tone.

"Clever is starting to wear thin, Jude."

The screen flashed a picture of the gaming room. The tape was shot from above, and the room looked just as the high-limit pit at the Le Grande must.

"Notice the clarity," Ben said. "These are sequenced. The first exchanges are okay. See."

I saw the tops of my and Angel's heads and our hands. Angel pulled a deck from inside his sport coat and switched it for the one I held. Considering my aim was failure, I was surprised the exchange was as clean as it was. The sequence was repeated twice more, both similar in efficiency. Ben stopped the tape.

"The second three take place the first week." He started the tape again. "These are smooth, almost perfect."

Again, I was impressed. These exchanges were faster and fluid.

"But look at the last."

As the tape advanced I saw myself moving slower and bumbling exchanges.

"Jude, if I didn't know better, I'd say you were getting worse on purpose."

"I've been nervous."

"Do you think the Mob's gone, Jude?"

"I don't think about it."

"Well, do for a moment. Think about how hard it would be for the Mob to walk away from all this currency."

"Look, I just want to get this over with, get the copies of the tape, and get out. I'm not cut out for this."

"I understand. But you don't. We've got an investment in you—got you your job, helped you get an attorney when you needed one, turned you on to some easy scores. This is payback, Jude. And you're not holding up your end, and you can't up and walk away."

"What's next? I get fitted for cement shoes or something?"

Ben looked at the ceiling. "This isn't a joke, Jude. We're serious people," he said as he stood and walked to the television. He ejected the first tape and replaced it with another.

"I've seen it before. I know what you've got on me," I said.

"Wait." Ben sat down again and pushed the remote.

What I saw this time made me gasp. It was my car, and to prove it, the picture zoomed in on my license plate. I was parked at Beth's school. The passenger door swung open, and Beth got out. She reached inside, picked up her backpack from the floorboard, spoke to me, and backed away from the car. As she turned toward the gate to the school yard, the camera caught her face and zoomed in. The last of the video showed her meeting two girl-friends and walking up the steps. The whole tape was three minutes long. "We won't be keeping this video, Jude."

I bowed my head and wiped a bead of sweat from my brow. First from Blitzstein, now from Ben. I realized the full weight of the troubles I'd brought on my family and myself. When I looked up, Ben was walking out of the room. I closed my eyes and reeled off the images of me on video, the star in an absurd play, the buffoon in an opera with no music, and then a string of other images filtered onto the screen, two human shapes tumbling to a landing as the hotel belched smoke, a painting of Prometheus banished to a parched land, left there to struggle forever against the chains that bound him to his despair. What had happened to the man who'd handed it to me, and how was it I'd found an exit? Not from planning it. Now it seemed there was no exit. All doors locked.

The door latch clicked. I looked over my shoulder, expecting to see Ben return. Instead, Wade entered and walked calmly across the room. He sat on a chair opposite me. Since our first encounter, I'd seen him twice in passing. No one had explained his role, and I hadn't asked again.

"So, Jude, here's the deal." Wade took out a 9mm pistol and set it on the coffee table. He gazed at me, his expression blank. "Your cut just went down to twenty thousand, and we keep the tapes. Questions?"

I shook my head.

"Good. There won't be further negotiating. Now, go in the other room. Ben and Angel are waiting. Put those good hands of yours to some serious work."

He was more articulate than I'd expected. I stood and trudged to the door, then took a glance back at Wade, who was leaned back in the chair reading a copy of *House and Garden*. I felt as if I'd gained a great deal of weight in a short period of time.

39 I sat at the end of a table in the help's hall and laid my head on my arms. Gathered around the next table, several women watched spellbound as a soap opera blared sentimental theme music and two actors faced off in a scene intended to stir emotions in the audience. What would these women think if I shouted that drama exists but not how it's depicted on soap operas, that real drama is even more disturbing? What if I told them it's in every corner of the ordinary human sphere? What if I said its prelude may be a pair of gazing eyes and a soft touch of a hand on a cheek, and its aftermath four walls in an empty room? What if I insisted it's more the stuff of blues and country western music than afternoon soaps, and in real life none of it is entertaining? Would they listen? Would they believe me if I told them my story, which I wasn't even certain of yet? Would they take their eyes off the television?

"You okay?"

I lifted my head and squinted up at Norma. "Yeah."

"You didn't sit with us?"

"No."

"Mind if I sit here?"

"Go ahead."

She fished a cigarette from a pack and started to light it. I looked at it disapprovingly. She tapped it back into the pack and said it could wait, that she should quit.

"You can smoke," I said.

"No. It can wait. Really, I am trying to quit. Are you sure you're okay?"

"Yeah, fine. Do you have kids?"

"No. I wanted them, but it's a long story."

"Right now, a long story's fine."

"You ever hear of endometriosis?"

"Maybe, but I couldn't spell it."

She placed her hands on the table palms down. "It's a painful disease that comes on when a girl starts, you know what I mean. It affects the ovaries. At fifteen the doctors removed one of mine. I was twenty-two when they took out the second and some other stuff along the way. By twenty-three I was growing facial hair and working in a circus as . . ." She smiled.

"Funny."

"No, it's not funny. It's just easier if I . . . My husband wanted kids."

"You're married?"

"I should say 'ex-husband.' We divorced a year after the last operation. Now he has his family. How about you? Do you have kids?"

"Boy and girl. They're great. Smarter than me. Lucas got his degree last spring. Beth, well, she'll be a lawyer someday."

"They take after your wife?"

"Ex-wife. Why didn't you two adopt?"

She studied the backs of her hands and then turned them over. "I would have. He wouldn't. Life, huh?" She pointed to the television. "Bet their real lives have more drama than that crap."

I looked up at the television and saw an uncanny resemblance between the actress on the screen and Audie. "Who's that?" I asked, pointing to the screen.

"I don't know her name, but I think she's the evil one."

"Really. Funny."

"So, does your girlfriend like your kids?"

"No . . . ," I said and looked up at the screen again. "I mean, no girlfriend." I pictured the ring on Audie's finger, the ring finger of her left hand, and another picture came to mind. Her and Wade. One more part of the puzzle coming together. I had to call Biggs and see if he had a picture of Moser.

She rolled the pack of cigarettes over on the table. "Well, I need a cigarette before I go ride into that herd of buffalo out there. You sure you're okay?"

"Yeah. Thanks for asking. I'm sorry you didn't have kids. You'd be a good mother. And you probably wouldn't smoke."

"No, I'd be a great mother. You know, you just talked more than you ever have since coming to work here."

40 It was 9:20 in the morning, two hours and forty minutes before I was to report for work, an odd time to be summoned to Ben's or whoever's house it was. I rang the bell and turned my back to the door. When it opened, I looked over my shoulder and asked, "More practice?"

"No," Ben said. "Unless you think you need some."

"I'm fine. I'm ready."

"Do you have your tie and work apron?"

"In the car."

"Give me the keys."

I handed him the keys.

"Go inside. I'll be in," he said and left.

I did as I was told. I was resigned to the fact that I had no choice but to comply for now. Fear, reservation, even ethics, if I had any left, didn't matter. But when this mess was all over, I intended to sell the house and leave. All that might keep me from doing that were my children.

A door down the hall on the left opened. Wade stepped out and signaled to me. "Come in."

The door was ajar. I peered inside. Other than a captain's desk, a chair, and a couch, the room was empty. Wade stood beside the door. He grabbed my arm and pulled me in.

I shook my arm free. "What the hell?"

"Get undressed."

"I don't think so." I backed away and started for the door.

Wade blocked my path and closed the door. "Undress and toss your clothes over."

"You're kidding."

"No."

The door opened. Ben stepped in and stood behind Wade, in his hand my apron and tie. "Jude, we can't go in the other room until you do."

"Get 'em off," Wade said.

Feeling a bit like I was playing a role in a cheesy Hollywood film, I unbuttoned my shirt and tossed it to Wade. I unzipped and let my trousers slip to my ankles. I stepped out of them and kicked them to Wade.

"You're a boxer man. I'm one myself," Ben said.

"That makes me feel better. Are you going to strip now and show them?"

"Take the shorts off." Wade held my shirt to the side and dropped it on the floor. "Shoes and socks too." As he searched my pant pockets, I unlaced my shoes, slipped out of them, and pulled my socks off. Then I stood and stepped out of my shorts.

"Turn around," Wade said.

I showed my backside and said, "Anyone turned on?"

Wade ran his hands over the pant legs. He flipped the pants to me. "Get dressed."

They walked me to the gaming room. A man sat on a couch, his back to the door.

"Hello, Jude," he said. "Glad to have you on board."

I recognized the voice as soon as he spoke. "Mr. B. How's your luck?"

"Getting better, I hope."

Linus Berman stood and crossed the room. It came together—his losing to me, his generosity to the dealers. The ultimate gypsy move, like all of them, required deception. Lose a little, win big. Berman offered me his hand to shake. Everything else was now obvious as well, especially the blonde with the pleasing backside.

"Your house?"

"Sort of. I rarely use it. Isn't that right, Ben? Ben, fix us some of that mint tea, will you?"

Berman pointed to a chair and motioned for me to sit. He took a seat, leaned back, and crossed his legs at the ankles. "Ben says you have reservations."

"Had some," I said.

"Now that you're with us, you may use the place if you ever need it. Who knows, a reception for your son or daughter if they ever marry? You do hope they'll marry?"

I got the message. I nodded. "That's generous."

"We're a sharing bunch."

I figured one of the things they shared was Patty Lane, and another was Audie. "Thank you."

"If you're curious about any of this, now's the time to ask. Curiosity later won't do."

"I'm not."

"You'll be taken care of. You have my word. How much have you been told?"

"It started at fifty thousand, but now it's twenty."

"I assume that's not twenty dollars." Berman looked at Ben, then Wade, and shook his head. "It's now sixty thousand."

I looked at the wall of windows, the drapes pulled back. Sunlight poured in. I noticed a galaxy of swirling dust particles. "I do have one question."

Berman walked to the blackjack table. "Join me over here."

I walked to the table.

"Your question, Jude?"

"Is Hefty in on this?"

Berman chuckled. "A dim-witted suck-ass, Jude. Last three jobs he's gotten as a casino manager have been because he brings me in as a customer. Humorous, isn't it?"

I smiled to show my appreciation. "So you told him to fire me at the Monaco?"

"Why would you say that?"

"No good reason."

"Someone close the drapes and turn on the lights. Let's get to work. Jude, get behind the table. Ben, give him the tie and apron."

Wade closed the drapes. Ben turned on the lights and said, "Offer the deck in the shuffler to Linus." I put on the tie and apron and bumped into a chair as I slid behind the layout. I pulled the deck out and offered it and the cut card to Berman.

"Hold it," Ben said. He straightened a chair and realigned it, using a ruler. "Start over."

An hour later I left, still in the dark about when the scam would go down, but wise to the rest. Ben would insert a digital image of Berman's cut to replace the image of Angel handing me a cold deck. It reasoned that Audie's role would be to leave with the house deck in her purse, as she'd done at the Monaco, the night I was an unwitting witness.

41 The knock came as I was dressing for the day. I grabbed the pistol and peered through the peephole. Detective Beardsley stood at the stoop. I stuffed the gun under the seat cushion and opened the door. He was writing on a business card.

"Officer, uh, Beardsley."

"Yep, me. Thought I'd come by. If you got a minute, I got some pictures. I mean, I can come by another time, or you can come downtown, take a look. Up to you."

"How many? I'm getting ready for work. But if it won't take long."

"Three pictures."

I let him in. The detective looked around and asked, "Mind if we sit?"

"In here." I walked into the living room and motioned him to the couch.

Detective Beardsley slipped some photos out of a manila envelope, thumbed through them, and handed me one. "That's Blitzstein."

I took a perfunctory look at the photo and shook my head. "I still don't know him."

"That's the before." Beardsley handed over the second photo, a larger shot in color.

It was of a full nude body, decomposing, the face beaten beyond recognition, hands severed. I swallowed back some bile that rose up in my throat.

"That's the after. The lab identified his DNA yesterday."

I shook my head. "This doesn't help. I didn't know him."

Beardsley nodded and handed a third photograph upside down. "Ever see this guy?"

I turned it over. The face confirmed what I'd suspected. I wouldn't need to call Biggs. It was Wade, a few years younger, twenty pounds lighter.

"Name's Joel Moser. Ring a bell?"

I handed him the pictures. "Never saw him."

"Well, if you do, you should avoid him. Nasty guy. Spent the last few years pumping iron in Indian Springs Prison. He cheated a few casinos, but that only scratches the surface. Before he went to prison on his last conviction, he's supposed to have ripped off some substantial cocaine dealers around Lake Tahoe and Marin County. A man and woman, a couple, were found dead in a cabin up at North Shore. Washoe County Sheriff's Office bungled the scene and wrote it off as a homicide-suicide. Circumstances say otherwise; so does some information from Blitzstein's personal papers. I can't tell you any more than that."

The detective slid the photos into the envelope. "I won't take up more of your time, Mr. Helms. But I did want to say that I checked with my cousin, and that money in the envelope you said was tips doesn't make sense. Now, why would you tell me that?"

I'd forgotten that from his previous visit. I said the first thing that came to mind. "It was an envelope from the Monaco. I hadn't opened it."

The cop nodded and stood. "Okay."

I stood. "I've got errands to run."

"Sure." Beardsley looked at the cushion. "The lump in your chair—that a gun?"

I looked down. The bulge was obvious. "That's where I keep it."

"Best be careful you don't shoot yourself in the ass. You wouldn't do that, would you?"

"No."

"Good, good. Hey, one more thing. I checked with some neighbors of a woman name Audra, uses the last name of Moser. You know her, right?"

"I met an Audie. The mother of my daughter's friend."

Beardsley tugged at his collar. "Yeah. Well, that Joel's her husband. He got released eight or nine weeks ago. After years of appeals, he got a cheating conviction overturned by a federal court. Thought you might want to know."

"Why would I want to?"

Beardsley grinned. "Oh, maybe because you were fucking his wife." The detective walked to the door. "You're into something that you shouldn't be. What it is, I don't know yet, but I will. You decide to start telling me the truth, I'm willing to listen. We'll pretend these lies didn't happen."

I shut the door behind the detective, my hands trembling as I latched it. Slow down, think, this isn't the MGM going up in a blaze, and you survived that, didn't you? Of course, I could just as easily have argued that it was luck and nothing more that led me to a safe exit. I sat weighing my options and came up with one. I needed someone on my side. There's time. I went to the kitchen phone, took a business card out of my wallet, and dialed the number. Biggs answered gruffly.

I said, "This is Jude Helms."

"Jude Helms?"

"The guy who came to Big Dog's and you knew who Joel Moser was. I need to see you after work tonight."

I gave him the number of my new cell phone. He said he'd get back to me, that he might have to break an appointment.

I DROVE THE NEIGHBORHOOD just to get out of the house. As I neared Edowski's, I saw him stepping out of his car. He mouthed something to me. I smiled back and cruised by. I looked in the rearview mirror. He'd moved to the sidewalk and was giving me the middle finger. It was the first light moment of my day.

I turned the corner and took the next street north. My cell phone buzzed. I pulled over to look at the caller's number, but didn't recognize it. I pressed the answer button, hoping it was Biggs calling.

"Hello?"

"Jude?"

It took a second to place the voice. "Mr. Friece."

"Yes, Jude. Good news. The insurance companies, hers and yours, got together, and the new offer is twenty-two thousand."

"My insurance company?"

"It's my policy to go after everyone who's liable."

"Take it." It could have been half that and my response would have been the same.

42

I stepped out into the parking of Big Dog's at noon, two hundred dollars poorer, but with a telephone number and the name Masters on it. I'd asked Biggs a couple of times, who was this guy Masters? He'd refused to say. He said that his only advice was to call the number he'd given me. I turned the ignition and dialed the number Biggs had written down. The line rang twice before a man answered. "Masters here."

"Hello. I'm calling because I was referred to you."

"Who referred you?"

"Biggs. He wouldn't tell me anything else. My name's . . ."

"Jude Helms. It came up on my screen. Great gadgets, these cell phones. Problem is we can't get free of them. Why don't we meet, say, in three hours?"

I looked at my watch. "About three?"

"Yes. Keep in mind, I know why you called."

I'd met too many cryptic people these past weeks. Now another? The first question I had to answer was why I should trust him. The answer was because of Blitzstein's ugly death and Joel Moser, Audie's husband. These were incentive enough to meet the devil. "Where?"

"Border's Bookstore on Rainbow."

"How will I know you?"

"Don't worry about that."

The line went dead. Don't worry? On the whole, what was one more absurdity in a pile of absurdities? One more layer of nonsense? But then, if life made sense, my uncle and I would be laying block walls. What, I wondered, were Uncle Frank's last thoughts. Bad timing? What does a good man think when life cheats him at the end? I was in over my head, but at last I *knew* what I was in. I was in my own dark bar as it was being robbed.

Again I drove residential streets and watched for a tail. Who, I wondered, is Masters? For years, with the exception of my kids, I'd pushed people away, preferring solitude. Now strangers were corralling me, and none of them friends. In case the worst happened, I needed someone to confide in, someone who'd let the police know. Norma came to mind, but I didn't really know her well enough. Besides, what would I say? That bad people might want me dead? That I was part of a cheating ring? That I'd slept with the wife of a man who might well be a murderer? No, I couldn't, in good conscience, involve Norma. I had to accept that I was alone in this.

I POURED MYSELF A GLASS OF WATER and sat on the recliner in front of the television. The TV station showed video of a city street in Baghdad devastated by a suicide bombing. I turned up the volume. The announcer reported the news in a near-frantic voice, detailing a recent spate of suicide bombings in the Middle East, this one being the latest. A camera taking video from a helicopter panned over the scene, images of a destroyed three-story building, its facade nothing but rubble. Using the building as a back-drop, a reporter on the ground began interviewing a witness, who was also a survivor. The man's anger as he struggled to tell his account in broken English and the sight of the crumbled structure evoked a reaction in me similar to how I'd felt two years before, following the collapse of the Twin Towers.

In the dealers' room, virtually every break for two days, I along with a dozen others had sat stiff as wax figures as we watched over and over the same approximate images repeated on the screen, planes striking the towers and vanishing in flames, smoke rising, and the sides of the buildings break-ing apart and masses of steel and concrete collapsing. A craps dealer, who couldn't take watching it any longer, had stood and shook his hand at the screen, then released a string of profanities that expressed for all the rage that boiled inside each of us.

I'd been no less stunned and angered by the calamity, but the images became, for me, a replay of events of November 21, 1980, and I'd felt a nearly resistless need to be alone—any empty chair in any isolated spot. I knew, before the first interview was aired, precisely what the survivors felt and how deeply they felt it because I'd felt it too. I remember thinking that if they and I could make it through the infernos we'd survived, we could make it through anything. I needed that reminder, even if it amounted to nothing more than seeking comfort in another absurdity.

The kids, or at least Beth, would be coming over for the night. I'd not slept well for days. A short nap would do me well. Besides, I knew by then what devastation a bomb could do. I'd witnessed enough calamity to last a lifetime. I didn't need to see any more, whether here or in the Middle East. I turned off the television and dozed off. When I opened my eyes, I was a bit disoriented. I sat upright and cleared my head, then looked at my watch and realized I'd have to hurry to make the meeting. It was 2:55. Even if traffic was thin, I'd be at least three or four minutes late.

I was six minutes late. The parking lot was nearly full. Hoping Masters had waited, I parked in a space close to the street and double-timed it to the doors, realizing as I did that I hadn't taken precautions driving here. Then it occurred to me that Masters had picked an ideal meeting place. If Beardsley or Joel Moser had followed, they would see me buying a book. I held the door for a woman talking on a Bluetooth while carrying a child in one arm and a bag in the other.

I looked around. For what or who, I had no idea. It just seemed like I should be looking. I walked the aisles, checking out books. I pulled one off the shelf at random, opened it, and read the first line—"In the long unfurling of his life . . ." I didn't recognize the author's name, but then I wasn't much of a reader. I took the book to the register and lined up behind four others.

I felt a tap on my shoulder. I looked back and came face-to-face with the Honda man. I stopped in midbreath. My face flushed.

"Surprised?"

"Masters?"

"Yes." He looked at the book I was holding. "Great book. Buy it. I'll wait over there." He pointed to the espresso counter. "Are you ready to tell a story?"

"Tell me first, exactly who are you?"

"Gaming Control. You want to see some ID?"

I shook my head.

"So you'll know, I'm here to throw you a lifeline. Don't throw it back."

"Okay. Yeah, okay. I guess I've got a story."

"What better place to tell one than a bookstore?"

EVEN BEFORE I LEFT MASTERS, the plan I'd been looking for started coming together. I headed first to the bank. After that I figured to call Friece for the name of a good attorney to draw up a will—in case. Everything from then on hinged on those two words.

43

Lucas reached across the table and hooked a bun with his fingers. Beth told him that was rude, that it was appropriate to ask.

"Damn it," I said. "I'd like some peace."

They stared at me, mouths agape.

"Haven't you ever noticed when it is that you two fight?"

"We fight when he's rude," Beth said.

"When she acts ten years older than she is?" Lucas said.

"No. When we're at the dinner table."

Lucas put the knife down from buttering his bun. "Dad, it's the only time we're forced to talk to each other. It's logical. Didn't you ever study Aristotle?"

"No, Dad didn't," Beth said. "And you slept through philosophy, so what do you know?"

"That's right," I said. "I've never studied philosophy. I never studied much of anything, but I wish I had. Yeah, and I wish I'd done better by you two and better for myself, but I am what I am." I stood and gathered up my plate and flatware. "I'll eat elsewhere."

"Jesus, Dad. We didn't mean anything," Lucas said.

"It's not you." I walked into the living room and sat on the recliner, facing the window, my plate on my lap. I looked out on the lawn. It was wintering outside. Neighbors had Christmas lights up. How much time had passed since Edowski's dog messed on my yard? It seemed forty or fifty years ago. I wondered, had I not followed him home, would things be different?

"Dad?"

"Yes, Beth."

"We're sorry, Dad," Lucas said. "We didn't mean to hurt your feelings."

"You didn't." I pointed them to the couch. "Come in here, the two of you."

They sat opposite me. I was exhausted and had been for longer than I knew. I couldn't explain it to them, so I had to trust that they would hear what I had to say and follow directions. I leaned forward and rested my elbows on my knees, rubbed my face with my palms, and began.

"I don't know philosophy. What I do know is that you two have been my blessing. A dad needs to remind himself of that. Ever wonder if life is like an honest shuffle and you play the cards you get and your decisions matter? Or maybe the deck's fixed, and no matter what decision you make, the outcome's inevitable, every card placed in a predictable pattern?"

Lucas shook his head.

Beth shrugged and said, "You're being as weird as Mom."

"Beth, do you still see Katie?"

"At school. I don't like to go to her house, since . . ." She looked off.

"Since what?"

"I promised."

"And you should keep it. But I think I know. Is it since her father moved in?"

"He gives me the creeps, Dad."

"I know. It's okay. In the kitchen, Lucas, in the bottom drawer, you'll find two cell phones. Get them."

Beth's face lit up. "Did you get us cellulars?"

"Lucas, go. I'll explain when you come back."

Lucas returned with the phones, pumping them up and down as if testing their weight.

"Sit down and give the smaller one to Beth," I said.

He did as told.

"Those are yours. I've paid for them." I took five hundred-dollar bills from my wallet and handed them to Lucas.

"Where's mine?" Beth said.

"Don't ask questions. I won't answer them. Do you understand?"

"Dad, this is getting too scary," she said.

"Don't be scared. Just listen. The money is to hold for now. It'll see you through a few days." I looked at Lucas. I felt as I had the first night I brought him home from the hospital and watched his tiny chest rise and fall. Emotion rose in my throat. I choked it back and waited until it waned, then said, "If I call and tell you to get Beth, you're to call her and immediately pick her up, no hesitation. Here." I handed him a business card from the Pine and Thistle. "It's a bed-and-breakfast in Pine Valley, Utah. The number's programmed into your phone. I've paid for rooms. You're expected whenever you show up. You following me so far?"

He nodded, then said, "I've got a job. Got to go to work, Dad."

"Quit if you have to. You've got a degree. It's time to think beyond waiting tables. Consider this a good reason to stop." I opened my wallet again and handed him five hundred more. "That'll more than tide you over."

"But I make almost two hundred a night on weekends."

"I don't care. I've never asked anything of either of you. Now I am."

"Dad, you're really scaring me," Beth said.

"Sorry, honey. Lucas, if I call . . ." I pointed to Beth. "Pick her up and drive to that lodge. Stay 'til I call. And wait until you're at least as far as Mesquite before you let your mother know the two of you are together. Don't say where you're headed. Instead, tell her you'll be driving to San Diego." I pointed to Lucas's cell phone. "Beth's number's programmed into your phone, Lucas. Call and make sure it rings through."

Lucas did as I said. Beth's phone buzzed. She answered it and said, "It works."

Lucas said. "Dad, what's going on?"

"I can't say. You have to trust me on this. And Beth, don't say a word about this to anyone, especially Katie or your mother."

Beth sat on the arm of the recliner. "Dad? Can't you tell us anything?"

I patted her hand. "Let's go out for ice cream. We'll do the dishes when we get back."

Lucas said, "Are you in trouble, Dad?"

"I never told you before and neither has your mother, but I survived the MGM fire."

"Really?" Beth asked.

"Dad doesn't lie," Lucas said.

"How I wish that were true. Well, let's go get some ice cream, then buy a Christmas tree and decorate it. We'll do the dishes later."

44 I wondered, as I had for weeks, if this, the last day of the year, was going to be the day. I couldn't be certain. Ben hadn't yet said, but I sensed tonight or the next the scam would go down. Over Christmas, business had been so slow bosses and dealers outnumbered the players. It would have been impossible to run a deck in. No shade, as the expression went.

Norma was standing by the time office. She said this could be the craziest day she'd ever worked. "Up to three hundred thousand out on the Strip partying."

"Well, if I don't get a break with you or see you later, Happy New Year," I said.

"Thanks. You too."

I punched in. "Hey, let's go fight the hoard," I said and held the door open for her.

"Jude, I was wondering, uh . . . ?" I waited for her question, but she shook her head and said, "Gonna be a long shift."

"If we're lucky, we'll get home before everything busts loose."

"Do you have plans?" she asked.

Every day since Ben dropped the bomb was a potential plan. "No. Not really. Why?"

"I was thinking we might have a drink after work."

"Aren't you going to any parties?" I asked to deflect the question.

She stopped. "Maybe. Look, I wasn't at the door on accident. Maybe, me parking and . . . What I mean . . . I think you and I should . . . I mean, why do you always sit with me?"

I'd never heard her stumble over words before. "You make me laugh. You're funny."

"That's me, funny girl. Okay, here goes nothing. I'm invited to a party, and you should go with me. You might even have a laugh or two."

"A party?"

"Let's plan on it. What else is there to do? It's New Year's Eve."

"Thanks. I'd like to. I'm not sure I can. Can I get a 'maybe I will' out of this?"

"Sure. A maybe, whatever that means. Just thought I'd ask." She looked at her heels, then said, "This quitting smoking is a bitch," and walked off.

I called for her to wait. She stopped, but didn't look back.

I caught up with her. "It's not you."

"I know I'm not pretty. And I'm not petite like the cocktail waitresses wearing butt floss."

"You're wrong. You are pretty."

"Don't do that, okay?"

"Really, it's not anything to do with you. I just might not be able to tonight. But I'm a good cook. Maybe you could come over sometime. I'll cook up some pasta with Italian sausage."

She looked ahead as we walked. "I knew it was a bad idea. Forget I said anything."

"Stop," I said.

She stopped and waited, but she wouldn't look at me. Even when I circled around to face her, she turned away so that she wouldn't have to look at me. Bumbler, I thought, how could you not see she'd sought you out on breaks? Called you over or sat with you? Had parked near you in the employees' lot? Often was waiting at the time office when you arrived? Now tears.

I'd been so wrapped up in my own mess that I hadn't noticed that she'd been interested in me as anything but a coworker. "You know, you've got beautiful green eyes. Shouldn't smear your makeup."

"They're hazel. You really don't get around much, do you?" She turned away and wiped at her eyes with the back of her hand. "I've got to stop at the ladies' room."

I waited for her. When she came out, she seemed herself again.

Though everything depended on the unpredictable, I said, "I promise, after this weekend we'll get together. Just not tonight. But right now I need a friend. I wish I could . . . explain."

"Be honest. Are you with someone?"

I thought of Audie, her heart as empty of humanity as the moon. "No."

She nodded. "Don't make me start smoking again, okay?"

"You did yourself a big favor." I touched her shoulder. She didn't pull away. "Be proud."

"Thanks. Let's go ride into that herd of buffalo, Wild Bill."

By the time we reached the help's hall, she was elbowing me and telling Michael Jackson jokes. She asked if I wanted coffee, and I said yes.

"Then, don't be a rube. Get up and go get us some," she said.

I glanced back over my shoulder at her. I liked the way she smiled, sly and content.

ON MY FIRST BREAK, I stepped through the doors to the hallway and came face-to-face with Ben. He told me to follow him and led me to an empty stairwell. Heart thudding, I stepped over.

He looked up and down the stairs and said, "It goes down your next-to-last break. We'll time the game for a new deck right before you get off the table."

Now that the scam was given voice and ready to happen, it took hold of my throat. I'd planned for this, but did so believing I'd have a day or so to notify Lucas. Now I faced calling him immediately, and I couldn't risk using the phone outside the employees' cafeteria. I coughed until I could speak and managed a weak, "I'm ready."

I turned to leave.

"Jude?"

I looked back. "Yeah?"

Ben paused for effect, then said, "Don't bungle it. Wade knows where your daughter is."

If not for the picture of Blitzstein, I might have thought it was a bluff. I felt the threat seep into my joints. "I understand. I'll be fine," I said, my voice as clear as his message.

We weren't allowed to have cell phones at work, and because cameras surveyed the hallway, I couldn't risk going directly to a phone. I found Norma in the break room seated with Johnny and Luby, two other dealers. She was about to light a cigarette. My options limited, I had to take a chance. The cigarette gave me a good excuse. I dropped into the seat across from her, took the cigarette out of her mouth, and said to the other dealers, "She's quitting."

Norma, at first stunned, quickly recovered. "I'll smoke if I want to."

"You don't need to." I broke the cigarette in half. "I want to talk to you. Okay?"

"That was my cigarette," Johnny said. "A perfectly good one. You owe me one now."

I stood and tossed a dollar on the table. "That cover it?"

Norma seemed confused, but followed me to the hallway.

"I can't believe what you did in there."

I took her arm and looked into her eyes to show I was serious. "I need a friend. Please. I don't have time to explain. I want to, but I can't. I need help. Will you help? Please?"

Her face knotted. "Jude, are you putting me on?"

I shook my head. "I need you to make a couple of phone calls. Do you have a pen?"

"Yes."

I pulled out business cards from my wallet and read off the numbers. She copied them down and looked at the cards before handing them back. Three crap dealers approached. I moved aside and waited for them to enter the help's hall. "Call the 385 number first. Tell him you're a friend of mine and that I can't call. He'll understand. Tell him also that my son will be looking for her."

"Beth. Is that your daughter?"

"Yeah. You remembered."

"What am I supposed to tell the other guy?"

"That'll be Lucas, my boy. He's a good kid. Tell him you're calling for me and that it's time to pick Beth up wherever she is."

"Jude, are you in trouble?"

"Not exactly. I'll tell you over a slow dinner. Soon, I promise." I reached in my pocket and drew out some change for the phone. "Here."

"Okay, I'll go along." She closed her hand and said, "I've got coins. Besides, I want you to owe me." She backpedaled toward the pay phones and said, "Jude, why me?"

I would tell all later if she gave me a chance. "It's the hazel eyes," I said. "Believe me."

I returned from break to find my game empty. I'd calmed down enough to appear my normal self. All I could do now was play out the hand. The rest was up to Masters's people and the Metro Intelligence Unit. And, of course,

Lucas, who'd agreed to walk away from his job when and if the call came, even on the busiest weekend of the year. He'd tried to return the money I'd given him, but I insisted he keep it, explaining that they might have to stay in Utah a few days. For Christmas, he'd given me a trowel, said that I'd invested in his future by paying half his college tuition and the mason's trowel was his investment in my future. I'd talked about starting a masonry business on a few rare occasions, spoke of it whimsically, never for the kids' benefit, but for mine. I never thought either of them heard me.

Eric clapped out, and I settled in behind the layout. My table was the only one with a reserved sign. A player was complaining to the pit boss about my game, saying that he bet five hundred or more a hand and didn't appreciate being treated like a five-dollar player.

"I'm sorry," the pit boss said. "Reserved tables on New Year's Eve require a ten-thousand minimum bet, ten to twenty-five thousand."

When a player's irate, the best thing a dealer can do is be invisible, or, short of that, mute. I didn't want to be drawn into the argument, so I stood like a highland guard and stared off.

Twenty-five grand! Jesus, I thought, they're aiming for two million on the busiest night of the year. It wasn't as if Patty Lane could just walk in, bend over, flash her Dow Chemical chest, and draw every eye to her cleavage. Berman needed serious shade, someone in the pit. I wondered who else was in on the scam. I decided that it didn't matter. What did was Norma's call to Lucas getting through and Lucas and Beth's being safely on their way.

I'd filled in most of the blank details I wasn't privy to. Ben had the eye in the sky under control. Running cameras from three angles at once, he'd filmed dozens of images of Berman cutting the deck as I held it. An hour to get images enough to cover any condition, the best of which he preserved as files. Once the deck was planted, he would splice the best substitute into the actual surveillance footage. If a question arose, if the Gaming Control Board wanted to review the table action, if someone on the floor detected anything unusual, all they would see was me removing a deck from the shuffling machine and offering it to Berman, who cut the cards—digitalized evidence, every step following house procedure.

The man and the pit boss were still arguing. Finally, the pit boss picked up a phone and called Hefty. Hefty arrived, all smiles and handshakes, and took the man aside. A minute later he walked the man to my game and took the reserved sign off.

"A thousand-dollar minimum for him," Hefty said, then to the player,

"You have to give it up by five o'clock," then to the boss said, "Go ahead and deal to Mr. G and treat him right."

The player said to the pit boss, "See? No harm. How about a drink?"

I scooped up the deck on the layout and placed it in the shuffling compartment and took the other out. This was a bad turn. If he caught a run and refused to leave the game, that would freeze the scam.

THE BREAK ROOM BUZZED with human voices. I sipped water nervously and waited. Five minutes, ten. Norma didn't show. And if she didn't pass on the messages? What if the deal went sour and Moser had Beth? My mouth went dry. I felt the onset of a headache and left the room early to look for Norma. I looked around the casino, noting with unexpected clarity the dealers, their expressions flat as an off-pitch note, the gaudy opulence, bodies packed in the aisles or on stools in the pit, and the clamor, as if noise and light and only those confirmed life. Between being hired and retiring on Social Security, was this all there was? Daily tips, help's hall food, insults. Keep the head down and the cards in the air. I was struck by the sense that beyond being able to deal hand after hand without giving a thought to it, I understood none of this and never had. There was something desperate in all of it, and it had controlled me for more than half of my life.

I spotted Norma's game in the main pit and strolled by as casually as I could. I slowed to gain her attention. She looked up, nodded, and gave me a wink. She came through for me, and I felt better, not good, but better. Assured, I headed for the high-roller pit. Three breaks to go, I thought. Did Masters have his people ready? I looked around for him, then remembered how he'd vanished when I last saw him in the casino. The casino floor of Le Grande was a five-acre tract of meandering slot machines and gaming tables. People everywhere. A man could hide in a dozen places, watching from behind a bank of slots or from the mezzanine. He wouldn't be obvious. Like Ben, Masters was a no-loose-ends guy.

A guard was posted at the rail to keep noninvited players out of the pit. The aisles were crowded, people lined up to get in the buffet and the four restaurants. Mr. G had lost seventeen thousand and left. Idle again, I watched the nearby games. Action everywhere, markers handed from pit supervisors, bets paid or scooped up. Three bosses, two women and a man, and one relief boss, one for each game, managed the high-limit games. Ben couldn't have picked a better or a worse night. All shift long they would work in rotation, buried in writing markers and scratching figures down on rating slips, with little time to actually watch a game. It followed that whoever ran the pit when Berman landed would be either the least competent of the lot or in on the scam.

A player strolled into the pit and said he'd never seen anything like it—the Strip was packed already with tens of thousands of celebrants. Whenever the front entrance doors opened, the noise of the street crowd roared into the casino. I remembered downtown on New Year's when I broke into the business. Back then I would have thought it crazy to cold deck the house on New Year's Eve, but it made sense now. One distraction was sufficient to divert a boss's attention. One deck out, one in. If anything went awry, Angel could dissolve into the crowd as he had at the Monaco.

I recaptured as best I could the sequence of events the night Berman won the million at the Monaco. Presidents' Day, a long weekend, slower than expected. Ben hadn't planned on a dealer's game being dead. Mine was. Gus shuffled slowly, looking around as he did. Then, when he was about to offer the cut card to Berman, I was warned to keep my eyes on my own game, and Angel appeared in an overcoat acting drunk, spilling a drink on Manny, who grabbed a towel to dry off his jacket. I, an unwitting witness, had been distracted, not by Angel, but the backside of a blonde walking up beside Berman, who said something about "Lady Luck."

BY THE FOURTH BREAK, I couldn't stand the suspense of not knowing. I walked to the back entrance and told the guard at the time office that I'd left my work card in my car.

"No one checked it when you came in?"

I shrugged. "Guess not."

"Not s'posed to let you go out," the guard said.

"Gaming agents are in the casino. Boss says they might start checking cards."

"No one tells me these things."

"Five minutes. You can smell my breath when I come back."

"Hell, what makes you think I'd want to?" The guard laughed at his joke. "Go on."

I grabbed my cell phone out of the glove box and dialed Lucas's number. There was no answer. I dialed again. And again. I felt under the seat where the magnum lay, touched the cold barrel. If anything has happened to them, I knew who to target first. It was an infraction of rules to carry a cell phone at work, but I slipped it in my trouser pocket anyhow and walked to the entrance at the time office. I showed my work card to the guard.

"Good thing I'm here to keep you out of trouble."

"Sure is," I said.

Berman was just sitting down at the table when I entered the pit. Beside him was Patty Lane. She pretended not to see me, much the way she'd never noticed me when I'd worked with her. The boss had been replaced by Danny Waite, who usually supervised baccarat. Waite, a pretty-boy type promoted after two years in the business, couldn't tell a card switch from a soccer goal, but was good at telling high rollers, with a straight face, how wonderful it was to see them. I tapped Eric off the game. He finished the hand and slid the top card facedown to the center of the layout for me to bury.

"See you in an hour," he said. "Be good to him."

"Hello, Mr. B." I looked at the rack, filled now with five- and ten-thousand-dollar chips.

"Hello." Berman squinted as if trying to read my name tag. "Jude. Jude, of course. This lovely lady with me is Patty."

"Pleased to meet you." She smiled, then looked demurely at Berman.

"Let's hope you bring me luck," he said. "A marker, two hundred thousand."

I called out a marker request to Waite. For the time being, Berman would play a normal game, lose a few and win a few less, all in timing with the scheme. I would deal as usual. Patty Lane would be every male boss's fantasy. Jokes, the three of us in a badly scripted comedy.

I buried the card Eric left and dealt out the first hand, my thoughts on Beth and Lucas. I was again concerned this might turn into another of Ben's tests. In that case, my hand would be tipped. I'd started all this. My pulse climbed. Had I misread Norma's look, interpreted it as one of assurance? What if the deal went bad? My imagination took off. My kids, Moser holding them at gunpoint. My mouth went dry. My recourse was the revolver. I knew where the door to the eye in the sky was. I'd put the barrel to Ben's head and tell him if I didn't hear my children assuring me they were okay, he'd go first. Ben, then Berman. Audie? Her too. Then I'd find Moser.

As we waited for Danny Waite to fill out the marker, I took the deck out of the shuffler, hollered, "Cut!" and offered the cut card to Berman. Waite didn't look up, just hollered, "Go ahead!" A turkey roast, I thought, everything jake, nothing tom.

I looked at Berman, the man behind this, and smiled. He smiled back. Conspirators ready to rip off a casino. It was quite a leap from dumping dog shit on a man's shoes. Could I kill? Hell, if I did, why stop with Ben and the Mosers? Go berserk. Take out Hefty if the frog face happened to be around. I had to reach my boy on the next break before I did something irrational.

The shoe was neither kind to nor hard on Berman. As it ended, he was up forty thousand. When the cut card showed, I looked at my watch. I would deal two more of these, but the timing had to be right. Angel had to show on time, but not too soon. How will they ensure the timing? How had it been factored in? As I was wondering, I got my answer.

Berman stepped away from the game and motioned Danny Waite over to the table. "I'm going to take a breather. I'll be back in a few minutes. May as well spread the deck." He offered his arm to Patty Lane. "Come along."

She entwined her arm in Berman's and smiled at him as if they were lovers. Waite told me to spread the deck, a grand decision, considering that was what I was doing. Their leaving would delay the shuffle until the exact moment. Smart. I looked around for any sign of Masters or his people. It was all but impossible to single out one face in the milling crowd. I felt like a soldier hunkered down alone in a foxhole surrounded by the enemy. Somewhere in the slot area a woman shouted. The operators paged names. Players shouted in the crap pit. Business as usual.

To occupy my mind, I counted the bank in my rack, $1.7 million in $10,000 checks and $400,000 in $5,000 checks. The table would require at least one more fill if they were aiming for $2 million. It would, under ideal circumstances, take sixteen minutes to finish a shoe. I figured Ben was clever enough to place a few losing hands in the deck. I glanced at my watch again—three and a half minutes to my break.

It was time, but where was Berman? And Angel? What if Eric came back early from his break? Dealers were unpredictable that way. That's something Ben might not have calculated. At two minutes to go, Berman returned to the pit, alone. He sidled up to the game and took the seat he'd sat in when we'd filmed the cuts. Still, no Angel in sight. This might be the test I feared. I was losing confidence that it would go down or that Masters was in the house. I steadied myself by holding my hands behind my back. Patty Lane strolled in and stood near the table at an angle to block Waite's view, and Berman said, "Let's go."

I scooped up the deck that was spread out and loaded it in the shuffler, then pulled the shuffled deck out.

A man hollered, "Fuck you!" and another man tumbled into the pit and landed on his back, blood spurting from his nose onto the carpet. His assailant pushed his way into the crowd. I recognized the wig as the one Angel had worn. There was no time to consider any of what was happening. Wearing tortoise-shell glasses, her hair bleached, Audie stepped out of the crowd and entered the pit. Unnoticed, she approached the game, unsnapped her purse, and nodded to me.

Audie? Of course. I announced, "Cut!"

Waite, who along with the guard went to the aid of the fallen man, glanced back over his shoulder just long enough to shout, "Go ahead!"

She barely brushed the back of my hand as she took the house deck. I reflexively grabbed the other, the one from her purse, the cut card in place. Before anyone was aware of what had happened or even that she'd been there, she had slipped the house deck into her purse and was walking by the security guard. Done, the timing impeccable. I watched her lovely backside as she blended into the crowd.

Eric walked in the pit as I placed the cold deck in the shoe. He stepped behind me.

"Good luck, Mr. B," I said.

"Thanks. I'll need it."

Motioning with his head toward the fallen man, Eric asked, "What happened over there?"

"Someone decked him."

Patty Lane placed a hand on Berman's shoulder as Eric buried the first card. On my way out, I stepped around the fallen man, who was reeling in agony. I figured Ben had already planted the doctored version of the cut. I wondered how much a man got paid to suffer a broken nose. Well, it was more effective than dousing a boss with a martini. I looked over my shoulder. Eric was in the middle of the first hand of a $2 million deck.

I looked around for Masters or anyone who might be watching the action, but saw no one. On my own now, I hurried to the hallway to the break room and stepped into the men's toilet. I dialed Lucas's number. The line buzzed. There was no answer, not even a recorded one. All that mattered now was getting to my children before Moser or Angel. I mumbled a curse as I headed for the time office. The guard asked where I was going this time. I didn't answer, just kept walking straight to the Nissan. I opened the door and reached under the seat. The gun felt heavier than I remembered. Shaking, but resolved, I slammed the door and turned toward the stairwell to go up. I could use the executives' back entrance and climb the stairs up to the eye in the sky.

I hit the speed dial as I neared the staircase and held the cell to my ear with one hand and the revolver to my side with the other. The phone buzzed. Lucas answered on the third ring.

"Where have you been?"

"Dad, you won't believe . . ."

"Is Beth with you?"

"Yeah, Dad. Don't you trust me?"

I leaned on the fender of some executive's Jaguar and closed my eyes. "Of course. Yeah, I trust you."

"The cops stopped us in Logandale. Do you believe it?"

"Were you speeding?"

"No. We're here with them now. They said a car was following us. They put the driver in handcuffs. Dad, what's going on? Beth's scared."

I looked at the gun in my hand. "So am I, but everything's okay now." I closed my eyes and said, "I'll explain everything later. Come on home. I love you both. Let me talk to Beth."

"All right."

I couldn't find my full voice. I whispered a throaty, "Yes, thank goodness."

"Dad, you're weird," she said.

"I've got to go. Give the phone back to Lucas." I took a deep breath, then said, "Lucas?"

"Yeah."

"What did you say to your boss at the restaurant?"

"That I had a family emergency. He said, 'On New Year's Eve?' and said I was fired if I left. I told him that was fine, family comes first."

I stared at the wall. I couldn't talk for a time, then he asked, "Are you okay, Dad?"

"I can't describe how okay I am."

I walked back to my car and slipped the gun under the seat. I sat down, buried my face in my hands, and cried. Norma had come through. What if she hadn't? But she had and it was over. As I headed back to the casino, three men intercepted me at the time office. One flashed a badge.

I nodded. "I've been expecting you. I just needed to talk to my kids."

"We'll have to cuff you," one said.

I put my wrists out and said, "Okay."

Patty Lane and Berman sat beside me on a bench in the security office, both in cuffs. None of us spoke or looked at one another. A moment passed before Masters pushed Ben inside the door and told him to take a seat. Two steps behind Masters a male and a female cop entered, holding Audie by the arms. Another cop followed, Audie's purse in hand. She looked at me as she took a seat beside Ben. I resisted the urge to smile when her eye caught mine. After all, we *did* sit through teenage karaoke together. It was a strange feeling, this mixture of fear and relief. I felt human and oddly hopeful.

45 The assistant district attorney placed the form in front of me. I picked it up and began reading. Masters sat beside me, holding a voluntary statement I'd given some weeks ago. In it I confessed to switching cards on a blackjack game at the Whiskey River with a man I knew as Angel.

"You can have an attorney read it before you sign," the assistant DA said.

"No need. I trust you and him." I pointed a thumb in Masters's direction.

"Still. Let's go over it just to reiterate the agreement that was discussed when you came forward. You understand that no one will file charges against you with a stipulation that you can still be prosecuted if you don't testify or if you commit perjury."

"I will testify. And I won't lie."

"If you want, we'll move you out of state to a safer environment. We have limited funds for such moves, and we can't guarantee work."

I'd already resolved not to leave town so long as my children lived here. "No. I'll stay." I signed my name to the document and laid the contract atop the desk.

"Also, keep in mind that if you go crossways with the law, we won't bail you out. Besides, you'll risk undermining your credibility as a witness and lose your value to us. As it is, their attorneys are going to attack your credibility, painting you as nothing but a cheat."

"Before this, I never did anything dishonest. I won't be a problem."

The assistant DA signed his name to the agreement and handed it to Masters to witness, then to the woman, a notary who stamped and certified it. The lawyer asked her to bring back a copy in a few minutes, that we needed to be alone.

"Jude," the attorney said, "don't take the threat lightly."

"I said I'd behave. I'm not a thief."

"I mean, the other threat. Moser. The man who was assaulted in the pit didn't see his attacker, and every eye and camera were focused on the table, so none of the investigators can identify him either. We all suspect he was the culprit, but we have no way of holding Moser accountable in this case. He remains free, out there on bond without an ankle monitor, pending appeals for retrial for the cheating scams up north. In short, he should be of concern."

"But I thought he was following . . ."

"No," Masters said, "Angel Mozello was the one following your kids. Even there, we can't nail him for anything except the card switch, which requires your testimony. Too bad you destroyed the video. We didn't turn one up in our searches."

That came as a shock, the idea that I'd had the only copy. Then I remembered that Ben had once said no tapes, no snitches. Had he destroyed the original, or was that what he gave to me? They'd bluffed me. I found the final irony amusing.

The attorney came around from behind the desk and leaned his haunches on the front edge. "We're taking it to the grand jury. The indictments are a slam dunk. I'd say the case is close to won. You did the right thing. If you need something, we'll help. But there are limitations. Anything we do for you will be brought up by the defense attorneys. Questions?"

I shook my head.

"Okay then. When the girl comes back with a copy, you can go." He started around the desk.

"Wait."

"What is it?"

"Can you do something for Katie Moser?"

The attorney looked at Masters, who said, "She's in Child Haven. Her grandmother is—"

"She's my . . . was my daughter's friend. A good kid. We don't pick our parents. Beth has asked about her. I'd like to tell her something positive. She's got to deal with what her father's done. That's enough worry for a teenager."

"Tell your daughter we'll make sure Katie's fine. Her grandmother's asked for guardianship. She'll likely be fostered out in the meantime."

A knock came at the door. All three of us looked in that direction. He told the woman to enter. I stood as she handed the copied form to the lawyer. He handed it to me.

"Good luck, Jude."

"Yeah, thanks."

Outside Norma waited in the reception area, reading a magazine. She set it aside, stood, and offered me a hand. I took it and squeezed gently.

"How'd it go?"

"Okay, I guess. Yeah, it went fine."

In the courthouse lobby she pointed to vendor's stand. "Ice cream always made things better when I was kid," she said.

A good idea, I thought. A double scoop.

46 Vegas's optimism, sparked by a surge of January visitors, had long since subsided, supplanted by a cynical sense that the worst was yet to come. In March the Dow spiked up and down like a bad EKG, and by May it again plummeted. Occupancy rates on the Strip dropped to below 70 percent, and early-summer vacationers began canceling reservations. The casino business slipped into a near coma following Memorial Day, and profits, down 4 percent in the first quarter, were anticipated to sink lower the remainder of the year.

And it was hot.

I was unaffected by the cynicism or the season. I'd given notice at the Rampart Casino and was looking at my last two days pitching cards. The trial, scheduled to start in five days, two and a half years after the scam, had come slowly, as expected. Pretrial motions were out of the way. Though apprehensive, I was prepared for the coming week. I awoke, as I had now for the past seven months, at four and dressed in a pair of jeans, a cotton shirt, and steel-toed boots. The longer I kept this early schedule, the more I'd come to understand how my uncle had managed waking up at dawn, laying block for four hours, then doing a shift in a casino.

Life had become an unexpected present opened anew every day. Now that I had custody of Beth and Anne got her for two days every second week, the house seemed full. I immersed myself in the rituals of daily life and work and took pleasure in small things, such as the smell of coffee brewing in the morning. As I poured some into a thermos, I looked at my forearm and hand, both tanned. I poured the remaining coffee in two cups, took a sip from one, set the pot down, and rubbed my calloused palms together. Then I dialed Papillon on the cell phone.

"Good morning, Pap. I'll meet you at the site in forty minutes."

"Forty. *Si.* For breakfast my wife make you a burrito, *carne* and *frijole.*"

"Your wife wants me to be a fat man."

"You got no one to cook for you."

"Just me. Norma's not allowed to even boil water. Tell the wife thanks," I said.

"My wife, she like Norma. Make her laugh, and Lupe, she don' speak English so good. You think it's maybe *un milagro*?"

"What's that?"

"*Milagro*. A miracle that my wife understands jokes in English."

"Yeah, sounds like a *milagro*. See you at the job." I said good-bye and hung up.

I went to the bedroom, where Norma lay on her side, facing the opposite wall. I walked around and set her cup on the nightstand. "You awake?"

"Go away. Go to work. Go do anything."

"Coffee's fresh."

She lifted her head and squinted at the cup. "Smells good."

"You'll like it. Will you pick up Beth at Anne's?"

"Sure. Give me a kiss, Jude Helms."

"Okay. I have one to spare."

DRIVING OUT IN THE CALM PREDAWN and seeing the desert burst to life stirred my blood. The morning was cool and cloudless. In an hour the sun would creep over the peaks at an angle that turned Frenchman's Mountain from shadow to alabaster and pink. For now the stars were still out, but fading. The freeway north was clear as I drove to the project, our first subdivision contract in the booming developments, our foot in the door, so to speak. Although casino business was slow, construction was still booming, though predictions in some circles claimed it wouldn't last the decade. I wished Uncle Frank had lived to see it. He would be rich by now. Rich and content to wear denim and a Stetson hat.

I'd loaned the pickup to Papillon so he could transport the crew. I leaned back in the seat and enjoyed the drive. The Nissan had turned 140,000 miles, but wasn't ready to retire anytime soon. It was hardly the shiny Mustang convertible I once coveted, and it had its crotchety ways, but we were used to each other.

I couldn't make the drive without recalling how the area had been in my youth—desert, dirt roads, scattered houses with low-pitched roofs and horse stalls in the yards. Tourists back then had asked how locals could stand to live here, hot summers, no trees or grass. Now the tourists were invaders and occupiers. The sweltering Southwest deserts were the new century's theme—stucco houses with tiled roofs and tiled floors and tiled shower stalls.

I hummed to Pink Floyd's "Dark Side of the Moon." As the state's case against Linus Berman, Harold "Ben" Benjamin, et al. kept getting delayed, I'd pushed thought of it all but aside. Norma had been with me since the day after New Year's, two and a half years now. First as a friend, then as the woman who filled my days and nights, even when we weren't together.

She couldn't cook, so she never tried to take over the kitchen. As I prepared meals on our days off, she was content to sit with Beth and cook up jokes at my expense. She'd quit smoking and gained fifteen pounds that she blamed on me. She talked to the television, sometimes argued with it. She squeezed toothpaste from the center of the tube, sang off-key, and wrote sentimental poetry that she'd read aloud in bed. Mostly, she made me happy, and I'd come to call it love.

We'd had one disagreement when she'd reached under the pickup seat for some spilled change and found the revolver. She'd asked me to get rid of it, said guns terrified her. I'd fired it only once, just enough to understand someone's fear of guns. After a bit of back-and-forth on the merits of self-protection, I removed it and secured it under the front seat of the Nissan.

Of course, a long trial loomed ahead. The others, the accused, as prosecutors referred to them, were free on bail and monitored electronically. Though I wanted to stare in their eyes and tell my story, I still dreaded the coming week—my name and picture in the papers identifying me as an unindicted coconspirator, my kids embarrassed again, though both would deny it. The prosecutors would admit that I'd cheated the Whiskey River, and the defense lawyers would prey upon it, and I'd have to admit to even more involvement.

The DA maintained the outcome didn't hinge solely on me, that doctored videos found in the eye in the sky and other evidence might by themselves carry the case. Still, my testimony was critical to securing guilty verdicts. There was sentencing to consider. How long would they get? Two to five, then come out of prison, wealthy all the same? The Internal Revenue Service had taken a statement from me and was considering filing federal charges and seizing property for unpaid taxes.

There was one last and ongoing consideration: Joel Moser, also known as Wade. Three times now he'd prolonged any new trial for his cheating crimes in Douglas County. Though Detective Beardsley continued to work the case and Moser remained the primary suspect in Blitzstein's murder, any evidence was circumstantial. The prosecutor in my case kept me updated on him, and the latest news on him was that he hadn't been seen for seven months. His attorney assured the district court that his client stayed in touch and would show up for the new trial. Masters believed Moser had fled the country, most likely to South America, and wouldn't be seen again. Detective Beardsley thought otherwise.

Well, while Moser ducked the law and the others sweated and prepared for trial, I was a free man with a present and future, and I'd found something I'd not had since the fire. I defined it as peace or contentment, an acceptance that breathing was an immeasurable pleasure if you let yourself enjoy air.

Two miles south of the Kyle Canyon turnoff I drove east onto a gravel road beside a sign that read "Bella Nueva Villas." Everything had a name to conjure up a romantic notion of history. Some developers fused Spanish with Italian, never the wiser for their mistake, as was the case here. It didn't matter. There was no sense of real culture, no history in any of this. Two hundred yards from the highway the gravel road spilled onto a freshly paved street.

I liked to arrive before the work crew and walk the fence line to look at the footers poured the previous day. A fence wasn't just a barrier; it was work that would probably outlast me, a finishing touch to a house a family would live in. Footers must be exact, each row of block absolutely level, each corner squared, smooth hand-troweled stucco to add elegance to the yard. I told Norma that fences were what neighbors shared when they shared nothing else. "Corny," she's said, then used the line in a poem.

I was being romantic about my work, but I enjoyed it, every phase from bidding to final cleanup. And I had Papillon as a partner, who was himself a romantic. As I slowed the car, I was thinking how lucky I was to find him. He was among several blessings the last months had dropped on me. He was from Hermasillo, and the first time we'd met I asked how he'd gotten a French name. "My mother name me," he'd said. "In Spanish is *mariposa*, the butterfly, and is woman. But in French, my mother says it sound like a man who can fly."

This was the final week for this project, but because of the trial I wouldn't be there to oversee it. Papillon would bring it in. I parked in the driveway to the sales office, a temporarily converted garage, and poured some coffee into the thermos lid. I looked around for the security guard's car, but didn't see it anywhere. Well, maybe he beat the clock this morning. For what he was paid, I couldn't blame him.

I took the coffee with me and walked four houses down to the new footer. I checked the rebar for soundness. Everything was on schedule and looked good. I took a sip of coffee and headed farther down where the crew had stuccoed two walls. These were fine houses. Oversized lots. Maybe in time, if business went well, I figured to buy one like these. How much house did a single middle-aged man need? Was that same space better if shared with another? That too had been on my mind. Norma stayed over so often, she might as well move in. Though I thought about it, I'd never brought it up to her. Guess I was waiting for her to suggest it.

As I stepped out from behind the house, I thought I heard a rock turn.

"Hello!" I said.

No one answered. I listened and scanned the street up and down, but neither heard nor saw anything. People get lazy and leave things propped up, especially painters and Sheetrock hangers. Objects fall over. I finished the coffee and headed to the car for a refill. I figured to listen to the radio as I waited for Papillon and the crew. It was an hour too early for the Sheetrock and painting crews to arrive.

I opened the car door and snuggled in behind the wheel. I leaned forward to pick up the thermos, and as I did, I caught sight of fleeting movement in the side-view mirror. I looked over my shoulder, then on both sides of the car, but saw nothing. I would have heard a car coming, seen headlights, or if someone were already here, I would have spotted the car. I figured it was a coyote. They still lived out here. Or more likely a stray dog.

I uncapped the thermos and filled my mug, then keyed the ignition and turned the radio to the morning news. The announcer said Israel had suffered another rocket attack and that Hamas was taking claim for it. The world's no less crazy, I thought, and snuggled in to drink my coffee. I was leaned against the seat back, blowing steam off the rim of the cup, when I heard scuffing noise on concrete. Somewhere near. I rolled down the window and looked behind through the side-view and the rearview mirrors. Then to the right I saw a man silhouetted beside the tract office. He stood shaded by the wall where it was too dark to make out any features. A painter, I figured, or Sheetrocker. Maybe even a homeless man. Some find temporary shelter in houses under construction.

"Hey, you! What do you want?"

Still an indistinguishably gray silhouette, he stepped out of the shadow.

"Can I help you?"

He walked toward the car, advancing slowly, his hands in sight. He was five or six steps away when he reached back with his right hand. Before I could react, I saw a flash, and the force of a bullet slammed me backward. I rebounded off the seat and slumped forward. The blow numbed me. My head cleared as he circled the car, apparently to approach from the driver side. His footsteps crunched over the driveway, slowly, in no hurry to finish what he came to do. I felt blood run down my right arm, sticky and warm. The bullet had struck above the shoulder blade.

No, I thought, not now. Not when everything's working out. I tried to reach for the cell phone, but couldn't move my right arm. Then it occurred that I was in the Nissan. I groped under the seat with my left hand and touched the barrel. I turned the revolver until I could wrap my fingers around the grip. I wasn't left-handed, wasn't certain I could control it, much less aim it. I lay motionless as the man reversed direction and circled to the back of the car. This time he approached the passenger side. I waited, angled so I could see the side window. When the door cracked open, I raised the gun and fired three times in succession, then a fourth. The man collapsed and released a groan. Then nothing. Hoping it wasn't the night watchman, I sat up and slowly scooted to the edge of the seat. The door was open. I planted the soles of my boots on the driveway and looked down at the face of Joel Moser as he stared vacantly at his last thought. His chest rose and sank.

The blood seemed hotter now and sticky. I felt faint, but still aimed the gun ready to shoot. Moser's bowels erupted. I looked around as best I could to see if he had an accomplice. Satisfied he'd come alone, I leaned my head on the center post and closed my eyes until seconds later sunlight penetrated Frenchman's Peak. I set the gun aside and felt around for the cell phone. It was wedged in the cushion.

I dialed 911 and said to the dispatcher, "I'm shot."

"Where are you?"

I took a labored breath and gave her the directions to the Bella Nueva Villas. She said help was on the way and told me to hold on.

"There's a dead man here," I said.

A crew of painters arrived before the ambulance or the cops. I was sitting, as I had been since making the call. A painter took my phone. He looked at the wound.

"Man, you're a mess, but this fucker's talkin' to the devil. You do that?"

I looked up at the man and nodded once. It was light enough now to see clearly. Men, three of them all blurry, stared down at me. I sensed their confusion, average men who'd stumbled into the last act of a . . . what? A comedy. Yes.

"They comin' for you?" one of the men asked.

I nodded. The faint sound of a siren came in the distance. Assured that the machinery of the world would now work to save me, I closed my eyes. When the ambulance siren burped to a stop behind my car, I pulled myself up with my good arm. I didn't want to be carried. I wanted to leave with dignity. I looked at Moser's body, then northward, where Snow Mountain stood in relief against the blueing sky. I thought of the fire, the sky that day. The men's faces swirled before me. They grabbed me and sat me back down, and I surrendered any thoughts of dignity.

A paramedic placed a compress over my wound and wrapped it. The painters watched from the edge of the driveway. I raised my good hand and waved feebly as the attendants checked my pulse. When they lifted me into the ambulance, one said I'd lost considerable blood and was going into shock. As the ambulance bounded over the unpaved road, the paramedic started an iv. It took her several attempts to find a vein. I watched with objective interest as she took my vital signs. She said that the bullet hadn't hit an artery. The driver wheeled the ambulance south onto 95 and hit the siren. Our first big job, I thought. Papillon, keep working on it. Don't worry about me.

"Can you hear me? Are you okay?" the paramedic asked.

She tapped the tubing that led to my arm. She was young. I wondered how much death she'd already seen. Was she able to engage the harshness of the world without it damaging her? Without experiencing the actual shock of an experience, how could anyone know what it meant to survive it? Perhaps by witnessing it. I pictured Randy swallowed in flames, two desperate strangers tumbling to their deaths down the side of the outside wall of the hotel, falling again and again, the last moment of their life preserved in my mind until I died. Though I wanted to, I wasn't ready to forget it. Then I remembered filling my lungs with cool air and knowing I would live. Sometime after the trial, I'd tell Norma and the kids what it was like to follow a draft of air and rise up from death and rejoin the living. Rise up twice. No, not twice. Three times.

"I'm okay," I whispered and thought, hold on, remember the smell of fresh air.